the Step Don't

RILEY HART
DEVON McCORMACK

PEACH STATE STEPBROS, BOOK 2

OTHER WORKS BY RILEY HART & DEVON MCCORMACK

The Metropolis Series
Faking It (Book 1)
Working It (Book 2)
Owning It (Book 3)
Finding It (Book 3.5)
Trying It (Book 4)
Hitching It (Book 4.5)

The Fever Falls Series
Fired Up (Book 1)
#Burn (Book 2)
Whiskey Throttle (Book 3)
#Royal (Book 4)
Game On (Book 5)
Boyfriend Goals (Book 6)

Stand-alone Novels
Weight of the World
Up for the Challenge
Beautiful Chaos
No Good Mitchell

1

Ash

L AST NIGHT WAS wild.

Like…Top Ten Nights of My Life wild.

After claiming victory at the TaskFrat Challenge, the Peach State frats met back at the Alpha Theta Mu house.

And we partied. Hard.

Which explains the headache.

How fucking tired I feel.

And why I'm struggling to open my eyes.

I finally manage to force them open, and I notice a bulge in the sheets beside me.

Someone's sleeping in my bed.

Last night steadily comes back to me. There was the friendly girl I met when the party started—the one with the smile and hot ass. Then later, there was the blond guy with the chiseled jaw and the impressive biceps. Friends with someone in Delta Phi, the guy practically on my tail all night—and at one point, he grabbed my tail, but after that, I can only remember up until flip cup.

Maybe after, the blond hottie and I came up to my room. I'm naked, so it's possible we messed around, but with how drunk I got, I'm tempted to think we just passed the fuck out.

A pillow obstructs my view of that sexy jaw, but my dick's already getting nice and hard at the thought that the guy might wake soon so we can finish what we started.

A smile tugs at my lips, but then I notice a shirt on top of the sheet.

Wait a second…

That's not what he was wearing last night.

And this guy seems taller.

"You're up, aren't you?" a familiar voice says.

My heart sinks.

This isn't my blond hottie from last night!

I groan as Colin removes the pillow that's blocking his face.

My brother? Seriously?

"Hangover that bad?" he asks as all my excitement is sucked right out of me in a few cruel moments.

Colin's light-brown locks lie flat from the backward cap he wore all night, his eyes squinty, the way they get in the morning.

"I can't even convey how mad I am at you right now," I say, glaring at him.

Colin's eyes widen. "*Me?*"

"I thought you were a sexy man in my bed."

"I *am* a sexy man in your bed." He sports a cocky grin, but I'm so disappointed, it's hard to even be amused by that.

"It doesn't really work when the sexy man is your brother." I sit up and snatch the pillow at his side, pulling it close.

I know he's hot. Since our parents first got together, I've seen firsthand how guys and girls fawn over him. The way they glance at that sharp jawline and grab at his thick biceps and chest. But that's not gonna do me any good.

"Wait a second," Colin says as he sits up, eyeing me suspiciously. "Did you think I was that blond guy you spent half the night with?"

"His name was…" I say in as obnoxious a tone as I can manage, but—

Oh fuck, what was his name?

So much for my attempt at being a smart-ass.

"That guy was straight, though, right?" Colin asks.

I have to keep from rolling my eyes. I swear, sometimes Colin is so oblivious. "I'm pretty sure he wasn't feeling all that straight when he had his hand on my ass."

"Oh," he says, rolling his head back for a laugh. "I didn't pick up on that at all. But, I didn't with you either, so…"

"Yeah, I think I might have broken you as far as figuring out who's queer or not."

"Maybe you did. But don't be an Ash-hole this morning." Colin scoots close and throws his arms around me, pulling me in for a hug. He doesn't normally wind up in my bed with my naked ass, but considering how close we are, it's not really much of a thing for either of us.

"My bro's sad he didn't get some *strange* last night?"

"I feel like you're weaponizing the slang I taught you."

I nudge my shoulder against Colin, and as he backs off, I run my fingers through his bangs, messing them up in the front. That only makes him grin even more.

Even when Colin's trying to get under my skin, he's still the big, lovable Labrador he's always been. Playful. Loyal. And loves to catch a ball—namely, a football, but really, any ball will do.

"You are just living for this, aren't you?" I ask.

"Don't be like that. You slept with Peach State's star tight end. You know how many people would kill to wake up to this?" He casually flexes his admittedly bulky bicep, the way he might for a girl he's trying to impress. "And the first guy to manage it? That's bragging rights for the rest of your college career." He's got this wicked grin on his face, trying to get all his digs in while he can. "Seriously, though. I'm sorry you woke up thinking you were gonna get some dick, and it turned out to be your straight brother."

"*Stepbrother,*" I say, which I normally use only when he's teasing me like this.

Colin puts his hand to his chest. "Ooh, I felt that one." He winks, making me laugh.

"Okay, I have so many questions about last night," I say, "but I'm also fucking starving."

"Come on." He pats my thigh. "Let's get some breakfast. At least you can put *something* in that horny mouth of yours."

And again, he's got me laughing, despite the combination of hangover and sexual frustration I'm currently suffering.

Colin rolls out of bed in just his briefs, grabbing his clothes off the bed and floor before he starts to head out.

"Hey!" I call after him, snatching his cap from between the sheets and tossing it to him.

He catches it. "Thanks, bro."

I toss on some clothes and my glasses, working my way through the events of last night, trying to fill in the gaps, but some things just aren't coming back to me. That's what happens when you fuck with hippocampal circuitry.

I head down to the kitchen. Several of my housemates are eating in the adjoining dining area, while Lance—my buddy and Alpha Theta Mu president extraordinaire—sits at the kitchen island in a tank top, eating his usual Froot Loops, his gaze on the TV, playing some reality show I don't recognize. As I near him, he turns to me, and his eyes light up. "Alpha Theta Mu TaskFrat victors!" he exclaims.

A few of the guys holler from the dining area.

Lance and I are both regular players in the Peach State TaskFrat Challenges—a year-round task-based competition between all the frats—because I do enjoy a challenge. And Alpha Theta Mu totally kicked ass last night.

"How you feeling this morning, bruh?" Payton calls out from the dining area, snickering in that way that assures me he saw some wild shit.

I fist-bump Lance before retrieving the container of grits from the pantry. As I start fixing a bowl, I ask him, "So…exactly how bad was I last night?"

"Why don't you tell me what you *do* remember, and we'll go from there."

"Up to flip cup."

"Yeah, why did the resident genius think playing flip cup with vodka instead of beer was a good idea?"

"Because the only thing that rivals my brains is my competitive streak—I thought we were good enough friends that you knew that about me."

Lance chuckles. "That sounds about right. So you don't remember dancing on the media console?"

"No." I groan.

"There was definitely some of that…for a while. Marty kept trying to get you to come down, first by saying this is not the behavior of a future professor, then under threat of your security deposit, so you'll probably be hearing about that again."

"I'm sure I will." Our housemate Marty is all about rules, which really, don't you need someone like that to make sure everything doesn't descend into chaos?

I pop my grits into the microwave. "Do you remember the name of that blond guy I was hanging with?"

Lance glances around like he's scanning his mind for the answer. "Greg…or Bailey? Or did he say he liked Bailey's?"

"He was Jeff Martin's friend," I say, "so maybe I'll check Jeff's and his friends' profiles and search for him there."

"I can text Jeff and ask."

"I wanna look cool, so let me aggressively stalk to find him first, and if that doesn't work, then we can resort to texting him."

"Yeah, because aggressive social media stalking is so much cooler than just straight up asking."

"Your sarcasm is noted, but really grating on my hangover right now."

Lance laughs. "I'm sorry. You really should have slowed down because you had that girl fawning over you the first part of the night, and then that guy on your ass the rest of it. My bi boy had the world at his fingertips."

"At least I was making some moves," I say, glaring at him.

"I still have a wounded heart."

"You broke up with Shannon forever ago."

"A few months." At my look, Lance adds, "Okay, more like five. I can't just hook up like you or Colin, though. But I can enjoy living vicariously through your stories, and given you had two viable options last night, you should have woken up with someone in your bed."

If only he knew, and nearly as soon as I have the thought, I hear, "He did wake up with someone in his bed." Colin rounds the corner, in sweats, a backward cap, and crocs.

"Oh really?" Lance says, his voice full of interest and curiosity. "And who was the lucky someone?"

"I was." Colin shrugs as he opens the fridge, leaving it there long enough that Lance's jaw drops. Colin doesn't seem to be thinking much of the bomb he just set off as he digs through the fridge, nabbing a cup of yogurt.

"Um…" Lance drags out.

"We woke up in bed together," I explain. "That's all that happened."

"It's not like it's the first time we've ever shared a bed," Colin tells Lance. "I'm sure you've shared a bed with your brothers."

"Not after middle school," Lance says. "And how did you end up in his room last night?"

As Colin fishes through the drawer for a spoon, he says, "When I got him off the media console, he wanted a piggyback ride to his room. Since he wore his contacts for TaskFrat, he started stressing about falling asleep with his contacts in and dying from an eye infection, so he made me swing by the bathroom so he could take them out before we actually made it to his room. Then he seemed to think I'd taken him to *my* room, and that he was kicking me out, and no matter how much I insisted that wasn't the case, he demanded I stay."

"Based on what I know of you guys," Lance says, "this is all adding up, especially the piggyback ride."

I have been known to demand piggyback rides from Colin. It's just one of those things we do from when we were younger that clearly other people find weird.

"I really don't remember any of that," I say.

"I've got video." Colin pulls his phone out of his pocket, keys on it for a moment, then passes it to me. A video plays of me dancing on the console. "Don't bother asking if my volume is low," he says, "because that's you when the music stopped."

"Oh God," I say, witnessing the horror.

It's not like I'm just bobbing around. I've got my hands in the air, really cutting up; the camera shifts, and

I see the blond hottie from last night glaring at me like I've lost my goddamn mind.

"Lance, look who it is," I say, flashing the video to him.

"That's the guy!"

"Guess we don't have to find out his name after all. Colin, we're staging our deaths and moving to Wyoming."

"Wyoming?" Lance asks, looking almost disgusted by the idea.

"Yeah, you have to come too," Colin says. "We can't risk you telling anyone the plan."

"He's right," I chime in. "It's too risky. We all have to stage our deaths together."

Lance bursts into a laugh. "You guys are so strange."

Admittedly, our senses of humor largely formed around each other since our parents got together, so we have a lot of inside jokes, like staging our deaths and moving to Wyoming when something bad or embarrassing happens. Really, it's a miracle anyone can understand what the hell we're talking about.

As I grab my grits from the microwave, Colin pops some yogurt into his mouth, and after swallowing, says, "Bro, you already humiliated yourself in TaskFrat last night. I don't know why you think the media-console thing is so embarrassing."

Lance chuckles. "Yeah, we were in a pair of Speedos,

tossing dildos into a bin in some weird-ass version of basketball just a few hours before that. That's the video my parents are gonna see on TikTok and call me about."

"Hope you're not too worried." I set my bowl on the counter. "'Cause they're probably gonna get that from my TikTok account. We looked hot in those Speedos, so I obviously posted it."

If only Lance knew, the kind of video he would find embarrassing not only doesn't bother me, it excites me.

More than he or any of the guys in the house could know.

Or even Colin, which for me, is fucking huge.

"It's more the acting like a fool afterward in front of the guy I was interested in that bothers me," I explain.

"And you were definitely acting like a fool," Colin says, shooting me a look, smirking, and I don't even try to fight my smile before his attention shifts.

"Troy, Troy, Troy," he calls out, breezing past me and tackling his buddy. He and Troy have been besties since they were on the same football team in high school.

After a friendly greeting, Troy asks, "Did your brother get with Bryan Crainers last night?"

"Bryan! That was it!" Lance says.

"Greg or Bailey?" I ask.

Lance shrugs. "I was drinking too."

"A few minutes too late for that," I say, glancing back at the video.

Troy pulls a face. "What is all this about?"

"Ash thought he went to bed with this hottie from last night," Lance says, "but when he woke up it was just Colin."

"No one has ever told me they have woken up with *just* Colin," Colin says.

Troy rolls his head back for a laugh. "Oh, wow. That's great. You are never living this one down, Ash Ketchum."

Troy's using the nickname I've earned around the house because of how many times I've cosplayed as the Pokémon Trainer during Alpha Theta Mu's themed parties.

What can I say? It's a simple costume to throw on, and every time I've worn it, I've gotten some action.

"To be fair," Colin tells Troy, "considering you're in a relationship with your stepbrother, do you really think anyone's gonna take that seriously coming from you?"

"Yeah, how is your brother's dick, by the way?" I tease.

Troy's eyes widen. "*Step* dick!" he insists. "Stop it! Fucking truce!"

We all share a laugh.

Troy and his stepbro, Atlas, are out and proud about their relationship, so really, he's the last person to judge our innocent morning.

"Did Atlas stay over last night?" I ask.

"Yeah, my A's tired, so I was gonna grab him some doughnuts and a coffee."

"Aww, that's sweet," Lance says. "Now all the step-brothers in the house are sleeping together."

Our housemate Marty's just rounding the corner, his eyes widening as he spins around, starting back into the hall, since I'm assuming he thought Lance meant all the stepbros in the house were banging.

"Don't be such a prude, Marty," Colin says. "Get back in here!"

2

Colin

Me: Do you want to bang for lunch today?

I text Ash as soon as I get out of my Constitutional History class. It's my only one of the day. He has a short break around this time, and it's often when he grabs a quick bite to eat. If I have time, I like to join him. Ash can get distracted by his studies, and it's important to me to make sure he eats and takes care of himself. Not that he can't do that himself, because he can, but doing this for Ash always makes me feel good.

Ash: Um...I know sometimes you can be the tiniest bit...and I say this in the most loving way possible...clueless...but do I have to remind you that you're straight? And we're stepbrothers? Though that one isn't as big of an obstacle as your sexuality is. Unless waking up with me naked in bed with you the other day has changed things...and if so, we should at least have a conversation before we get to the banging.

Banging? What the fuck is he talking about? He knows I'm straight and seeing his naked ass isn't anything new to me. We're cuddly stepbrothers. Usually it's with clothes on, sure, but it doesn't mean anything.

I scroll up to my message, before chuckling at myself.

Me: Hang. That was supposed to be: do you want to *hang* for lunch today?

I'm the worst with typos. He knows this. But that also won't stop him from giving me shit about it—not that I wouldn't do the same to him.

Ash: *laughing emoji* Well, just so you know, if you ever change your mind, I'm here. Brothers help each other out with things like that.

I almost stumble over a curb that wasn't there before, I swear it. Seriously, do they move those things? Or maybe I'm just shit at paying attention.

Me: Brothers help each other out with banging? Did Troy and Atlas start a trend?

Ash: I meant talking about your sexuality, smartass.

Me: Oh...my mistake...so...do you want to bang? Because you know that's gotta be something we keep using from now on. There's no way I can ever say hang to you again.

Ash: I'm sure that will help make us look like absolutely normal stepbrothers.

The thing is, we're not absolutely normal stepbrothers. Troy is my best friend, yeah, but Ash is my person. Literally my brother from another mother...well, and father, but the gist of it is the same. Most people see we're close—like the waking up naked in bed together—but they don't realize how truly close Ash and I are. That there's not a secret between us and hasn't been almost since the beginning.

Ash: I only have about forty-five minutes before my next class, but you're a quickie…

What's a few sexual jokes between brothers? It's all in good fun.

Me: You've never complained before. As long as I bring that good meat…

Ash: Good meat? That beaten-up rank sausage?

Me: Grade A sausage and you know it. You've seen my dick.

I chuckle.

Ash: Only if the A's for Asshole.

Me: A as in Ash-hole, you mean? So it sounds like you know what you're bringing.

Dude. That was a good one. I'm quite proud of myself. I automatically picture his mischievous half-grin. I've seen it too many times to count, and it's comforting in a way that probably doesn't make much sense. It's hard to think about it without a smile of my own.

Ash: Would be the best hole you've ever had. Now are you going to feed me or what?

Me: Obviously. Meet me in the dining hall.

I chuckle to myself as I head over. I can't imagine what people would think if they saw some of the things Ash and I do or heard some of the things we say to each other. To some people, that might seem weird, but then, others might not understand why it wasn't a big deal for him to wake up naked in the same bed as me either. We're just…close. We bonded in the beginning over the changes in our lives and dealing with them all together. Ash was a lot shyer when we were kids, though no one would believe it now, but he's come out of his shell so much over the years. Sometimes I sit back and watch him, amazed by who Ash is.

The dining hall is basically a cafeteria they call a dining hall, as if that will trick us into thinking the food is better than it is. It's between the law buildings where I am and where Ash will be coming from, so it's perfect. It doesn't take me long to get there, and when I arrive, Ash is leaning against the brick building, looking at his phone, his dark bangs hanging over his forehead. He's in an Alpha Theta Mu jacket that matches the cap I'm wearing backward. He has on his, and black-rimmed glasses rather than his contacts today. He prefers his glasses, but he'll wear contacts when he's doing something physical like the TaskFrat challenges.

"What's up?" I say as he stands up straighter and slips his phone into his pocket. Ash is more twunk than twink, words I only know because of him. He's about two inches shorter than me, and though he hits the gym and has great muscle definition, he's not as thick as I am. I keep in shape not only because of football, but because I like working out. My body isn't anything to sneeze at. Not that Ash's is either. We keep up with each other when we're working out together.

"Hey, you. How was class?"

I open the door and hold it for him. "Good. We're learning about some really interesting shit. Professor Wilkins was telling us about this precedent where…" I ramble on as we approach one of the build-your-own-meal style of food bars. Ash is a good brother who listens even though I'm talking about something he couldn't give less of a fuck about. My mom is a lawyer, and my dad used to be before he decided he wanted a change and became a writer. Ash's mom is a lawyer too, but unlike me, he has zero interest in law.

Ash glances around uneasily. "Careful, Colin. Someone's gonna hear you talking like this and realize you're a big nerd disguised as a jock."

"There's nothing nerdy about all this," I tease, though he's right about me being both a nerd and a jock. I love sports, am book smart as fuck—though not as smart as Ash. Brains aside, I'm aware that sometimes I can lack some common sense. Or…a lot of common sense.

"A big, mushy-hearted jock…who is kinda great," Ash adds, making me beam.

"Fuck yes, I am." He's not the only person to tell me things like that, and I know I'm awesome, but it feels better hearing it from my bro.

We grab Chinese food from the bar, then head outside. We're lucky enough to find a picnic table beneath a tree. It's a gorgeous March day, halfway through the month. After spring break, the school year always seems to fly by.

Ash inspects the table. "Bug check complete. No sign of Coleoptera, Hymenoptera, or Arachnida. You're good, Big Guy."

"I hate you sometimes." Though, really, I'm fucking grateful for him. I've always hated bugs, but I also don't like the thought of killing anything, like, at all. When I was thirteen, right after our parents moved us in together, the spider incident took place. I screamed like a six-year-old girl. Ash ran into the room, ready to defend me from a psycho killer...that wasn't there. When he realized it was a bug, he grabbed a shoe to squash it, but I tackled him before he could.

"Can you...take it outside?"

His nose had wrinkled in confusion. I'd expected him to make fun of me, and then I'd have to kick my new stepbrother's ass, or you know, get really mad at him because I'm a lover not a fighter, but Ash had just nodded, got the jar I kept in my room, and took it out for me.

He's been doing it ever since.

Which maybe isn't a good thing. Why do I need Ash to be my bug protector? That's not normal, is it?

"Stop that."

"Stop what?" I ask before biting into my egg roll.

"How are you so full of confidence in some ways but

all overthinky, unsure of yourself, and clueless in others?"

"Because I'm super hot and everyone wants to fuck me?" I pump my brows. "Also, wow…ouch…"

Ash glares at me. "You know damn well I never would have said that if I thought it would hurt your feelings. You know you're goofy and sweet and my best friend."

My pulse runs a sprint at his compliment, and at the fact that he can read me well enough to know my feelings weren't really hurt. "Aw! You really do love me!" I tease. This banter we share is the best. No one knows me the way Ash does.

"You once got a splinter out of my ass cheek, Col. How could I not love you?"

"What about your ass?" a voice comes from behind me. I recognize it instantly. It's Atlas's friend Brenner, whom I never really had a problem with until he started flirting with Ash. I don't know why I care if he does. They're both bi, sex is fun, we're young and dumb, so we should enjoy all the fucking we want, but lately it's been rubbing me wrong. Not just when Brenner does it, but when anyone does. I chalk it up to being a protective brother. Ash keeps me safe from creepy-crawlies and doesn't tell anyone my scaredy-cat secret, and I spoil him and make sure anyone he hooks up with is good to him, and if they're not, I might suddenly be okay with violence.

"Just that it's the best on campus," Ash flirts. "That and my dick, depending on what someone's in the mood for."

While Brenner never used to annoy me, we're not super close to him either. Since Troy and Atlas started dating, Brenner and Taylor are around more because they're Atlas's friends. Hell, I didn't even know Atlas had friends before he fell in love with my best friend.

"I mean...I'd have to test them both out to say for sure." Brenner sits beside Ash, who smiles at the compliment.

"His ass is cute. All tight and round," I say, and Brenner's mouth drops open. "What? It is."

"Um..." Brenner looks back and forth between us.

"Colin didn't mean it like you think he does. And it's not you. We're just weird," Ash replies, which kicks my protective stepbro instincts in again.

"Also, keep your hands off Ash's butt."

"I'm so confused. Did something change between you?" Brenner scratches his head.

"No. Why?" I ask.

"Because you're telling me what his butt looks like?"

"No, I've been seeing that for ages. This isn't new."

"Not sexually," Ash throws out.

"Obviously," I reply.

"I'm not saying I wouldn't be interested..." Brenner interrupts us. "Might be fun being between two stepbrothers."

"We don't have sex with each other, or with the same person at the same time," Ash says in unison with my, "I'm straight, and I said hands off Ash."

"Are you sure you're straight? And are you even connected to reality right now?"

"Fuck off, Brenner." I dig into my food, taking a bite, then point to Ash with my fork. "You need to eat. We spent a lot of time talking, and you have to go to class soon."

"I'll do what I want, thank you," Ash replies playfully, but he does start to eat. I think he likes that I pay so much attention to him, which works because I like paying attention to him. It was an interesting dynamic when he had a crush on Troy. I had to work harder not to let it show that I'm protective of him, but for some reason, I also knew that Troy and Ash would never happen.

"Anyway, I don't want to interrupt this brotherly lovefest. Hit me up." Brenner nods at Ash, stands, and takes off. I feel Ash's gaze on me, but I don't meet it on purpose.

"You know I could have sex with Brenner if I wanted to, right?"

"I know." And really, I don't care. Much. But sometimes I wonder if I do...or why I would. "Do you want to have sex with Brenner?"

"That's beside the point." Ash takes another bite.

"Want me to go get him for you?"

Ash glares at me, the hints of gold and green in his hazel eyes sparkling in the sunlight.

"Aren't brothers supposed to protect each other's honor and shit?" I ask. "I'm just trying to do my job. We look out for each other."

No one else would see it, but I think Ash melts a little. While his parents love him, they're not the most attentive people in the world, and lucky for him, I am. Well, lucky for both of us, since I enjoy it too.

"You're too sweet for your own good." Ash gives me a cocky grin. "Take me to class?"

I roll my eyes, pretending it's the last thing I want to do, when really, I'm here for it. "Just halfway."

We dump our trash, and then Ash climbs on my back. I spoil my stepbrother by carrying him the whole way...and feel strangely proud of myself when I do.

3

Ash

THE FOLLOWING TUESDAY, after I finish my classes, I head back to the Alpha Theta Mu house. I hurry through my usual routine—snack, brush my teeth, shower up. I get dressed, then let my gerbils out of their cage and spend some time with them on my love seat while watching TV. Sagan's crawling around on my chest while I roll Darwin up in the hem of my shirt— she'd spend her life this way if she could.

There's a knock at my door, and I answer it with Sagan on my shoulder and Darwin still rolled up in my shirt.

"Oh, you got the mice out," Lance says.

"You know they're not mice."

"Yeah, Darwin and...what's the other one?"

"Sagan. I would've expected them to be great friends, but Sagan nips at Darwin a bit. Don't you, girl?"

Lance pulls a face before smiling. "Okay...some of the guys were gonna head down to the rec center for pickleball, if you want to come with. I almost texted, but then I was like, I can get off my lazy ass and knock next door."

"I would, but today's my meeting with Mom."

He chuckles, closing his eyes. "That's right. Maybe I was trying to block out the fact that you have to schedule your meetings with one of your parents."

"I'd complain, but since our therapist suggested this, it's actually been a lot better."

I have a strange relationship with my parents. They aren't like Steve, Colin's dad, who's very present and attentive, and who's been as good for me as Colin since they entered my life. Mom and Dad aren't really affectionate or emotional people. Highly intelligent, yes, but the qualities that have made them successful in their careers have made them struggle with parenting. And that Mom sets aside this time for me means a lot.

"Yeah, no, I wasn't meaning to criticize or joke," Lance says quickly, like he's horrified I might have mistaken his playful remark for anything else.

"I knew what you meant. But it's a no on pickleball for today. Maybe next time?"

"Of course." He starts like he's about to come in for a hug, but after eyeing Sagan, offers his fist for a bump.

I watch some more TV before my allotted four o'clock with Mom. Usually, she calls, but she can be a few minutes late, so I give her five before ringing her up, keeping her on speaker so I can manage Darwin and Sagan.

"Lauren Fuller speaking—oh, no, it's you, Ash. Sorry, I saw your name come up. I'm just in the middle of something and can't think straight."

I tense up. "In the middle of something? You remember this is our scheduled time, right?"

Yes, she has a difficult job. *"Criminals don't lock themselves up"* is always her joke at a party when it comes out she's a prosecutor with the DA.

Mom's not one for jokes.

Obviously.

But she is one for sticking to a tight schedule, so to say I'm stunned by this would be an understatement.

"Didn't Sarah get ahold of you?"

I grind my teeth. Sarah's Mom's personal assistant, who's probably responsible for more than a few of Colin's and my birthday and Christmas presents.

"Why would I talk to Sarah about our meeting?"

"She was supposed to call and reschedule because we have a deposition we couldn't get to until…right now. They're still parking, but they'll be in soon, and I'll have to go."

I run my hand through my hair. "And you couldn't text me to let me know?"

"I always get Sarah to change it. Is that wrong? Are you upset?"

It's true. I really shouldn't be surprised, and I can tell by the way she asks that it's a sincere question. She cares, but sometimes there's a real disconnect. "It's cool, Mom. So you've gotta go?"

"I have a few minutes. Is it something important?"

"If it was important, I'd just call whenever. I wouldn't need to schedule with Sarah."

"Are you being passive aggressive again?"

"What's passive about that?" Now I'm raising my voice. I take a breath. "I just wanted to tell you about my week. And hear how your week was going."

"But you can see why that's less of a priority for me than the deposition to put away a murderer, right?"

Is that even a fucking question?

"Just tell Sarah to make time to call me so that you can make time to call me."

"With how much time we spent on this call, I feel like I should have just asked you how your week was." She snickers, and I'm sure she thought that was funny. And it could be funny if this wasn't typical for her.

"I'd say you could call Steve," she says, "but he's at the golf course with a friend from college. What about your dad?"

"He's at a conference in Tokyo. And it's not like I have to talk to someone about my week. I wanted to talk to *you*. I'll figure it out, but thanks, Mom."

"Okay, Ash," she says like a goddamn robot.

"I'll talk to you later. I love you."

"Talk to you later. I love you too." I can tell she's forcing herself to say the words. Mom is not the show-your-feelings type, so fortunately, this is an area where therapy has helped us.

After we hang up, I'm on edge. I take Sagan in my hand and pet her to soothe myself.

Colin's out of his last class, and he's not working today, so I call him to tell him about the stunt Mom pulled. When he answers, he says, "I don't think Marty's gonna do well on his test tomorrow."

"I can hear you!" Marty says, which makes me laugh.

This is typically how Colin and I answer each other's calls. Not much "hey, how's it going?" We jump into whatever's going on.

"What are you guys up to?" I ask.

"Marty has a chem test tomorrow he needs to study for, and it's not going well."

"No offense, but he asked *you* to help him with chem?" I'm the unofficial tutor for all the guys at the frat, which I love, so I'm thrown.

"It's flashcards and memorization," Colin says. "Trust me, he'll be hitting you up too."

I chuckle. "Let him know I'm here when he's ready for me. Sorry it's not going well, though."

"Eh, it's Marty. Who cares?"

"Asshole!" Marty says.

"Oh, whatever. You love it."

The guys laugh before Colin's attention returns to me. "So really, what's up?"

"It's nothing. I can tell you later."

"You were talking to Lauren, weren't you? It's just past four, so that has to be it."

He knows me too well sometimes.

"Yeah. She bailed. She had a good excuse, but you know."

"I'm sorry about that. You want me to ditch Marty, come right home to cuddle you and hear all about your day?"

"You can't ditch me," Marty says, sounding stressed. "I will fail this test, lose my scholarship, and then some prick is gonna move into my room and make all your lives hell."

"Yeah, 'cause you make all our lives so much easier. You know, come to think of it, let me have a minute alone with these flashcards…"

"You big shit," Marty says.

"I'm teasing," Colin tells Marty. "I'm not letting you fail this test. I got you."

And he won't let him fail; that's the kind of guy Colin is.

So funny how a few minutes on the phone with Colin can cheer me right up after that bullshit with Mom.

"How about when I finish up," Colin says, "I come back, we get some takeout, and you tell me all about your week? Then maybe a movie?"

"Oh," Marty's voice comes from the background. "You didn't tell me I was keeping you from a date with your brother."

Getting his in, I figure.

But Colin and I have gotten enough jokes about our relationship over the years that this sort of comment doesn't really faze us.

"That sounds good," I say. "Get going. I'll be here when you get off."

"Get off? I feel like we're making more innuendos ever since we slept together."

We share a laugh. Marty groans, and Colin tells him, "You started it. Just wanting to hear about how I woke up with Ash's pretty lips around my dick."

"*I can't hear you. I can't hear you,*" Marty sings, and I don't have to be in the room to know he's got his hands over his ears.

"My lips are pretty?" I ask Colin.

"Shut the hell up. You know you have pretty lips."

Why does that make my cheeks warm? Kind of makes me think of last week when he was talking about my ass.

Whatever.

"Okay, get back to helping Marty. I'll talk to you

later."

After we get off the phone, I return Darwin and Sagan to their cage and use some hand sanitizer.

Even though I feel better knowing Colin will be around later, I still feel kinda shitty. But I know just what I need to take the edge off. I plop down on the bed and roll over, retrieving lube from my nightstand, when my gaze shifts to my phone, sitting on the edge of the bed.

A wicked impulse stirs within me.

I pick up the phone and scroll through my apps until I see the symbol for Manzturbate—a live stream site where men post amateur videos, usually doing sexual things to earn comments and tokens you can trade in for cash. I first discovered the app a few months ago when a guy I hooked up with was telling me my load was worthy of some Manzturbate attention.

I was nervous about posting something online, but most of the guys on the app don't show their faces, and after the idea kept coming back to me, it was hard to resist the temptation to give it a try.

Even harder the second time.

Am I really considering a third?

I hop up from my bed, heading over to my desk, where I set the lube down and rig my phone mount.

I toss off my shirt and sit in front of the phone, excitement rushing through me at the thought of getting the comments and the tokens just for showing off my muscles, cock, and load.

But there's something else there too.

A bit of guilt.

Back when Colin and I were first adjusting to the whole stepbrother thing, we made two lists to help us navigate the situation. In one column was Step Dos. In the other, Step Don'ts.

Step Dos are shit like "do be respectful of each other's time," "do communicate if there are issues," "do take turns cleaning the bathroom." Step Don'ts are things like "don't throw the other under the bus with our parents" and "don't hog the TV." But the most important Step Don't was "don't keep secrets," something that came from the fact that our parents had kept their relationship secret from us. We only found out when the work scandal broke—prosecutor and defense on the same case. We heard about it at work events, parties…even kids at school were talking about it. Fortunately for Mom and Steve, no one could prove it, so they didn't lose their jobs, but Colin and I knew the truth, and we knew our parents were lying to save face.

Not that they're terrible people, but the scandal wasn't great for two middle schoolers who had enough to deal with.

So when we said "don't keep secrets," we weren't talking about what we did in private. We didn't chat about intimate details after we became sexually active with our girlfriends.

Colin doesn't want to hear about my sex life. Hell, he can barely tolerate Brenner flirting with me. And I'm sure the only reason he was cool with me crushing on Troy was because he knew his bestie wasn't into me.

No, what I'm about to do isn't something he would need to know about.

But then, why do I feel a pang of guilt?

I shake my head, pushing my worry aside the way I have the other times it's come up. Then I pull up my account on the app, aptly named fratwiz20. I log in and adjust my camera to catch my body, keeping my face out of the shot and setting my glasses on the desktop.

Excitement pulses through me.

Of course, there are nerves too. What if no one comes into my live room?

But apparently, I'm not too nervous because I press the Go Live button and lean back in my chair so that my chest and abs are on full display.

My cheeks are warm.

This is so naughty. So dirty.

I wonder if I like it so much because no one would suspect I would be into something like this. Just innocent, nerd-boy extraordinaire with an impressive GPA, who happens to love equations and helping a bud out by tutoring him for an upcoming test.

A few moments pass, my nerves intensifying before the first couple of users enter my live room. Then a few more before the comments start.

feralmanho1e: saw this guy last time he was on. sexy bod.

th1rstyb0ywantzluv: LOVE tht chst.

sweetslibrarian78: im here for this.

I figure some of these might be from my new followers whom the app notified I was on. Pretty good for this only being my third time.

I fondle my chest and flex my arms for the camera. I wish this came more naturally for me. I'm sure a lot of the guys on here are sex studs who are so slick and suave. But I'm just starting out. Hopefully I'll get better.

Get better? Am I already considering doing this more?

I run my finger around my nipple before trailing my hand down my abs, past my happy trail, playing around the fly of my jeans.

th1rstyb0ywantzluv: yesss...

As the number of viewers increases, a barrage of compliments eggs me on, so I stand up, positioning myself so I can remove my pants.

The token ticker increases as I'm lauded with more compliments.

But I'm not just gonna give them this dick.

No, they love the tease. And so do I.

I pull my pants down, kicking them off, so I'm just

in my boxers. As I rub my crotch, my dick's so fucking hard. Painfully hard, which is making the comments go wild as they beg and plead for more.

feralmanho1e: wait til u see the guys load.

Warmth radiates in my chest and cheeks. I love a compliment.

I tuck my boxers down, placing the waistband under my balls, revealing my cock for them.

noobPup85: Jerk it.

cumGuzzzl3r: jack it.

Live4theapplause: shut 4 us, fratwhiz!

After I remove my boxers the rest of the way, I sit in my chair, leaning back to display my naked body for them. I'm grinning ear to ear as I pump some lube, then take my cock in my hand and play with myself. As I stroke the shaft, I continue fondling my body.

feralmanho1e: Ur killing me!

sweetslibrarian78: *heart emoji*

It's hard for me to pin down why I enjoy this so much. There's something about it being naughty. About them being willing to pay and beg me for this. About getting myself off.

But mostly, the praise and attention. Not of my brains. Of my body. I just want to be an object. Their worshipped object.

It feels so good to have all these eyes on me, of people wanting to see me pleasure myself fully. And I want to give it to them.

As I jerk myself, I play with my chest with my free hand, massaging my pec, stressing the form in my bicep for them—they fucking love that shit. I leave my mouth hanging open just enough so it's in the frame.

They're begging for me to come, and I'm ready to give it to them, when I think of my texts with Colin. *"We can bang later."*

I smirk at the ridiculous thought and his comment today—*"You know you have pretty lips"*—but then suddenly there's this jolt rocking my entire fucking body before I'm shooting all over my abs and even up to my chest.

It doesn't stop—I keep dumping my load across myself, a thick, juicy mess. It glides down my body, streaming through the grooves in my muscles.

I always come a lot, but this is even more than normal, and I know it's because of how much I fucking enjoyed doing this.

I peek to see the chat group going wild with excitement over it.

Then I lean back in my chair, reveling in the delicious satisfaction.

Weird to think that one minute I'm worried I could be committing a Step Don't, and the next I'm thinking about Colin right before I come.

Bet he'd give me hell for that one.

4

Colin

"WHAT'S UP?" I head into Troy's room and collapse onto his bed. I just finished up in class for the day, and I have a small break before I have to be at one of my jobs. I should probably get started on my homework, but I'm pretty good at getting it done quickly. This shit comes naturally to me, like somehow it was ingrained into my DNA because I have lawyers as parents.

"Nothing. Finishing up homework." Troy is sitting at his computer desk, wearing a crop top and jeans. I can only assume Atlas is busy since he's not here.

"Yeah, I have work to do too. Where's your boy?"

Troy gives me a sharp but playful look. "We're not together all the time."

"I never said you were." I chuckle, walk over, and pick up a tee on his desk. There's no doubt in my mind it's Atlas's. "But when he's not here, you always have one of these." I pull it to my face teasingly, before Troy pushes out of his chair and tackles me to his bed so he can wrestle it away.

I laugh, enjoying these times with him. When his elbow accidentally lands in my gut, I make an *umpf* sound and let go of the tee. "I give up."

"No one is allowed to smell him but me." He balls up the shirt and tucks it close to him.

"You're so weird."

"It's hot."

I shrug, not really getting it myself, but not one to kink shame.

"Where's Ash?" Troy sits back down in the chair.

"He's in class, and I'm chillin' before work."

"Atlas ran into him in the dining hall earlier. He said they had lunch together."

"Look at our stepbros bonding." I pick up the football Troy keeps by his nightstand, twisting it around in my hands. We played together in high school, and I loved it, but an injury sidelined him from playing college football.

"I definitely didn't see that coming."

It's not like Atlas and Ash are besties. This is the first time they've done something like have lunch together, just the two of them. I would know otherwise. But Atlas has softened toward Ash over the past few weeks. Since Ash used to have a crush on Troy when he was tutoring him, he'd playfully flirt with Troy, and he even bid on him in an auction. No one knew Troy was hooking up with Atlas at the time. I've since learned that Atlas got a bit stabby about Ash because he used to want to bone Troy.

In some ways I get it. Like I said, I'm protective of my stepbrother too, though we clearly don't have the same relationship as Atlas and Troy. It's strange how it never really bothered me when Ash liked Troy—or maybe not so strange since I trust Troy wouldn't have ever hurt him. If anything had gone down, it would have been a hookup and then that's it.

"Atlas is practically a docile kitten now that he's with you." He is actually the opposite of that, but I also know there's a softer side to him that he mostly only feels comfortable showing to Troy.

Troy lets out a laugh. "First, he absolutely is not, and second, don't ever let him hear you say that."

"I'm not scared of your boyfriend." I flex my biceps, earning myself a shake of the head from Troy. "Hey, if you have time, you should come to the park with me." Along with my part-time position at a local law office as a legal assistant, I teach small-group football lessons to middle schoolers. Ash had a hard time in middle school, and in a lot of ways, I did too. It's when my parents separated, and Mom moved to North Carolina. I made the decision to stay in Georgia, and not long after, my dad and Ash's mom were together. Getting close to Ash helped, but I know he had a harder time. I think he felt alone. Even though my mom moved, we're still close and talk all the time. I spend holidays with her and my sister, Emily, and visit in the summer. My parents are the type who hug us all the time and make sure we know they love us. Ash's parents love him, but they're both hands-off. On top of that, he had bullying issues around the same time, and yeah, like I said, middle school wasn't easy on him. I like the idea of being there for kids around the same age—giving them an outlet so they know they always have someone in their corner, like Ash might not have had if it wasn't for me.

Troy's eyes light up. "I can do that."

"Bet. Get ready. We leave in ten."

He nods, and I go to my room to get changed. Ash will be out of class soon, but he has to intern for a few hours at the biomedical research lab on campus.

Troy and I head out a few minutes later. The park is within walking distance of Peach State, but we take my car because of all the supplies.

When we pull up, the six kids who take the lessons are already there. Troy and I grab the bags from the back and head over to the kids. Their parents are all waiting at picnic tables, most of them glued to their phones.

"Hey, crew." The group is made up of four boys and two girls, which I think is fucking awesome. It's cool that we have girls who love football so much that they're here, even though they would never be able to play on their school teams. Some of them have started playing in girls' flag football programs, which I would love to see become a more widespread thing. "I brought my friend Troy with me today. He's not nearly as good as I am, but he might have a little knowledge to impart to you."

My joke earns me snickers from the kids and a playful scowl from my friend.

"Okay. Let's set up for drills!" I clap my hands together, and we jump into our warm-ups and then offensive drills. The two hours go by in the blink of an eye, and before I know it, the kids are helping pack up and their parents are coming over to thank me and say goodbye.

"That was fun," Troy says. Despite the spring nip in the air, we're both a sweaty mess.

"Yeah, I fucking love it."

My phone buzzes in my pocket, and I pull it out.

Ash: How was practice?

I can't help smiling. I love that he knows I just finished and is checking in. Ash knows how important this is to me, and it means the world to me that he cares.

Me: Great! They were, of course, still amazed at my talent.

Ash: As they should be. He adds a wink emoji, and I feel my grin grow. Why does everything about Ash make me smile?

"I recognize that smile. Did you meet a woman?"

Troy asks, and my nose wrinkles.

"What? No. That was Ash, and I don't have an I-met-a-woman smile." But when I think about it... "Though it has been a long time since I've met and hooked up with anyone. I miss sex."

"You were with Hannah, like, three weeks ago."

"That's a long time. Great, now I'm horny."

We grab all our shit and pile into the car.

Me: Troy got me horny.

Ash: He has that effect on people. So now you can't get on me about how much I had the hots for him last semester. *laughing emoji*

I frown. What? *Oooh.* I roll my eyes.

Me: Not like that. I'm not attracted to him.

"Will the two of you be busy long?" Troy breaks into my thoughts while I'm watching my phone and waiting for Ash to reply.

"Shit. Sorry. You know me. Easily distracted."

I toss my phone into the center console and drive us back to our house. Troy doesn't even come inside, heading straight for his vehicle because he's staying at Atlas's tonight.

The house is empty, everyone else off doing their own thing.

I take a quick shower, then remember I left my phone in my car and go out to grab it.

Ash: Of course not. But you're missing out. Men are hot too.

Me: I can appreciate a good-looking guy. Just never had one get me hard.

I've gotten a boner when I've landed on gay porn once or twice during my searching, but who wouldn't get hard watching anyone fuck? It had nothing to do with the guys; it was the sex.

Ash: They can do a lot more than get you hard. *wink emoji* Want me to bring home dinner?

Me: Is there a reality where I would ever say no to food? Are you going to the gym first?

Ash: I went this morning.

Me: Good because I'm starving.

I do some homework, then log in to play *Final Fantasy* before Ash gets home. I'm not sure where everyone in the house is, but I'm kinda glad they're out.

When I hear his footsteps on the stairs, my stomach automatically growls. Ash pushes open my door with a large pizza in his hands, and I can't help moaning in response.

"Fuck yes. Best. Brother. Ever."

"Surely, you can't just now be realizing this."

Ash sets the pizza on my desk. The T-shirt he's wearing showcases his firm, cut biceps he worked on in the gym this morning.

"Is that a new shirt?"

Ash plops a few slices of pepperoni on a paper plate and frowns like my question surprises him. "No. I've had it for a while."

Hm. I don't remember seeing him wear it before.

Though it's not like I have every piece of his clothing memorized, so it's logical that I wouldn't remember it.

Ash hands the plate over before making one for himself, then going to my mini fridge to grab drinks for us. We're so comfortable in each other's space that neither of us would think to ask before doing something like going into the other's fridge.

"Fuck, this is good." I take a bite, and Ash sits on my bed and does the same. "How was work?"

We chat about our day while we eat, then end up playing video games, until doors begin slamming downstairs, alerting us that people are getting home. "What time are we going to Mom and Steve's?" Ash asks. We're heading there next week, and I figure he's mentally working out his schedule. My dad is better at keeping me in the loop than his mom is. Lauren is so fucking smart and ambitious, and I know how much she loves Ash—loves both of us—but she's not one to show it, even if she wasn't so busy all the time.

I've always felt lucky in that respect, and for what it's worth, Dad does soften some of Lauren's rougher edges.

"Dad said four. Did Lauren tell you why she couldn't make it to your last phone call?" I've wanted to ask, but the last thing I want is to remind Ash of something painful, and I guess I'm holding out hope that it was for a good reason.

"She had a deposition. Sarah was supposed to reschedule but didn't." He picks up his phone and looks at something before saying, "Wanna watch a movie?"

"I'm down." I stand up and tug my shirt off, making my hat fall to the floor. I pick it back up and place it on my head.

"You and those damn hats."

"I look hot in them."

Ash shrugs. "Truth."

We strip down to our underwear, and I hit the lights. It's late, so there's no doubt one or both of us will fall asleep before the movie is over.

I grab my laptop, the two of us settling on an action movie. Ash sets the computer on my nightstand, then lies on his side, and I snuggle in behind him, with my arm around him.

Leaning down, face close to his hair, I inhale.

"Did you just smell me?"

"I like the scent of your apple shampoo." I breathe it in again.

"We should really evaluate how often we're in bed together."

"I mean, who doesn't like cuddling?"

"Most stepbrothers."

I smile into his hair. "They don't got nothin' on us."

Ash chuckles like he does when he doesn't know what to do with me. Right before I fall asleep, I'm pretty sure I hear him reply, "No, they don't."

5

Ash

"ASH, I KNOW this is gonna sound like a dumb question..." Angie says as she enters our shared cubicle.

Angie's another new intern, working with me at Peach State's biomed research lab. Right now, I'm only doing data analysis and familiarizing myself with the tech, but being part of this exciting intersection of technology and health is why I became a biomedical engineering major. I like learning the ropes, and I imagine really getting into the swing of things, fantasizing about the day something in this place triggers an idea for my master's thesis and eventually my dissertation.

Even just knowing Angie has a question for me gets me going. I'm armed not just with everything I've learned the past few months at the lab, but with the knowledge I've acquired in my own research outside of school.

"Lay it on me, Ang!"

"The new espresso machine. Where do you put the grinds in?"

"Oh…yeah, I can help with that."

Admittedly, a bit of a letdown, but I get up and head to the break room, navigating her through the new espresso machine, which I can understand might be confusing.

There are a lot of duties I perform as an intern that I feel like don't fully utilize my talents, but I get that this is part of paying my dues. And I'm eager to put in the work, even if that means explaining to most everyone on my floor how to use the new espresso machine.

After offering Angie a brief tutorial, I head back to my desk and finish up on my files for the day. It's just past six when I head out of the mid-rise building. Dad called while I was working, so I FaceTime him on my way through the parking lot.

"Morning, Ash," he answers. I'm about to correct him when he says, "Oh, guess it's late afternoon there."

"Yeah, I was gonna ask if you wanted me to call you when I get back to the frat. Just finished my internship hours for the day and heading back."

He cringes. "Actually, I have a tour of Kyoto in a bit."

After Dad's conference in Tokyo, he and some friends were planning to see the sights around Japan.

"That's why I called earlier," he adds. "I'm supposed

to meet the guys in the hotel lobby in five."

"You and Mom are real busy recently," I say through my teeth.

"She mentioned what happened last time you were supposed to chat. Not exactly Mother of the Year, is she?" As I tense up, he quickly adds, "Sorry, that wasn't a nice thing to say about your mother. I know I'm not Father of the Year, and she's been the one you've lived with for most of your life. I was just trying to make light of things."

Dad tries, but even when I was little, he tended to try to cheer me up by cracking awkward jokes to avoid emotional moments. He's gotten a lot better about making sure he's not dismissing my feelings. It's a process, and I appreciate both Mom's and Dad's work on our shit. Just like I appreciate he remembered to give me a call even when he's traveling.

I open the door of my Honda Civic and slide into the driver's seat.

"I'll call you another day, Ash. I promise. Tell you all about the trip. Sorry again about the timing."

"It's okay." But I can't disguise the disappointment in my tone.

We exchange I-love-yous before ending the call. I tuck my phone away and grunt out my frustration as I start the car.

The engine revs.

Then cuts off.

I try again with the same result.

Uh-oh.

COLIN AND I sit on a bench in the waiting area at the auto repair shop where Troy works.

After Colin showed up at the lab, he waited with me while the truck driver finished getting my car rigged to the tow truck. Then we followed him to the garage.

Fortunately, Troy's working today, so he's been generous enough to take a look to see if he can figure out what's wrong.

"Yeah, we're still waiting to see what's up," Colin says, holding up his phone with Steve on FaceTime.

I called Steve while we were waiting in the parking lot, but he called to check in.

"Okay, boys. You just let me know if you need anything. And text me when you find out what's wrong. Love you guys."

As Colin returns the words, I chime in, "Love you too, Steve."

After he hangs up, I tell Colin, "You really didn't have to come. AAA's taken good care of me. And I could have just Ubered back to the frat."

Although, I'd be lying if I said I didn't prefer my bro

having my back.

Things are always better with Colin.

He glares at me because I know damn well nothing I could have said would have stopped him from heading over once he found out my car wouldn't start. "You just don't want me to keep you from flirting with Troy," Colin teases, setting his phone on his thigh. "*Do you have any more tests coming up in Thermo? I would love to tutor you.*"

"Why do I sound so dumb in your impersonation?"

Colin keeps on, without changing his tone. "*Oh, it's getting so hot in here, let me take this off real quick.*" He starts hiking up his shirt, revealing those bulky muscles that anyone would have to be impressed by…and slightly turned on. And yes, that includes me. I'm only fucking human.

I grab his wrist and tug it down so he won't strip right here in the shop. "You asshat. I've been good ever since he and Atlas got together."

Colin turns to the garage door. "*Big Troy, why don't you come in here and take me? Take me, Troy. I'm all yours.*"

"He might hear you." I can tell this isn't gonna deter Colin, so I snatch his phone off his leg, keying in his passcode. "Maybe I can text that Phi Kappa girl you hooked up with."

"Her name's Hannah."

"You remember her name? Oh, you must be in love."

"I always remember girls' names."

It's true. He's very much that kind of guy, but if he's gonna give me hell, I can give him some too.

"Bet she's in recent messages," I say. "Wonder what I could tell her."

"Two can play at this game." Colin reaches into the front pocket of my jacket, grabbing my phone. "I'll hop on Grindr and maybe start chatting up your last trick."

I know he's not intending to follow through with this any more than I'm intending to invade his privacy, but he keys into my phone and scrolls through my apps like he's about to, when his brows tug closer together.

"What's Manzturbate?"

I freeze.

The blood in my face drains.

My throat's dry.

I'm struggling to think straight.

"What? No, it's nothing," I say so defensively, I know now Colin won't have a choice but to question further.

"Is it a hookup app? Like Grindr?"

It would be so easy to say yes, but "don't lie" is about as big a Step Don't as "don't keep secrets."

I don't lie to Colin.

Ever.

I hand him back his phone. "Seriously, just let me

have my phone back."

He hands it over, eyeing me like I've grown a third eyeball, which makes total sense because this is not me.

Not us.

Like, at all.

Since we were kids, I've told him almost everything. He's the first person I told I was being bullied in middle school, who talked me into going to administration, and who confronted them with enough force that I was never bothered again. Hell, he knew when I had my first bi impulses, the moment I started feeling attraction toward guys as well as girls. I've told him about hookups, break-ups...

But not this.

I'm struggling to think how to make sense of what I just did without revealing the truth, when the garage door opens and Troy says, "Okay, looks like it's a bad starter. Common issue. I can get you set up in a few days, once I get the right part in."

I head to the main desk, and Troy and I go back and forth about the price because he's trying to give me labor for free, which doesn't sound fair, but he finally convinces me.

This whole time, there's this tension in my chest. Colin's trying to play it cool with his bestie, but he's looking like the time he was at the bottom of a tackle in the fourth quarter against the Bulldogs—out of it, in a daze.

I'm running through my head what the fuck I'm gonna tell him about that app…

That I've live streamed myself jerking off for people?

That I've done it more than once?

That I want to do it more?

That I don't know why?

After we finish up with Troy, we head to Colin's car, and as we get inside, he says, "Are we gonna talk about what just happened?"

"Can we please wait until we get back to the house?"

He grimaces. I'm sure he's trying to make sense of why I'm acting like this.

"Please," I beg.

"Yeah, totally."

I feel like shit all the way back to the house; in all the time we've known each other, the only time Colin's been this quiet with me in a car has been when he's passed out.

I'm hoping I'll have something to say by the time we get back, but I'm just spinning in my thoughts about the naughty things I've done on that app and the guilt of the big Step Don't I've committed.

I reflect on those twinges of guilt when I was recording.

He wouldn't want to know this, I told myself, but clearly, he fucking does.

But this is so private...

Yet when the hell have Colin and I ever done private?

I'm on edge as Colin leads me to his room, closing the door, his expression serious as ever.

"Okay, so I waited."

"I..."

I still don't know what the fuck to say!

"If this is that serious, you know I would never make you talk about anything you didn't want to," he says. "I won't even google it if you tell me not to. But you can understand why I'm confused, right? I find a hookup app on your phone, and you've shown me guys on Grindr, so I don't understand why this is something you feel you have to keep from me."

Which puts me in a weird-ass position. "Maybe this is just what a good boundary for us is," I say quickly, and his expression twists up.

"Boundary?"

He sounds sincerely thrown at the notion of a boundary between us, and I can't blame him.

"Yeah, like healthy relationship boundaries. You know, so we're not like some messed-up, codependent stepbrothers."

"But we're kind of codependent, right? That's what I love about us."

That's what I love about us too.

Fuck, he's making this hard.

"I just mean, I really don't want to answer this question, Colin. And I don't think you would like me to answer it either."

Judging by his expression, you'd have thought I stomped across the room and decked him.

And it's the hurt that stings the most.

Even worse, I know he has a right to be hurt.

"What about no secrets?" he asks. When I don't answer, he adds, "Whatever it is, I'm sure you're being safe, so I guess other than that, it's none of my business." He hangs his head. Despite wanting to give me my privacy, it's clear how much this pains him.

Fuck me. Right in the jugular.

I pull my phone out of my jacket, looking at the black screen, my face warming as I think about the glimpse he got into my dirty secret. This is so fucking embarrassing, but I can't do this to him. I'd rather endure any amount of humiliation than see him hurt.

"Okay, I'm just gonna say it, since you want to know. Just try to be open-minded."

His gaze wavers, as though he's trying to imagine what I could possibly be about to share, but I sincerely doubt he's gonna figure it out on his own.

So.

Here goes...

"So one of my Grindr dates," I say, my cheeks burning more and more as I go on, "he showed me this app he was on called Manzturbate. People can go on there and post amateur videos of themselves for people to comment on. They're paid in tokens, which convert into cash. And people watch this kind of stuff and—"

Colin chuckles, closing his eyes. "Oh God, Ash." He breathes a deep sigh of relief, as though he'd been imagining something far worse.

Not the reaction I was expecting.

As he reopens his eyes, he says, "This is what you were so worried about telling me? Seriously?" He rests his hands on my shoulders. "I totally get it, man."

I hesitate. "You do?"

"Dude, you should see some of the porn I watch. I don't care that you like finding guys on live video streams."

Oh… I realize there's been a little miscommunication.

"Why did you think I would freak out over that?" he asks, and he's got that beautiful clueless look in his eyes. It's that lovable Lab who thinks I'm about to throw the ball, not give him a bath.

A part of me wants to let him live with his delusion, but I've come too far to stop now. "Colin, I'm one of the people making videos on this app."

He smirks, eyeing me like he's waiting for me to say, *"Just kidding!"* When I don't, his expression turns serious. "Huh?"

"I've made a few videos for people to watch me do sessions…jerking off."

His brows shift subtly as he wears a familiar expression—like in high school when I was helping him with precalc. "Oh…" He releases my shoulders and turns away from me, starting toward the bed.

It's a weird reaction from the guy who, when I came out to him, threw his arms around me and said, *"I'll always love you, no matter who you fuck around with."*

What does he think? Why isn't he saying anything?

"Colin…"

"Yeah, yeah. I'm just…"

"Are you mad that I did this?"

He turns sharply back to me, and again, I see the hurt in his expression. Like my Lab's coming home with a broken leg. It burns in my fucking chest. The kind of burn that makes me wish I could go back in time and redo this whole conversation, tell him everything the moment he asked.

"You think I'd be mad?"

I'm struggling to read his expression.

I, Ash Fuller, can't read Colin Phillips's expression?

The world is coming to an end.

"You're not talking," I say. "You're not telling me what you're thinking. This is weirding me out."

"Yeah, well, then you know how I'm feeling now."

Ooh, fuck him for being right.

"I don't understand it," he says, "but there are other things I haven't understood about you. I know it's not the same as something like this, but I didn't get you being queer; I wasn't mad at you about it, though."

"No, I didn't mean... I don't know what I meant, Colin. You're just acting strange."

"I'm not the one keeping this big secret. We don't do that. What about our Step Don'ts? We don't have secrets."

No, we don't. It's a sore spot for both of us because of Mom and Dad, and I'm sure this is digging at him, and I'm the reason he's hurting.

And it's killing me.

"I don't understand why you wouldn't trust me with this."

"It's not that I don't trust you, Col. It's just...I didn't think it was the kind of thing that my brother would want to know about."

It's more than that, but I stop there.

"I can wake up in bed naked with you and not have an issue, but you think I would draw the line at knowing you jerk off on camera?"

"Those aren't the same thing."

Colin stares off for a moment, and I wait for a reaction before he says, "I think I need to sort through some things."

"Sort through some things?" Why am I not understanding any of his reactions?

"I need to get my head around this."

"Let's talk about it. I'll tell you whatever you want to know."

It's like he's unintentionally waterboarding me, and now I'll confess to anything. Hell, if I could think of another secret I'd kept from him, I'd be out with it right now to end this agony.

Colin nods. "Yeah, I just…need some space."

"Space?" I ask, like it's a foreign concept.

He starts for the door.

Colin has never walked out like this before. Hell, I can't even remember us ever having an actual fight.

Not that this is anything like a fight to normal people, but when the fuck have we been normal?

He heads out, closing the door behind him, leaving me reeling in a big what-the-fuck before he comes back in.

"This is my room," he says, holding the door open.

This is all so much that I can't even enjoy the classic Clueless Colin moment as I step out into the hall.

His gaze meets mine, and I see something I don't recognize there. "I just gotta sort through this, Ash. I'll be fine."

As he closes the door, it's like I've been connected to an oxygen concentrator and he just snipped the cord.

The tension that started when he saw the app has

intensified, tight bands constricting my chest as my mind spins out, because my whole reality with Colin has just shifted.

Space?

I'm definitely too codependent for this.

6

Colin

OKAY, SO I can fully admit that a lot of the time, when it comes to stuff that's not book smarts, I can be a bit lost. This isn't one of those times, not really, but then maybe it is.

"Ugh!" I groan into my empty room, unsure of what I feel, much less if I have the right to feel it. This soft voice in my brain that doesn't always speak up tells me I'm overreacting. So Ash jerks off on camera. It's not the end of the world. To each their own and all that, but then...then that's not the part that has me in a tailspin, is it?

This whole situation is less about him doing it and more about the fact that he didn't tell me, that he *didn't want* to tell me. He would have actively tried to keep it from me if he could, and that's what has confusion going wild in my head.

Anyone else could keep this secret from me and I wouldn't bat an eye, but this is Ash. My Ash. My person.

RILEY HART & DEVON McCORMACK

The one who came to me when he was bullied, the boy who helped me hide stray animals when we were young and I tried to sneak them into the house. The one who talks to me about how stuff with his mom makes him feel. We're a team, and no matter how many mental gymnastics I go through, I can't figure out why he would commit this Step Don't with me.

Why didn't he think he could trust me?

Have I done something to make him feel like he can't come to me with anything? He's the only person who could say, *Here's this dead guy I just killed*, and I'd be like, *What time do we go hide the body?*

Despite that, Ash didn't tell me.

What did I do wrong?

If I could understand why Ash is into it, why he wanted to keep it from me, then all the pieces would fit together.

I think…

Maybe…

Who the hell knows because in the almost ten years we've been stepbrothers, this situation never occurred.

I plop down on my bed, unable to find it in myself to care that I'm pouting. I close my eyes, and the first thing that pops into my head is the dejected look in his hazel eyes. He looked like I hurt him, but the thing is, he hurt me too. I don't care if we're codependent. This is us, and it's never caused us any problems before.

But he's also my Ash…my cuddly bro. My favorite person to talk to and spend time with. A guy couldn't ask for a better brother, and I'm the lucky one who has him. I don't have it in me to hurt him, so even though my heart is still banging against my chest and my thoughts are still spinning out of control with questions like *why* and…well, just *why, why, and why?* I push to my feet, quietly grumbling while I walk down the hallway to his bedroom.

I knock, and a second later it pulls open. "I would hide a body with you, Ash."

His brows pull together behind his glasses. "Just to confirm, is there currently a body we're talking about?"

I huff, annoyed but trying not to smile because he's Ash and he knows how to make me do that. I squeeze into his room and fall onto his bed, looking at the ceiling. "Remember when I had those glow-in-the-dark stars over my bed when we were kids?"

Ash climbs onto the mattress beside me. "And one day, while you were gone, I wrote my name in them."

A stupid, annoying grin tugs at my lips. "Yes. I wouldn't let you change it afterward, and I bought more with my allowance and put my name on your ceiling too."

"Wow, we're definitely codependent."

"We're brothers."

Ash sighs. "We're not normal brothers, Col."

No, we're not. Even I get that, but. "I like us."

He cuddles close, setting his head on my pec. "I like us too."

"Then why didn't you tell me? I don't understand why you would try to keep this from me. Why you thought I would care. That's what hurts the most—that you didn't trust me or thought I would what, judge you?"

"*I* judge me."

I frown and sit up, and he does the same.

"Why?"

"I don't really... I don't know. Did you ever think that maybe I didn't tell you because I can't figure out why I'm doing it myself? If I can't explain it in my own head, how can I explain it to you?"

"There are a lot of things that go on in my head that I can't explain."

"That's not true. You're smart as hell. Almost as smart as me, but only almost."

The annoying Ash-induced smile returns.

"I'm better at law stuff."

"Don't sell yourself short. You're all right with a football too." We're joking, being playful, but then he looks away, eyes on his comforter as he draws pictures with the tip of his finger on it.

"What's wrong?" I hook my finger beneath his chin and tilt his head up.

"I don't want to fight with you, Col. And I don't want to make you feel like I don't trust you. I don't trust anyone more than you. It just…it feels good, and I don't know why it feels so good. Especially when I don't think it should."

Well, now I feel like an ass for being so hard on him. Funny how I can be hurt and annoyed but also feel guilty. "Maybe I would get it if I like…watched you do it?"

Ash's eyes go wide, his cute little mouth dropping open. "Excuse me, what?"

"I can be off camera. I'll see what happens, how you react and all that, and maybe that will help us both understand." I beam, feeling like the smartest person in the world. It's the perfect solution, and maybe I'll see something that clues Ash in on what the public jerkoffs do for him, which will help him but also help us understand why he didn't tell me. "I'm a genius!" I throw my arms in the air.

"Except for the small detail that you're asking to see me jerk off! Jesus, Col. That's a terrible idea."

I frown. "Why? It's not like it means anything. I've been naked in bed with you. Hell, I've seen you jack off before."

"That's not the same." He sounds exhausted by me. "And an accident."

"Well, me walking in was an accident, but the fact

that I didn't walk out and then watched porn with you while tugging on my boner was absolutely not an accident." It hadn't been planned, sure, and it's not something we ever did again, but this wouldn't be any different.

"We were horny teens, and half the time we were making jokes about what we were watching. That was totally different. Why would you want to see me jerk off anyway? You're straight."

Which is true, but this isn't about sex. This is about trying to understand something Ash doesn't get. I know him. He likes answers. He's always had answers, so for him, not getting where this is coming from is probably stressing him out. "It's like an experiment...a sexperiment."

"I thought this wasn't about sex?"

"It's not, but the play on words was fun."

Ash laughs like I hoped he would, before sobering. "I really am sorry I didn't tell you. I wish I understood it better so I could have talked to you about it sooner."

"I know." I wrap my arm around him and pull him close. We lie down on the bed together again, my fingers running through his hair. "I'm sorry I freaked out on you. I don't know why I did that. I just... This feels like a big Step Don't, and I'm not sure why."

Ash sets his hand on my abs, tracing each indent between muscles with his finger. "I feel the same. Maybe if I figured out why, I could either jump in full steam ahead or pull back."

"Maybe." I don't offer to watch him again. The last thing I want is to come off as creepy. He knows the offer stands.

"No more secrets," Ash says.

"Deal."

We're quiet for a moment. He's drawing stars on my stomach, maybe because of our conversation earlier. I let him be, knowing Ash needs that sometimes. Plus, I like sitting in the quiet with him, feeling the soft strands of his brown hair fall through my fingers.

"Can I think about it?" Ash asks a few minutes later.

"The offer to watch? Of course. No obligation either way, but maybe it will help us get to the bottom of it."

Ash laughs, but I'm not sure why.

We lie there together, close. This isn't out of the ordinary for us, but we're soaking it in a bit longer, a little differently because of our argument. It's a territory Ash and I aren't familiar with navigating.

Music starts playing downstairs as our roommates and frat bros get home.

"Fuck. I forgot we have a frat meeting tonight." Ash lets go and rolls away from me, my body feeling…funny.

I jump to my feet and stand in front of him. "Climb on."

"You can't take the stairs with me on your back."

"Yes I can."

"Well, I'm not going to argue."

I chuckle. "I had a feeling you wouldn't."

Ash climbs onto my back and wraps his legs and arms around me. This started out as a joke when we were kids—me wanting to show how strong I was, betting how long I could carry him around. Then we'd try for longer and longer each time, before we realized we both liked it. It feels good to be something, anything, for Ash.

I carry him, Ash jumping off when we get downstairs.

The house is busier than usual because of the meeting—more people than just our roommates are packed into the living room. Lance is standing in front of the TV at this wooden podium he bought, and he bangs his gavel on it. It's wild that he's our president. I remember when his bid was a running joke, which got out of hand, but since he won, he's really stepped up to the challenge. He's the best prez since I've been here.

"Now that the brothers are here," Lance says, "we can get started."

"We're all brothers," I say.

There's a space on the couch, really one that's too small, but I force my ass between Troy and Payton, then pull Ash down onto my lap.

Lance ignores me and gets started on the meeting. We go over finance, which Payton gets up to talk about, then volunteer and charity ideas, and parties, before landing on TaskFrat Challenge, which is where Ash perks up, before we get back to parties again.

I'm not sure we actually make any decisions, but I think we all feel more responsible when it's over.

Everyone hangs out at our house for a bit, and I'd be lying if I didn't admit to spending most of my time watching Ash. What does he get out of anonymously jerking off online? It's not the money; we have plenty of that. Our privilege isn't something I'm blind to. It's not the sex; he can get that anywhere he wants. So…what is it? I'm missing something. I must be.

By the time I'm in bed that night, it's still on my brain. Is Ash in his room doing it now? Will he do it before he decides if it's a good idea for me to watch? And then my dick starts feeling neglected, so I shove my underwear off, lube up, and stroke my cock. A guy's gotta come, right? It has nothing to do with Ash. Who doesn't get horny thinking about anyone jerking off?

I tighten my hold with my right hand, while tweaking my nipples with my left. I fucking love my nips getting fucked with, love a girl worshipping and paying lots of attention to my pecs.

I squeeze my right one, my slick palm sliding over my cock.

A camera flashes in my mind's eye, and I try to find in my imagination that place Ash has found in real life—

working through what it's like to be watched as I writhe on my bed, fucking my fist and squeezing my nipples. Before I know it, an explosion goes off inside me, a kaleidoscope of pleasure shooting colors around inside me while my spunk hits my chest.

Well, fuck. Post-nut clarity didn't come through. I'm no closer to knowing what Ash gets out of this, but I sure as shit released more pent-up tension than I'd even realized I'd built up.

7

Ash

I'M TAKING NOTES through Systems Physiology, my last class of the day.

I'm usually an attentive student, but today I'm distracted. Have been the past few days since my chat with Colin about Manzturbate.

"You're gonna need more lube, or you'll rub yourself raw."

I smile at the memory of him passing me the lube before taking some for himself during that playful moment when we were younger, when we were both exploring ourselves. Even though my attention should've been on the porn, there were moments when I remember wishing he would have turned and watched me. At the time, I chalked it up to my horny-ass teenage brain, but I guess it's not a huge surprise that a few years later, I'd find myself live streaming on an app for people to watch me.

I doodle a star on the corner of the page of my notes,

RILEY HART & DEVON McCORMACK

thinking about Colin's reaction to my secret. About how he went from worrying me to offering to sit and watch me jerk off in front of strangers. Why that gets me smiling, I can't figure out, considering I was stressed as fuck during the brief time he needed to wrap his mind around all this.

But I'm glad it didn't become an issue; if anything, it makes me feel even closer to him now that he's the only one who knows my naughty secret.

After class gets out, I see a missed call from Steve and a text from Colin.

Colin: You haven't been messing around on that app without me, have you? *eggplant emoji*

I burst out laughing, to the point where I search around to see if anyone noticed the big-ass reaction.

Since last week, Colin and I had playful text exchanges about it, and I notice most of his jokes are about how he wants to be present the next time I do it. Not poking fun or giving me a hard time about it.

That's so him.

A part of me thinks maybe he suggested watching me to let me know he's totally cool with it, but then there's this other part that wonders if he really is interested.

What's that about?

Me: No. And I'll let you know when I do.

He's probably still in class because my Systems Phys professor always ends class twenty minutes early because he gives zero fucks.

I plan to swing by the student center and grab one of their jumbo chocolate-chip cookies, so I'll have it for my study time at the library. I would've grabbed it earlier this morning, like I normally do, but apparently thinking about my stepbro has distracted me enough to throw me off my routine.

En route, I head into the main courtyard and give Steve a quick call to see what's up.

"Hey, bud," Steve answers, asking about my day, telling me about the riveting chapter he just wrote at Starbucks earlier.

"That's great," I tell him. "Happy to hear it's going well. I like these conversations more than the ones where you get stuck."

"I'm learning that I'm a plotter, not a pantser. Can't seem to figure my way out of a jam once I get myself into it. So how's the car been since you got it back from the shop?"

"Running, fortunately," I say with a laugh. "Troy took good care of me."

"Glad to hear it. I'll tell your mom when she gets home later. Speaking of…"

The way he says it, I know where this is going.

"…she said I should talk to you because you wouldn't reschedule with Sarah."

I grit my teeth. "I said I was busy. That's all."

"She told me what happened last time you had your

scheduled chat, and she's very sorry, but I can tell you she has been killing herself over this case. She's hoping she can intimidate the defense to a plea, so it's been all-consuming."

It'd be more compelling if I hadn't heard this before. "Yeah, and the last case was all-consuming, and the one before that, and the one before that, and I'm assuming the next one won't be a cakewalk either."

He grunts. "Yeah, I wish I could argue with you there."

"I also can't help noticing she's not the one calling me right now. Sending you on her behalf. She's even delegating her apologies."

"Bud, I'm sorry. She thought you might prefer to talk to me about it, but I don't want you to feel like I'm stepping in where I shouldn't. I can tell Lauren that you would prefer to talk to her."

Steve and Colin are so much alike—so considerate and thoughtful. After all these years, none of it has rubbed off on Mom? Really?

"Steve, I appreciate that you're trying to keep Mom and me on good terms. I'm frustrated with her right now, but we'll be fine. Maybe when she wraps up this case, we can have another therapy session."

He chuckles. "I'm sure Lauren would appreciate that."

He moves on to other subjects, and despite calling

him on trying to smooth over my beef with Mom, I love that he cares enough to check in, unlike either of my biological parents. By the time we get off the phone, I'm near the library, so I head in. I'm halfway up the stairs when I realize I was supposed to swing by the student center for my cookie.

Fuckin' A.

Oh well. I'm already on the fourth floor, so it's a lost cause, but I text Colin.

Me: I forgot my cookie this morning. *sad emoji*

Me: Might have something to do with how you've had me thinking about you sitting in on my app time.

I'm sure he'll get a laugh out of that when he gets out of class.

As I start through the fourth floor of the library, I notice a familiar face at the tables set up by the Literary Criticism shelves.

"Atlas?" I say as I approach.

He's working out a problem, his textbook open next to him, and he glances up, offering a warm smile.

"Ah, hey, Ash."

"I don't think I've ever seen you in the library before."

"I've been getting my ass kicked in Physics, so I've needed extra time to study. And Troy is distracting as fuck."

"Yes he is," I blurt out. "I meant, I…I…" I'm rebooting.

From what Colin's told me, Atlas and Troy were getting together around the time I was making a fool of myself trying to get Troy to go out with me, and Atlas wasn't exactly the friendliest with me, so in the times we've gotten together, I try not to talk about how hard his man used to make me.

But Atlas surprises me with a laugh. "It's cool, Ash. I know how hot my T is, and I insist everyone knows it too. As long as you know he's mine."

His comment emphasizes how confident he is about what he and his stepbrother have. And it's nice to see him smiling so big; from what I've heard about his and Troy's family situation, it hasn't always been so easy for him to smile.

"Sit down," Atlas says. "You know anything about physics?"

"I—"

"That was a joke, Ash. I know you do."

I chuckle as I sit down beside him, setting my bag beside the chair.

"I'm tempted to ask you for help," he says, "but last time my stepbrother did that, it lost me a bet."

"I'm sorry," I say, which makes him laugh.

"Best bet I ever lost," he says, something wicked in his expression now.

"I don't really get that, but Troy never told me about a bet."

He laughs again. "Um…he probably wouldn't tell you about this one. But I figure one day we'll tell the world. For a bet I lost, it earned me major bragging rights for the rest of my life."

"Now you're just a tease," I say, but I don't think he really wants to share, so I change the subject to his physics difficulties.

He gives me the rundown, and I watch him work through a few problems.

"This is pretty common," I say once I've pinpointed the issue. "You're getting tripped up because you're used to seeing similar word problems and equations in algebra and trig, but they're flipped around in physics."

As I'm walking him through a problem, he eyes me curiously. "You really are very good at explaining things."

"Thank you. I enjoy explaining them. I feel like I'm good at having an objective view and seeing where people get tripped up. Then showing them where that is. I like to think of it as my superpower."

"I didn't know Ash Ketchum had any superpowers," he teases.

I laugh. "I do look good in my Ash Ketchum costume. But in that case, maybe it's not a superpower, but like my strongest Pokémon."

His gaze shifts. "Oh, well, look who it is."

"Atlas fucking McCallister," Colin says as he approaches. "You having secret study sessions with my bro?"

"I might have to start," Atlas says. "Think he might have just unstuck me with this problem I kept running into."

Colin sets his backpack on the corner of the table and unzips it, revealing a brown bag I recognize from the student center cafeteria. I can't disguise my enthusiasm as he plops it down in front of me, wearing a broad grin like he just made a touchdown.

"You fucking spoil me," I say, sneaking a peek at my six-inch cookie.

"Damn right."

"Okay, you guys have a very different relationship than Troy and me."

Colin's forehead creases. "Yeah, we're not boning."

That one really gets us all laughing, earning us a few strange looks and frowns from the students studying around us.

"Oh shit," Atlas says, and as I turn to him, I see he's looking at his phone. "I gotta get out of here and get to work. Thanks for the free tutoring session, Ash."

"No problem. Hit me up if you want to meet some other time. Happy to help."

"I might just take you up on that."

After he heads off, Colin settles in the chair next to mine. "That was a sight I wasn't expecting to see today," he says with a smirk.

"I was surprised to see him in the library. He said his stepbrother was too distracting for him to focus on his work at home. I can attest that sometimes stepbrothers can be distracting."

Colin's brows tug closer together. "What does that mean?"

"Seriously, after the things we've been talking about, how can you be that clueless?"

"Are you saying I've been distracting you because of that talk we had?"

"Maybe." I fish into my bag, pick off a piece of cookie, and pop it in my mouth.

This is my preferred way to eat my jumbo cookie—savoring each bite. I close my eyes, thoroughly enjoying the chocolatey, doughy goodness and humming to myself. "Thank you, bro."

"Anytime."

He's wearing this playful smile, those intense blue eyes right on me. And I'm smiling too.

I'm not a mind reader, but I swear it's gotta be about that text he sent earlier, and he confirms this when he says, "So…you haven't been playing around on any apps since we talked?"

I glance at the nearby tables. Feels naughty to even allude to this here. But these days, I'm really enjoying feeling naughty, so I roll with it. "I've played around on several apps."

He tilts his head, offering an overdramatic glare.

"Not that one," I assure him before enjoying another piece of cookie. I swallow before saying, "Speaking of which, I've been thinking."

"You're always thinking."

"Pfft. Not about, like, normal things. More…" I lean closer, lowering my voice. "The kind of things brothers may or may not do in private."

My cheeks are warm. Even though there's no way anyone could know what I'm referring to, I can't help imagining one of the guys at the nearby tables standing up and saying, *"Holy shit! These brothers are talking about one messing around in front of the other?"*

Colin searches around, and I'm wondering if he'll change the subject, or just tell me this isn't the place to get into it, but he turns back to me and lowers his voice as he says, "That's funny." When he whispers like this, his voice is all deep and sexy and…yup, feeling that in my pants. "I've had the same thing on my mind recently."

"Really? I couldn't tell from the texts," I tease. "I just meant, I wanna make sure you're serious. Because I was thinking I wouldn't mind you watching." That's so on the nose, but I remind myself no one around us could know what he would be watching.

"I am," he says. "I imagine I'd enjoy seeing what you get out of it, maybe more than you realize."

I snicker like a fucking goofball; why is this making me react this way? I know I'm a dork, but Jesus fucking Christ. "Meaning?"

"I like seeing you happy, and this is something that clearly makes you happy. But I get if you don't want me to be there when you do it. It sounds private. Well, *private* might not be the right word, considering..."

I grin. "Yeah, not much private about it."

I take another bite of cookie and realize I'm popping these in so fast, I've already eaten a third of it.

I glance around again. Everyone's so into their work, no one's realizing that two stepbrothers are talking about potentially having one jerk off on camera in front of the other. The thought sends a rush of adrenaline coursing through my veins.

Wild to think that I kept this from Colin, but now that he knows, it feels even more exhilarating than before.

I whisper to ensure no one hears me. "I've been thinking more about what I like about it since we talked." A lot more. "I enjoy the attention. And people not caring who I am or what I think. They see me as this object, you know? They don't give a fuck about anything as long as they can watch me."

"I'm sure they want to watch you dump that giant load all over yourself."

I laugh, this time slightly too loud, drawing attention. My face must be bright red as I turn to him, and he's smirking, like he's pleased to be evoking this response.

"I can't believe you said that," I blurt out.

"Am I lying?"

"I'm not answering that."

"I was actually kind of jealous when I saw it back when we had our little…" He scoots his chair until his knee grazes my thigh. "Porn viewing."

"With that thick thing, I doubt you're jealous of much."

We both have these big, ridiculous grins on our faces. What would people think if they turned and saw us looking like this? They'd think we were sharing the best inside jokes ever.

But the more I think about that experience when we were younger, and how much fun it is even just joking around with him about it, the more fun it seems like it would be to have Colin there. I've enjoyed doing it on my own, but as I've learned plenty of times in my life, things are just more fun with Colin.

But I can't totally shut down my logical brain either. "You know people will give you hell if they ever find out."

He leans forward and takes the piece of cookie between my fingers into his mouth. He runs his teeth gently against my fingers, sending sensation rippling through me. Takes me by surprise.

He chews and swallows before his gaze locks with mine. "When have we ever cared what people said about us?"

My logical brain starts to go a very different direction…surely assisted by the excitement racing through me right now.

Because of what we're talking about doing.

Because of where we're talking about it.

Because of whom I'm talking about it with.

"So you're considering it?" Colin eyes me like he already knows the answer.

"Shut the fuck up. You don't know what I'm thinking."

"Maybe I do a little bit." He wears a cocky smirk, like he's so damn proud of himself for being able to read me so well.

"Well, if you want to watch, you might need to come back to the house with me, because after this conversation, I'm gonna want to hop right on my phone and get to it."

Colin's lips are inches from mine, his hot breath hitting my face as he says, "Guess we'd better get back to the house."

My face is on fucking fire, in a way that assures me I'm right: things are more fun with Colin. Just like that day when we got off together.

Maybe it's weird. Maybe it's wrong. I don't really give a fuck right now, and neither does he.

Like so much around this app, I don't get it, but right now, my dick's telling me we need to get back to the house ASAP.

8

Colin

SO...IS IT A Step Don't to get hard in the library while maybe kinda flirting with your stepbro and talking about watching him jerk off? I adjust my dick, hoping Ash and anyone else walking by don't notice the tent in my track pants. This is...different. Ash and I talk about shit all the time, we tease and play around, though not how we did today. It's never given me such a raging boner before—something that would likely be a Step Don't for others, but somehow, it's not off-limits for me and Ash.

The frat house is within walking distance from the library. Ash's legs are moving much faster than they usually do, and while I'm in a hurry too, I'm lingering behind, following him like a puppy.

Why is it that I've seen Ash naked a million times, but this one has my pulse speeding up in a whole new way? Has my thoughts spinning so quickly that I can't settle on one other than *yes* and maybe, *I can't fucking wait.*

This is about Ash, I tell myself. It's about understanding this thing he enjoys but is unsure of. It's about supporting him because we always do that, and about seeing him happy, but like, when does seeing someone happy get another person's dick hard? Do I have a happiness kink I didn't know about? Is that even a thing?

"You're being quiet." Ash turns around, walking backward.

"Just thinking." *About seeing you jerk off. About my boner...about seeing yours spurt a big-ass load that definitely had me curious last time.*

"Are you sure you're—"

"Yes."

Ash's gaze darts to my hard-on.

"See? Very okay. Come on." I grab his hand, and now it's me leading Ash, tugging him along toward the house like if we go too slow, he might change his mind.

Ash laughs. "In a hurry, are you?"

"Just being a good big brother."

"You're the best brother."

Totally not going to argue, though considering the situation we're about to head into, calling each other brothers might not be the best idea.

We turn down Sugar Maple Street, our house the second one down. We're lucky that the area is full of students from Peach State, who have a partying agreement and don't ever complain about each other. It can get loud here on the weekends.

I say a silent thank-you after unlocking the door to a quiet house. Everyone should be at school or work. Hell, I should be at school right now too. How the fuck did I forget I had a class? I swear I have Ash-brain. When it comes to him, nothing matters as much as Ash.

I take the stairs two at a time. "We should do this before anyone gets back."

Luckily, my dick has deflated on the walk over, so I don't have to explain that to any of the guys.

We head straight to his room. I close and lock the door behind us, in case anyone comes home. "Here." I start taking his backpack off him.

"You don't have to take that off. I'm not helpless."

"I know." My cheeks heat, and I'm not sure why. "I just like to do things for you."

"I like to do things for you too." Ash gives me a grin, and oh, ugh. Why oh why does Ash have such pretty lips? Not that it matters to me.

We each take our own packs off, then stand there looking at each other like a couple of idiots.

I open my mouth, close it, and we burst into laughter, the two sounds dancing together.

"Why are we being weird? You've seen me naked. This is nothing new." Ash pulls off his shirt. He works hard on his body, and it shows. While he's not as thick as

I am, his muscles are hard and compact. He's lean, every groove of his abs distinct.

I pull my shirt off too.

"Wait. Why are *you* getting naked?"

I freeze. Oh fuck. Why am I getting naked? No fucking clue. *Think, think, think.*

"I…wanted to take off my shirt?" I say ridiculously. Ash squints in that cute way he does sometimes, but then just chuckles without calling me on my dopiness. "Where do you usually do this? And get those pants off." I toss my tee to the floor and make it a point to keep my fucking pants on.

"In the desk chair."

I nod and go to his backpack to pull his laptop out. I hear noises behind me, and a quiet voice in my head is saying, *Ash is getting naked, Ash is getting naked, Ash is getting naked.* Of course he's getting naked. How else is he going to jerk off on camera? What is wrong with me?

I turn around with the laptop, and yep, he's naked. I'm thicker than Ash, but he's longer. He's half hard, his balls plump with the big loads I remember him making. "Wow, don't even have to get worked up much, do you?" I tease.

"I'm naked in front of a hot guy and about to jerk off on camera. Just thinking about those things gets my balls full."

I frown. "You think I'm hot? I mean…I *am* hot. I

just didn't know you thought that."

"Anyone who can see you knows you're hot, Col."

I nod in a way that feels a little dumb, then blurt out, "I'll be right back," and leave the room before Ash can say anything. I don't go far, just to my room, rolling my computer chair across the carpet until I get back to him. "I figure I can sit off camera, but I want to angle it so I can see you, but also what people are saying. I think that'll help me get it."

Ash cocks a brow.

"What?"

"You're taking this seriously."

"When do I not take important things seriously?"

"Good point."

Ash grabs the lube while we get everything set up. He turns on the camera, and we find a spot where my chair won't be on-screen but I'm close enough to get the full picture about everything.

Ash sits down so his torso is all that's showing.

"You can't see your cock," I tell him.

"I know. I'll show it." Ash chuckles. "I usually start this with my pants on. You seemed eager for me to get them off, so I went with it."

"I wasn't eager."

"I seem to remember a very pointed *get those pants off.*"

Why does he have to remember everything I say?

"Again, just trying to be helpful."

"I can't believe we're doing this."

I don't reply because really, I'm not even sure how to.

Ash logs in to his account—fratwiz20. It's such an Ash name.

He plucks at his nipples the way I do to myself, while watching the online room, waiting for people to show up. My gaze darts back and forth between him and the screen, and I see the changes in him—how his teeth dig into his bottom lip as he waits, the way his eyes won't meet mine, staring at the computer, his thoughts on display for me in a way I don't think they would be for anyone else.

Holy shit. Ash is afraid no one will show up.

My fingers twitch to reach for him. I try to find the words to tell him he's fucking hot, and people will show up, and fuck them if they don't, but then the first name pops onto the screen, quickly followed by another and another.

BiGuyFker: fuk yea. Ur back.

UzeMyHole33: Cant wait to see you shooooot.

CockChaser86: would do anything to taste your load.

Okay, come on strong much? Simmer down there, guys. It's on the tip of my tongue to tell them that's my brother they're talking about, but then my gaze snags on Ash, on the sparkle of gold in his intense gaze. His teeth no longer biting into his lip, his skin flushed with desire as the compliments roll in.

He likes this. He fucking *loves* it.

Why does that knowledge make my dick twitch? And maybe even makes me tingly in a way that's more than just being turned on?

UzeMyHole33: show us ur dick.

Ash's smile grows. His hands run down his muscular chest, to his dick that's already hard as fucking stone, then back up again to his chest, clearly playing with the viewers.

BiGuyFker: Dont tease us.
CockChaser86: want to see you jerk it.
cumGuzzzl3r: Ur here to get us off not tease us.

Again, I want to tell that motherfucker to fuck off too, but I'm not here to worry about him. I'm here for Ash...whose cheeks pinken more as they continue to pay him attention and talk at him like he's just there for them to use.

He stands up, a bead of precum at his tip, the sight of it making my cock throb. He plays with his balls, keeps teasing them, and I hear the sound of tokens coming through, but I can't pay any attention to them anymore. Ash has me in a trance, flicking his nips with one hand and massaging his nuts with the other.

He pumps lube into his hand, wraps it around his cock, and for the first time, his gaze flicks to me as he strokes. I swear I fucking see the pulse throb in his neck, see him light up with how much this does it for him. I can't deny that it's doing something to me too, the tornado in my head gaining strength. If I pushed my hand down my pants, it would probably take one stroke for me to bust a nut, because seeing Ash enjoy something this much, seeing how it makes him fucking glow and fills him up in this way I've never seen, is sexier than I expected. But more than that, it makes me feel good. Seeing Ash happy has always made me feel good, but now it's entwined with this unfamiliar desire that's confusing the fuck out of me.

His gaze flicks back to the computer, and mine does too.

CockChaser86: want to bury my face in ur balls.
cumGuzzzl3r: Hope ur load is even bigger than last time.

Ash jerks himself harder, faster. The muscles in his chest and arm tighten when he does. I press my palm to my dick, massaging it through my track pants, needing release something fierce.

When Ash glances my way again, pupils wide, mouth parted slightly, and looking like he feels like he could fly, I can't stop myself from pushing my hand beneath my waistband, my underwear too. I'm slick with precum, body pulsing with the need to come.

Ash nods at me, which is all the confirmation I need. I shove my pants down, pull myself out, spit in my hand, and jerk off with him. Why does seeing him like this go to my head? Does things for me nothing ever has? All I know is I've always been Ash's person. I make him smile like no one else does, make him laugh, make him feel good, and while I don't begrudge him getting it from this site...I want to make him feel this good too.

His body tightens, and I know he's close, know he's going to give all these people the load they're looking for, and I can't help wondering how it will compare to the one I've seen him shoot. My thighs begin to shake, my vision blurs slightly as my balls draw up, and as embarrassing as it is to come this early, I can't stop myself from falling over the edge.

I shoot stripes of cum up my chest, empty my balls in front of him for the first time in years. Slick cum slides down my cock as I keep stroking myself through it, spurt again as I begin to come back to earth.

Ash groans. I lean forward...close...making sure I'm not on camera but needing to see. He looks at me, at the screen, then back to me. They're telling him how hot he is and how much that turns them on, but for whatever reason, Ash glances at me too.

His balls draw up, arm muscles taut when the first pulse of his cum jets out of him, hitting his chest and stomach. His cock jerks again and again, cum all over his hand and cock, running down his stomach in what is definitely an impressive fucking load.

BiGuyFker: Fck yes.
CockChaser86: So hot.
cumGuzzzl3r: eat it.

Ash grins and uses his other hand to end the feed. The second it's turned off, he looks away, his spine not as straight as it was before. He grabs his shirt and begins wiping himself off. "That wasn't in the plan."

He's trying to sound light, but I know him too well for that. He's unsure what I think. Getting off is one thing, but that doesn't mean I understand him. Ash needs that as much as I do.

"You're beautiful when you do that."

His head snaps my way. "What?"

"I don't know why I said it like that. I meant, it clearly turns you on. It does something for you up here." I almost tap my temple but then remember I have jizz on my fingers. Ash chuckles as I bend down and pick up my shirt. "I like seeing you that way."

"You like seeing me jerk off?"

"I like seeing how it makes you feel." Which I strangely get off on. I've always known I like seeing Ash happy, but it's never gotten me off before. Huh. Interesting. "I wouldn't mind doing it again."

"You wouldn't?"

I shake my head.

"So we're...good?" Ash asks, a quiet vulnerability to his voice that he only shows me.

I stand and pull him into a hug. "We're always good."

"We're also naked and covered in cum."

Shit. Yeah. He's right. I guess I shouldn't naked-hug my cummy stepbrother. "Clean up and go out to dinner?" I suggest, wanting to find a way to get back to normal—for Ash and for me. My thoughts have been doing some weird things today, and I want to show him everything is okay.

Ash grins. "Your treat."

"Or you could use some of that jerk-off money."

I pull my pants on, even though I'm still a mess.

"Fine. My treat," he replies playfully.

It's not until I get into the shower that I realize I'm still smiling.

9

Ash

"WE'LL HAVE THE twelve-inch, half pepperoni and half meat lover's. And the big guy here'll have chicken wings." I turn to Colin and wink, and as the waitress heads off, I tell him, "As always, if any of your sausage touches my half, I'm gonna be pissed."

"You didn't seem that squeamish about my sausage earlier. Besides, you're gonna need some extra meat to replenish your protein after that load you dropped."

How can I not laugh? We're sitting at our favorite pizza place, making jokes about what we just did.

Sometimes after I jerk off, I want to take a nap, but this time, I've got adrenaline surging through me like when I'd get all worked up about Math League competitions. It was wild, and strange, but mostly hot as fuck.

Despite being playful, Colin's been quieter than his usual self since we did that, but it's not like the other day when he was surprised about my secret. It's that look he gets after he's won a big game. Or after a particularly hot night with a girl.

Just seeing that satisfied expression has me thinking about how he looked when he was playing with himself. How he wanted to get off, looking to me like he wanted my fucking permission. I love feeling in control with what I do on Manzturbate, but with Colin looking at me with those eager eyes, I felt like I had him wrapped around my finger. I was in charge of his pleasure, and I could shut it down or let him play.

But, Colin, I would never fucking shut you down.

Then seeing him stroking his thick cock, how it pulsed as he came in two distinct streams, his eyes rolling back as he gritted his teeth… It reminded me of that first time we jerked off together. I don't remember being turned on as much as shocked by how he shot his load, since we don't come the same at all—at least, we didn't then or during the live stream. But now, thinking about it has my dick shifting again in my pants.

After the waitress brings us our drinks, I ask him, "So what did you think?"

Colin smirks. "I didn't feel like I left much to the imagination."

"You obviously had fun, unless you're that good at faking a good time. But I meant the live stream part."

Colin's shoulders tense up—a similar reaction as when the comments were rolling in on the feed. "Some of those guys are fucking demanding," he says, and his body language—tight fists, tense jaw, hunched shoulders—reminds me of when I'd tell him about the bullies I was dealing with at school. "I got a little worked up when I read a few, felt like I was memorizing the names in case I needed to track them down."

Though he says it half-seriously, there's something behind it; Colin's protective like that. And I like that he is.

"Yeah... I guess there's no point being coy about it after that, but that's what I like about it."

"Really?"

I widen my eyes as I nod, a grin expanding across my face. Strange to think I was keeping it from him before, and now that he knows about it, I want to share it all. "I like that's how bad they want it, you know? Like it's driving them wild."

"You were definitely doing that."

"And you thought you might have to step in and protect your little bro?"

Colin winces, but then raises his hand, demonstrating the size with his finger and thumb. "That much."

I laugh, a big one I have to cover my mouth to stifle.

He beams. "Glad to know my being there didn't keep you from being able to perform."

"Nope. It helped, actually," I blurt out, which catches his attention. "I mean, clearly, I enjoy being watched, so having someone there in person...it made it even better than just with the people online. *A lot* better."

Fuck, why am I saying this? Am I that determined never to commit another Step Don't again?

"Even though it was your stepbrother watching?"

I shrug. "Maybe because it was you."

"What?"

"We get each other. I feel comfortable and safe around you. It felt easy and chill…and hot, if I'm being real. You're hot. I'm bi. That shouldn't be a huge surprise."

I'm downplaying it because I've never felt as turned on by Colin as I was when we were doing that, never been thinking about the things I wanted to try with his dick…or what it would be like if he shot that load across me before feeding it to me. *Okay, now I'm getting carried away…*

"I should be asking what *you* were getting out of it, unless you're gonna tell me you were imagining a hot girl going down on you, in which case, don't hurt my feelings like that."

Is it weird that I'm nervous Colin would say something like that?

Of course it is! This is all weird.

Colin's brows jump. "Is that what you think got me to finish?"

"I'm still trying to make sense of that part. I mean, you're straight. And it was just me and this app. I thought maybe it was a combination of the voyeurism and it being a sexual thing."

"It was incredibly hot watching you do that, but I'm wondering if it's like what you just said. That it was hot *because* it was you."

He's putting it out there, and I shouldn't be surprised, considering what went down, but I am.

"What do you mean?"

His brows tug closer together. "I was hard because it was you, Ash. I was enjoying watching you enjoy it. It feels...*different*."

"I—I—don't even know what to say to that."

For as long as I've known Colin, he's been my big straight stepbro, but now between what happened and what he's saying, I don't know what to think.

"Aren't I supposed to be the clueless one between us?" Colin asks.

I really shouldn't let myself go there. Like, sure, I thought a few times during it that it was all pretty queer, but I know Colin so well, and he tells me everything. If there was any inkling that he was curious, he would have said something to me...his bi bro.

Fuck, here I've been thinking about how hot it was, when he could be struggling with this or confused.

"Colin, do you think you could be queer?"

He hesitates for a moment. "Maybe. I saw some gay porn and got hard before, but I figured that's just because it was sex, not because of the guys. I've never really thought much about it until today. What's happening is definitely outside the realm of straight, but again, part of me wonders if it's just because it's with you."

I consider this. "But you've talked before about noticing when guys are attractive."

"I've never wanted to jerk off with them before, though. Like I said, I notice things—guys in porn or whatever—and maybe this was simply a physical reaction, but it felt different. That's the only way I can think to explain it."

He has a point there. It's one thing to notice someone's attractive, another when it makes you question your identity.

But now that a floodgate of questions has opened, I'm starting to worry. "Have I not been paying enough attention? Did you need me to bring it up? Or should we just drop it? You know, I think I'll shut up and let you tell me what you need. You know I'm here for you if you need to talk about anything, right?"

That gets him chuckling. "Now you're the one who's concerned about me. What is wrong with us? Maybe because I've known you as bi for so long, it seems like if that's what it is, that's what it is. I'm not going to stress about it, but I think it's adorable you care so much."

I can't shake my uneasiness, though. Not about him

questioning why he's feeling this way, but that I—who proudly know him better than anyone else in the world—missed something.

Now I get why he was so rattled when he found out about my Step Don't.

Colin must see the anxiousness in my expression because he reaches over and takes my hand. It's not unlike something he would have done with me before, but it feels warmer than usual, and our gazes meet. I'm waiting for him to pull his hand away, but we both just start snickering as heat stirs in my cheeks.

"Is that doing anything for you?" I ask Colin.

"I don't know. Is my face as red as yours?"

"A little pink."

We're still snickering when the pizzas arrive. I'm annoyed they finished them so quickly because I was enjoying Colin's hand in mine. As the waitress finishes setting the food and plates up for us, we're grinning at each other.

Because where the fuck do we go from here?

When she finally heads off, I just spit it out. "This is so strange."

Colin shrugs. "What about today has been strange? I can't imagine what you're referring to."

"Why don't we call Marty and put him on speaker, tell him, and then gauge his reaction to determine how normal it is?"

Colin slides his phone out of his pocket. He's got one distinctly raised eyebrow.

"You would never."

"Oh, a challenge?"

"Yes, a fucking challenge."

Because there's no way in hell. And when he starts pulling up his contacts, I fold my arms. "If you think I'm stopping you, you're outta your goddamn mind."

Colin sets his phone down by the pizza so I can see Marty's name and photo as he places the call on speaker. The phone trills a few times. I doubt Marty will even answer, but we're both making eye contact. He must think I'm gonna snatch the phone and demand he not say anything.

The trilling stops, and Marty says, "Hey, man, what's up?"

"Oh, hey, Mart. Just wanted to reach out. Had something dirty I wanted to share with you."

"Oh really?" Marty's voice is full of interest. As much of a pain as he can be sometimes, the guy loves gossip.

"Ash and I just jerked off together, and I'm wondering if maybe that makes me queer? I'm certainly questioning things."

I notice he left out the live streaming, and I'm sure it's because that's my secret. Even when I'm fucking challenging him, he still goes out of his way to protect me.

I'm stunned that this is happening, but it's so us.

Marty's silent for a few moments. What the fuck is he gonna say? He's such a prude, he's gonna freak the fuck out.

But then I hear a deep roaring laugh, so loud that the audio blows out a few times. "What bet did you lose that you had to call and tell me that?"

"What the hell?" Colin says. "I call and share my innermost secrets with you, and this is the reaction I get?"

Surely he's saying all this because he knows there's no way in hell Marty's gonna believe any of it.

Marty's still in stitches. "Right, okay. Tell Troy I said hey. I get it. I need to lay off the stepbrother teasing. Got it. Noted. Now you know damn well I got studying to do, so I'll catch you later."

Marty hangs up, and Colin shakes his head. "Maybe I've actually tried to come out to my friends several times and they just don't believe me."

I'm fucking rocking about in my seat as I laugh. After what happened today and what he's shared, feels like I have a thousand questions, the most important being: Why am I into the live streaming? What's Colin experiencing? Could I be into my stepbrother? Could he be into me?

Whatever's happening, I'd never push him. Sure, everyone knows me as the guy who loves answers. But

Colin makes me feel like it's okay not to have all the answers right now. Like we can figure this out together.

"You don't have to figure anything out today, Col. And I'm here for you, no matter what."

"Like sitting-through-a-live-stream-for-me here for me?"

I snort. Fucking snort. Oh my God. "As long as I'm the one on camera?"

"Wouldn't have it any other way."

We share another laugh.

"We're so weird," I say.

I fucking love the way we're weird.

10

Colin

IN THE DAYS since Ash and I jerked off together, things have been both the same and not. I can't look at Ash without picturing his face when he came, can't forget the way his muscles moved when he stroked himself or what he looks like covered in a load. The memory has gotten me hard more times than I care to admit, but I'm not closer to any real answers. The logical one would be that I'm bi, but then, that doesn't explain why everything is heightened and so much more vivid when it comes to Ash. I guess it can be that I'm bisexual and have a crush on Ash.

Honestly, I don't care. I'm not the type to overthink my sexuality. Everyone is different, and while some people need labels, I don't. At least not at this point. Right now, I'm fine acknowledging that Ash makes me feel really fucking good. The rest of it doesn't matter.

So yeah, the fact that I'm imagining Ash naked is different, and so is the way we're a lot flirtier with each other. We've never had an issue throwing sexual innuendos around, but now a random eggplant emoji has a whole new meaning.

Remember when I spewed my load in front of you?

Do you think we'll do it again?

That last question I'm thinking about entirely too much, partly because it was hot and partly because I'm still trying to wrap my head around it. The pushy guys I wanted to punch in the face got Ash hotter. He likes knowing how much he's turning them on, so by extension, he would like knowing how much I get turned on too. The attention is what does it for him, knowing how wild he makes someone, and making him feel good makes me go wild, so really, it's perfect. We're like a can of gasoline waiting for the flick of a match to make us explode.

And just like the fact that it's Ash made things different for me, him knowing I was watching him made his pleasure burn fiercer too.

"That's it for today," Professor Rixson in my Morality and Law class interrupts my Ash-induced thoughts. My notes are not very thorough, which isn't like me, but I'll have no problem catching up and sorting my shit out later. I pack my stuff as everyone around me rises and begins filing out of the lecture hall.

This is my last class of the day. Ash and I are heading home to see our parents for dinner. Our last trip had been postponed, and Dad had called last night to set it up because Lauren has an unexpected day off, so he figured we should take advantage. Dad is good with stuff like that.

Even though there's not a doubt in my mind that Lauren loves Dad, on the surface she seems so different from him. He's always made sure to hammer home that there's nothing wrong with men having emotions and being affectionate. He's the complete opposite of the toxic masculine culture so many people push, and I've always been grateful I've had him as an example. I can kick fucking ass on the football field while also being the guy who talks about my feelings and can love cuddling and spoiling my brother.

Shit, why does everything go back to Ash?

When I get back to the house, Troy, Atlas, and his friends Taylor and Brenner are there, playing video games. Usually, that's something they do at Atlas's place, so not sure why they're here today.

"'Sup?" I ask, plopping into one of the beat-up, reclining chairs. It's seen a few too many parties. "Remember that time when Atlas used to not be allowed here?" I joke, adjusting my backward hat.

"Remember that time I didn't give a fuck?" Atlas replies, but I don't take it personally. Atlas can be a bit of a dick, but he's a cool dick who is crazy in love with my best friend and treats him well.

"That's cap." Brenner gives Atlas a pointed look. "You used to drag our asses to every fucking party here, making up dumbass excuses, and now I know it's because the whole time you wanted to bone Troy."

"You say that like you didn't want to bone Troy too," Taylor adds.

Atlas growls, and I laugh, but then I remember Brenner has recently started flirting with my brother, and I feel a bit growly too.

"Damn…all the boys want me. Who knew I was this irresistible?" Troy teases, earning a laugh from all of us.

"Now you belong to me." Atlas nips at Troy's throat.

"Welp, they're gonna go upstairs and fuck in three…two…one…" Brenner counts down before Atlas attacks Brenner and the two of them wrestle around like idiots.

"Why did you start all the fun without me?" Ash says, coming into the room. I hadn't even heard him get home over the sound of everyone. He gives me a grin, and I pull him to my lap. Ash follows my lead, sitting on my thighs.

"It started with Brenner and how he used to want to fuck Troy, and this is where it landed," I reply.

"I give! I give!" Brenner says dramatically, voice full of all the energy that's always radiating off him.

"I was just about to jump in and defend our honor," Taylor teases, holding out his hand for Brenner and pulling his friend to his feet.

"Just about, huh? My fucking hero."

We all let out another chuckle, my hand coming to rest on Ash's thigh.

Troy shakes his head at our friends. "What are you guys doing today?" he asks me. "Wanna chill?"

"Nah, me and Ash have to go see our parents, so we're gonna bang."

"Motherfucker! Missed out again! *Whyyy?*" Brenner throws his hands up playfully.

"Hey, me and Troy did that at our parents' house too," Atlas adds, earning another shake of Troy's head.

"That's how we say hang out." Ash adjusts his glasses.

"Sure it is. I bet that's how Atlas and Troy say it as well. When I banged a girl last week, we were really 'hanging' too," Taylor says, air quotes around *hanging*.

"Think what you want." Ash shifts on my lap, and...oh...*oh*. I'm feeling some twitching action in my pants. We've been sitting with each other like this for years, and that's never happened before.

My face heats. "We should get going." I start to stand slowly so Ash can get to his feet. "Rock, paper, scissors?" We both like to drive and jokingly argue about who gets to do it each time. Since I'm a year older, I got my license before Ash and used to tease him, holding my driving status over his head.

"Sure...or I could just drive." Ash snickers.

"Where's the fun in that?" We each hit our fist on our opposite hand two times before choosing a shake. "Rock smashes scissors." I tap Ash's scissor fingers with my fist. "I win." I tug my keys from my pocket, and Ash tries to get them from me as we work our way toward the door.

"Have a banging good time!" Brenner calls out in a really bad British accent.

"I'm not sure how I feel about us inheriting Brenner and Taylor when Troy fell for Atlas," Ash teases as we go out to the car.

"Do you think there's a return policy?"

"I assume it's already expired."

We climb into the car and head to our hometown, which is only about a forty-five-minute drive but also like a whole different world. Peach State is in a college town, this artsy bubble people in the burbs complain about.

"Fun fact: I started to get hard when you moved on my lap earlier." I turn onto the freeway. "I figure that's something I should share with you."

"Have you ever before?"

"Nope."

Ash shrugs. "I guess it makes sense, considering what we did last week. You're okay with it?"

I love that he's checking in with me again. Ash

knows me well enough to know I'm not having an identity crisis, but it's nice to have someone to talk to. He had me when he came out as bi, but I probably wasn't able to give him everything he needed because I hadn't yet realized I'm queer. With Ash, I have someone with firsthand experience. "Yeah, I'm good. It's funny how it feels like a shift for me but also not." Again, I think that's because it's Ash it's happening with. Everything between us has always felt as natural as breathing.

"Is that why you jumped up so quickly?"

I chuckle. "I didn't want too much to happen. Plus, I don't ever want to make you uncomfortable."

"Colin, it would be impossible for anything with you to make me uncomfortable. That's not how we work."

No, it's really not. "Dad said Lauren is ordering Chinese. She knows how much you like it," I change the subject.

"That was nice of him to ask her to ask Sarah to do that."

"Ash…" I hate that he thinks of it that way, like he's an afterthought, when really, that's not the case. Lauren's love language is just different—not that that changes how it makes Ash feel. If I'd grown up with Lauren and his dad rather than my parents, I might feel the same.

"It's not a big deal. She's busy. She has to work harder than men who do the same job."

Fact. Still, I have a feeling Ash doesn't think he's as important as her job. Or at least, she doesn't put as much effort into being the mom Ash needs as she does in her career.

"Plus," Ash says, "she's really had to prove herself since the drama when our parents got together."

"She's a badass lawyer. A so-so mom," I say.

Ash nods. "She is. I'm damn proud of all her accomplishments."

"As you should be, but if you ask me, you're even more badass." I wink, and Ash shakes his head as if I'm being ridiculous, but I know how much he loves it. Giving him that makes my insides tingle. Makes me feel...important?

"I'm lucky I have you," Ash says.

"Truth," I tease, both of us snickering.

We don't talk about anything important the rest of the ride. We pull into the driveway of their gray house— the front done with a lot of expensive stonework. Both Dad's Beamer and Lauren's Lexus are in the driveway. Ash and I have grown up privileged, something we both acknowledge and which inspires us to give back.

Dad opens the door, giving a goofy wave like he hasn't seen us in years. It's so him. We're similar, he and I.

"Hey, boys! Glad you could make time for us!" he teases, pulling me into a hug.

RILEY HART & DEVON McCORMACK

"It was hard, but we managed."

Dad snickers, then hugs Ash. "Hey, bud."

I don't know why he calls Ash that. It's not something he says to me, and clearly, Ash isn't a kid, but my dad has always done it.

"Hey, Steve."

Lauren steps into the doorway next. She has the same dark hair as Ash, only hers reaches her shoulders. She's wearing a pencil skirt and a nice blouse, looking like the shark she is.

She tries to emulate my father, but the hug she gives Ash is stiff and unsure, closer to a pat on the back than comfortable affection. "I got your favorite. General Tso's."

"Thanks, Mom."

Dad wraps his arm around her and squeezes her shoulder as if to say good job and make sure she knows he's proud of her.

"How is school going?" she asks as we file into the house. We settle in the living room, Ash talking about his classes and his internship. Lauren glances at her phone from time to time like she worries she's going to miss something while also trying to stay in the moment.

We make small talk for a while. Ash finally had a chance to catch up with his dad about his adventures in Japan, so he shares a little about that.

When dinner arrives, Dad rushes to say, "I'll grab

dishes!"

"I'll scoop everyone's plates!" Ash adds.

"I'll…" Fuck. What will I do? "Damn it!" I hate being the last one to offer to help.

"What…?" Lauren's looking at the three of us like she's not sure what's going on.

"It's just a silly game, dear. The last one to offer to help has to do the dishes." When she frowns, maybe wondering how she missed out on that, Dad adds, "We don't do it all the time. It's pretty random."

"Oh." Lauren shifts uncomfortably.

"Looks like it's me and you for cleaning up," I say, to pull her into the game with us.

Dad grabs plates and silverware, and we head into the dining room. Dad and Lauren have chairs at each end of the table, Ash and I across from each other.

Ash begins opening the containers and adding a serving spoon to each. Just as we're about to sit down, Lauren's phone buzzes. Everyone goes quiet. Her gaze darts toward it like she wants to answer, like it's killing her not to, but she knows she shouldn't.

"You can get it before we eat," Ash tells her. He knows she wants to, and he likes to pretend it doesn't bother him. He begins adding chicken to my plate first.

"Five minutes. Then no more interruptions. I promise." She swoops up her cell and leaves the room.

"Anyone want to hear about my new book?" Dad

asks.

"Absolutely," Ash tells him, and Dad rambles the way he does—and, okay, maybe the way I do sometimes too—but I can't stop worrying that Ash is disappointed his mom chose to take the call.

I pull my cell phone out, keeping it beneath the table. I remember him saying he liked it when he saw how much the guys wanted him. I'd seen it before he told me, felt it in the pulse in the room, and I want to make him feel good again.

Me: Is it weird that we're at our parents' dinner table and I can't stop thinking about what you look like when you shoot your load?

It's true. Maybe part of texting him right now is for Ash, but I'd be lying if I didn't admit it's for me too.

"One of the characters is a law student." Dad turns to me.

"Oh really? What happens to him?"

I shoot a quick glance at Ash, see him look down, checking his phone. Dad keeps talking, oblivious to what's going on around him. I nod and ask questions, leg bouncing beneath the table in anticipation of Ash's reply.

"I'm back!" Lauren sits down just as my cell vibrates. "Let's dig in!"

Ash: It's hot that my big bro loves seeing how much I can shoot. You'd come when I did, wouldn't you? Stroke that thick cock and empty your balls as soon as you saw me come.

I swallow a lump in my throat. My skin tingles as blood rushes to my groin.

This is wrong.

And dirty.

And a little weird.

It's also hot AF, and I don't want to stop.

Me: Hell, yeah. I'd be just like those guys online, begging to see you unload. You're so fucking hot when you do.

"Are you not hungry?" Dad asks, and I realize I must have been sitting like this longer than I thought.

I glance at Ash when I say, "Starving," then hit Send. Holy fuck, this is fun—the thought of sending messages around people who have no idea what we're saying. I take a bite of my food, Ash's jaw tense across the table.

I turn to Lauren and Dad. "I want to ask you about the case study we're working on in school." They both light up. While I explain it to them, I know Ash is reading my text, coming up with a reply.

When Lauren and Dad start discussing aspects of the case study between them, I'm pleased. Operation Create-A-Diversion is a success.

Ash: Starving for my load? You wanna taste it next time?

Do I? Yes, yes I do. But…are we being serious or not? Is this just some game we're playing? Because it's hot and we're clearly pervy fuckers, but either way, it makes my dick throb and I don't want to stop.

Me: Yes...I'll go wild for you just like those guys online.

Fuck, this is dangerous territory. I can't sort through why I'm saying these things, but I also know they're true. Our time in his room flipped a switch inside me, and now there's no turning back.

I want to be a part of what Ash is doing online.

Or maybe that's not it, and maybe I just want to give him what he gets out of it. I want it coming from me instead of randos who don't give a fuck about him like I do.

11

Ash

I MANAGE TO nab the keys from Colin so I can drive us back to the frat from Mom and Steve's place.

I'm slightly on edge, and of course, Colin knows this. "I'm sorry she took that call," he says.

"I should have told her I preferred she didn't. Just, sometimes I wish she'd choose me. Not need me to bring it up in therapy. Not need Steve to remind her. Or for me to ask."

"I hear that. She could have waited to return the call."

Fortunately, Colin's texts managed to keep me pre-occupied throughout our get-together. And not just the texts, but feeling his eyes boring into me, seeing the way he had to shift in his seat or turn away from his dad so he wouldn't notice he was getting hard for me.

Wild to think how much we've been around each other—fucking seen each other naked—and he's never been like this before. Although, I've never thought about him like this before either. Never thought so much about his cock and how he comes.

I haven't pushed to do the live stream again, but I've been enjoying our text exchanges—the tease, the promise of what comes next. Maybe I'm nervous because the live stream stuff has me a little confused. And so does whatever's happening between Colin and me.

But there are a few things I'm not confused about.

I know he's hot.

I know I want him.

And I know he wants me.

Fuck everything else.

As I pull onto the interstate, I say, "So did you like how slick I was with nabbing your keys?"

"I was disappointed you weren't just trying to feel me up."

I laugh, though I can tell he's serious. "Well, I apologize for that and for spoiling your cover."

"Cover?" Colin asks.

"I figured out why you wanted to drive there so bad. Then you have your eyes on the road and the speedometer. Not getting all hot and sweaty over your stepbro."

Colin slides his hand down his thigh, and I glance over quickly, noticing the bulge in his jeans.

"Just to be clear," Colin says, "I thought it might be better if I didn't have a raging boner around our parents, but now that we're alone again, I don't give a fuck."

"I know you don't." I reach over the console and take his girth in my hand, giving it a good squeeze. "Like a stone," I say, my chest swelling with pride. "I like knowing I'm the one doing this to you." I slide my hand under the waistband of his pants, tucking a little deeper to get under his briefs as I find his flesh…

Colin settles back into his seat as I massage it, feel it firm even more in my grip.

"Well, you definitely did that," Colin says. "But you're smart enough to know your hands should be at ten and two."

I burst into a laugh, pulling my hand back. As I sneak a glance at him, he sports a wicked smirk. I must admit, as hot as what we did was and the things we text about, I love that it's not just hot—it's fun.

I like seeing Colin's playful side when it's also a little naughty. Almost like he's been committing a Step Don't by not flirting with me sooner.

"It's nine and three now, not ten and two." I place both hands on the steering wheel. "As per the National Highway Traffic Safety Administration."

Colin snickers. "You're real proud of yourself for knowing that one, aren't you?"

"I am. And while I demonstrate safe driving, guess you're just gonna have to drink me in from over there. You don't have anything to distract you. You have to look at me all the way back to campus. Thinking about those things you texted me. How you want to watch me shoot again. How you want to taste me. How you want to do for me what those guys online do."

A low growl escapes his lips, sending a charge right through me. I don't know whom I'm torturing—me or Colin.

"Don't be cruel to me, Ash."

I can hear how bad he wants me in the way he says it. I know this guy nearly as well as I know myself. He's hungry for me, craving me.

I have to adjust in my seat because my cock is stiffening at an uncomfortable angle. I tug at it so it slides into the leg of my pants.

"But you like when I'm a little cruel." I sneak another look. There's that wicked smirk again. "I keep thinking about how you said you wanted to taste it." He's quiet, like he's waiting to see where I'm going with this. "I think you'd be good at it."

"Yeah? What makes you say that?"

"You remember when I was about to hook up with Chelsea?"

Chelsea was my first long-term girlfriend, and of course, I needed tips from my older bro.

"Yeah…" he drags out.

"You remember what you told me?"

"To take your time, explore and probe with your tongue and lips, listen to her body."

Fuck, my cock is painfully hard.

"Same idea," I say. "Only you know how to please your cock too. So you know what feels good."

He reaches over and rests his hand on my crotch, caressing the shaft with his index and middle finger. "I don't just know how to please my own cock," he says, which makes me gulp. "You think I didn't notice the way you twist your hand when you get to the head?"

God, was he really paying that much attention to me during the live stream?

My face is on fire.

"No fair. You've been taking notes."

"That's what I have to do to keep up. That said, yeah, I have a feeling I'd be pretty good at it too."

His words, his touch, it's all driving me wild, and I'm hardly thinking straight as I flip on the blinker and take the next exit.

"What are you doing?" Colin asks, though going by his suspicious expression, he already knows the answer.

"My stepbro's always been a man of his word," I say, pulling into the gas station at the main road. I find a spot on the far end.

Bright lights flood the busy station, cars packing the pumps and people coming and going from the convenience store. Why does having all these people around make this even more exciting?

I'm hardly even thinking as I unfasten my seat belt

and crawl into the back seat.

"What the hell are you doing?" Colin asks again with a laugh.

As I settle on my ass in the seat, I see his eyes light up, his expression all eager and excited.

"You think I haven't seen that look right before you're about to make a go for the ball?" I ask. "You think I don't know exactly what you want?"

He's so fucking curious. Reminds me of all these unanswered questions, and how sometimes the best way to solve a problem is through guess and check.

"Get your big ass back here," I spit out.

"Do I have to crawl back there with my big ass, or can I get out and use the door?"

"Crawl," I say. "I wanna see how much you really want it."

Colin rolls his head back, laughing, but then his expression shifts, turns serious, a determined look in his eyes. I've seen that look before too. Like when he's running down the field, knows exactly what he needs to do and where he's going.

He crawls over the console. This isn't some messy, fumbling crawl. He's focused, got his sights set on one thing—me—and he's gonna get me, however he wants me.

Soon he's got one knee resting on the seat and a foot on the floorboard. Sometimes I forget how big he is, but

I love the way he's towering over me.

As I toss my shirt off, he glances around, squinting. "You like it out here like this, don't you?"

"It's exciting," I confess. Because I don't feel like I have to hide anything from Colin—nothing about me or what I want. I'm not committing any more Step Don'ts anytime soon.

I haven't even set my shirt on the floorboard when I feel Colin's hand at my belt. He unfastens it and pulls it open. He's careful at first, but then he tugs down my fly and boxers, his gaze on my cock like he's been waiting to see it again since my live stream.

He licks his lips, as though thinking about what he suggested…how much he wants to taste it.

"Ready to show me how right I am?" I ask. "Show me how good you are?"

Colin's gaze locks on mine, and that wicked smirk returns before he leans down.

Then I feel the warmth of his tongue sliding under the head…

I roll my head back against the window, resting my hand on his head as his tongue explores, probes.

Is this really happening? Is my straight stepbrother going down on me?

No, not straight, but—oh, whatever the fuck, who gives a shit?

He follows those instructions he gave me years ago,

taking his time. I scan around at the windows, watching as people come and go. No one's noticing us, of course. Everyone's busy with their lives. They aren't thinking that two stepbrothers might be going at it in a nearby car.

It makes me think of the live stream. That naughty feeling. That rush I get from it.

I love this sensation—like we could get caught. Someone might see Colin worshipping my cock.

He gives a tender kiss right under the head of my dick before pulling back.

"Fuck, you can't stop now."

"Oh, I thought we were fine with being cruel," Colin says with a wink, making me laugh. "One sec." He grabs the waistband of my pants and boxers and slides them down.

He leans back, expertly pulling my jeans down to my ankles. He throws off my shoes and socks, then removes my pants and underwear, discarding them on the floorboard so that I'm naked beneath him.

I'm not like this when I fuck around—I'm more the messy goofball, trying to make this all look less awkward. But Colin makes everything look so damn cool.

"Much better," he says as he glances me over, like he wants to soak up every inch of me. He takes a moment, really studying me before his gaze meets mine again. "You really are sexy," he says, making my cheeks hot again, like his words are wired to my sympathetic nervous system.

He reaches back, grabbing his shirt and tearing it off. He tosses it to the floorboard with my clothes, then dives back onto my cock. His tongue and mouth get right back to work, as though they remember exactly where they left off.

I feel my cock expanding before he whispers, "There it is. There you are."

I must be precoming. Fuck, how could I not be when he's going at me like this?

He grips the base of my shaft, angling me up before sliding his lips on either side. Taking the head in at first, he moves back and forth, and I'm shocked with how quickly he drives down, taking even more of me, like he's trying to prove a fucking point.

With his mouth and tongue working my nerves, I arch my back, reaching out and grabbing the driver's seat with one hand and the headrest on the back seat with the other, bracing myself as he goes at it.

"Fuckin' A, Colin. Oh fuck, I was so right about how good you'd be at this."

And he keeps showing me how right I was.

Hard for me to enjoy my victory as he grips my thighs and really goes at it. He's made my body so desperate. I rock my hips with his movements as I climb higher.

He releases one thigh and raises his hand to my chest, taking my nipple between his finger and thumb, toying gently, reminding me of these notes he took during the stream.

Oh fuck, it's my goddamn kryptonite.

I'm trembling from all the excitement he's worked up, my body jerking about as the pressure mounts. He releases my other thigh and pulls off my cock, kissing my abs. With one hand, he continues playing with my nipple, and with the other, he strokes my cock as he looks up at me. I can see some of my precum just under his lip before he licks it up. His gaze locks with mine, but he doesn't stop working me. "Still as good as you thought?"

That's not a fucking question; it's bragging. "Amazing," I admit because it's the truth. "Col, I don't know how much longer I'm gonna last."

He chuckles. "That's kind of the idea."

I laugh, but then my body takes control again, these surging sensations overtaking me.

Colin doesn't take his eyes off me. "I told you I can go wild for you." He speaks in that low, sexy fucking whisper, like his voice is working up my ears while his hands are working up my body. "Make it all about you and your pleasure, Ash. I love watching you like this. Where you're so turned on that you're just letting go and enjoying yourself. Seeing the way your adorable lips curl upward, the way you moan. I want you to know that I'm the only one who can give it to you like this. The only one who knows you so well, your every shift and noise, the only one who will ever be able to pleasure you like this because I'm the only one who'll ever know you this well." He doesn't break eye contact or stop building me up.

The heat swells in my chest and face, the pressure in my hips becoming unbearable.

"I'm right, aren't I?" he asks.

"Yes," I reply in a breath.

I can't deny that everything he says is the truth.

I keep imagining someone coming by and seeing him, totally absorbed in me, totally lost in how fucking high he's taking me.

"I'm about to come," I warn him.

He smirks with pride before leaning close to my chest. He stops playing with my nipple with his fingers and licks at it as he twists the head of my cock just like I like it—like he was fucking memorizing it when I jerked off for the live stream.

I call out, practically screaming from the explosion tearing through me, and I can hardly think straight as I feel myself releasing, the warmth coating my abs.

I'm trembling as Colin's lips release my nipple and he dives to my abs, burying his fucking face in my cum.

With how feral he is, diving into it, lapping it up, it's

like he's not even thinking about what he's doing. Just going off this primal need to taste me. His tongue and mouth only existing to serve me.

I grab the back of his head, rubbing my thumb through his short hair. "Yes, get it all," I say. "Every fucking drop."

I glance around the parking lot, wishing we had a fucking audience to see what my stepbrother can do to me.

12

Colin

A QUIET VOICE in the back of my head tells me this shouldn't be as hot as it is, that we shouldn't be doing this where everyone can see us, but then a tingle lands at my nape and my cock pulses and throbs because holy fuck, part of what makes this so hot is the fact that everyone can see…which gets Ash hotter, which gets me hotter in return.

"So fucking good. I could get addicted to this." I run my tongue over his abs again, hoping to find some cum I missed, wanting to savor the taste of his pleasure, have it tantalize my taste buds for as long as fucking possible. "Here we go." I swipe my tongue over the only spot I missed, the salty taste going straight to my head, while also making my cock throb with need.

"You want me to feed you a load every day? Gotta get your protein to keep those muscles." He squeezes my biceps. "Or maybe I'll save it for when you're good."

Goose bumps race down my arms. Movement and

noise from outside the car snags Ash's attention, making lust flash in his eyes, which somehow lands right in my balls.

"You better hurry up and come, Col. We could get caught any second. Someone could walk over and see that you just ate a load out of your brother's balls."

Is it too much that I feel a little feral for him? That I want more of his jizz, want everyone to know I sucked it out of him. "Hell yeah. I'm gonna come all over you, and later, you better make another load just for me."

The muscles in his arms tense like he has to hold himself back from devouring me. I push up onto my knees a little more, shove my pants and underwear down, trying to get into position without my bare ass being up against the window.

I've never been so hard in my life or my nuts so full. I swear I feel like I'm almost blinded with my need for him. All those guys who annoyed me online? I almost feel like them, frenzied in my desire for Ash, but the difference is I know him. He's…mine. In some ways Ash has always been mine.

"Let me see you shoot, Col. I wanna see you stroke that thick cock."

"Fuck yes." I spit in my hand, wrap it around myself, and tug. I'm leaking so much precum and that, along with my saliva, makes it a pretty easy slide.

Ash's intense gaze is on me, his irises bursts of gold,

brown, and green, like stars orbiting black holes. I've seen these eyes so many times, but they've never had the power to cast a spell on me with one determined look.

I search around to make sure no one is close, but then give him my attention. He is…fuck, he's so goddamn hot—dark hair swept over his forehead, firm, sexy body, pecs I want to bite and taste.

"Shoot on me. Let me see how much you want me. Let me feel the hot splash of your cum on my skin."

For a moment I feel like I'm deprived of oxygen. I get dizzy, orgasm teetering on the edge, but then it has been since my first taste of Ash's cock. I'm going to be a goddamned fiend for it from now on.

The thought of it shoots straight to my balls, nuts drawing high, vision blurring while I'm swept under a surge of pleasure that makes me feel like I'm shattering apart. "Oh fuck!" I say as the first spurt hits his thigh. Another one, then a third swiftly follow, painting Ash's pretty skin with the proof of what he does for me.

"No one has ever made you shoot that hard."

"No." I shake my head. "Fuck. I'm dead. I don't even know if I can get dressed." I collapse onto the seat beside him, one of Ash's legs behind me. "Is it possible to come so hard you die? If anyone can make me do it, it's you."

Ash chuckles, but I'm serious, and I do think part of it is because of our bond. There's this connection that twines me and Ash together on this level I don't think anyone would understand, that I don't think is possible with anyone other than us.

"Well, I hardly think it's fair that you got to taste me and I didn't get to taste you. Let me taste you, Col."

My dick twitches again already as I scoop cum onto my finger and bring it to his lips. Ash sucks it into his mouth. I do it again, and let me just say…seeing him eat my jizz off my fingers is hands down one of the sexiest things I've ever seen in my life.

"All clean," I say, grabbing his clothes and handing them to him. He has to move so he's facing the front. We're quiet as we get dressed, and I can't help wondering what he's thinking. Does Ash regret it? But no, not a part of me thinks he does. I know him too well, know us, and while yes, this was a really big deal and we might need to work through it, neither of us will regret it.

Just as he finishes pulling his pants up, a car pulls in beside us. He lets out a soft moan.

"You wish we got caught!" I say, cluing in.

"After everything that's happened recently, this surprises you why?"

He has a point. "You're right. My mistake. I'm not surprised at all."

"Makes you hot too."

I push down on my already swelling cock. "Sometimes it's not easy having someone know me so well.

You're still gonna drive, right?"

"I was thinking you might want to drive," Ash replies.

"I mean, I'm game. I have a whole extra year of experience, so you need to try and catch up."

A few hours ago we both wanted to drive to our parents' house, and now post-orgasm, neither of us does. We burst into laughter, the way we always do with each other, the way we only do with each other.

"I'll drive," Ash says. "Gotta reward my big bro for being so good for me."

My skin tingles. "Yes. That. More of that, please."

We get out of the car and climb back into the front, where I take a blissful nap.

"Wake up, sleepyhead." Ash brushes the back of his hand against my cheek, making my eyes flutter open.

"Oh, are we home already? Sorry, I was sleeping so fucking good."

"Asshole." He winks.

"Don't be jealous that I got a post-nut nap and you didn't. I think we should do this more often—find some random place to get off, and then you can drive me around afterward while I sleep."

"Yeah, and maybe I'll kick you out of the car next time." We get out and meet at the front of the vehicle. "I love that we can joke about what we did," Ash admits.

My heart does this strange stumbling thing. "Me too.

I also really, really like what we did."

Ash leans against the hood. "Did you like it for you or more for me?"

I ponder his question. I can see why he'd ask. So many of my thoughts have always circled around Ash. "I liked it because of both of us. It's hot. You're hot. I keep wanting more of you. I think you're underestimating the effect you've had on me since I watched you jerk off. Doing it where we could get caught gave it an extra layer of naughtiness, and while I might not have known this about myself before, I really get off on it. But I must admit that a part of me gets off on it *more* because I know what it does to you. You're my new sexual fantasy."

Ash laughs, nudges me with his arm, then leans his head on my shoulder. "I felt like I could get you to do anything I wanted today. Like there's nothing you won't do to make me feel good, and that's an incredible rush."

"That's because there isn't anything I wouldn't do to make you feel good. I guess it's a good thing we both get off on that."

"I guess so."

We're quiet for a moment, resting against the car, when I hear a soft *meow*.

"Do you hear that?" I move toward the bushes at the side of the frat, Ash right behind me.

Meow. A soft, broken sound.

"It's tiny," Ash says while I get on my knees and crawl under the bushes, where I find an orange kitten tucked inside. It tries to hiss when I wrap my hand around it, baby kitten paws scratching at me.

"Shh. It's okay. I got you." I pull him close to my chest. Ash kneels beside me.

The kitty is dirty, too skinny, and he's got goop around his eyes. It's a fighter, though, tearing up my hands as I hold on to it.

"It doesn't look good, Col."

Fuck. Hearing that is like he drop-kicked my stomach, though all it takes is looking at the kitten to know that.

I've always had a thing for animals. I can't say how many times I've brought home a stray or injured one. Most of the time, Dad and Lauren didn't let me keep them. I could nurse them back to health, or we would bring them to the vet and they'd pay for them to get taken care of, and then I'd never see it again.

"I think he's alone. I need to check if there are any others." I try to still hold him while bending down to look, but Ash stops me.

"I'll look for others. You just take care of him."

I love that he doesn't treat me like I'm silly, that he doesn't mind getting messy and climbing into bushes to look for stray kittens for me.

"Shh," I tell the kitty again while Ash looks.

"There's nothing else here. I even did a bug sweep." I know he says the last part to make me smile, and it works.

"I can't believe I didn't make you do that first."

"Yeah, well, you're all heart, so it makes sense that when you heard something in need, you forgot about yourself."

Meow.

He doesn't fight as much this time, just curls against my chest.

Ash sighs. "Come on. I'll drive you to the emergency vet."

"Thank you. Frat Cat says thank you too."

"Oh fuck. You already named him?"

"Of course I did."

We head back to the car, Ash in the driver's seat while I hold the kitten.

"Don't get too attached, Col. You don't know what might be wrong with him."

"Too late." I rub the kitten's belly.

"Jesus, Col. What am I going to do with you?"

"I can think of some really dirty ideas, but Frat Cat is too young to hear that kind of talk."

Ash chuckles. "We're keeping that cat, aren't we?"

I smile at his use of *we.* That if I'm doing this, Ash will do it with me because we're always there for each other.

"Methinks you already know the answer to that. I'll blow you again later to say thanks."

He cocks a brow. "You'll blow me again because you like swallowing my load."

"That too. It's fucking delicious."

Ash groans, pressing his hand against his cock.

"No getting hard around Frat Cat."

"Then we're definitely not keeping that cat."

Good point. "Okay, we can get hard around him. I changed my mind."

We have to sit in the waiting room at the emergency vet for two hours before they see us, and Ash doesn't complain once. Frat Cat has an eye infection and is malnourished, but other than that, he seems healthy. They still want to keep him overnight to give him IV fluids and medication.

"Will you be keeping him?" the vet tech asks.

"Yeah, he's ours," Ash says, and I beam at his response.

"You have two new daddies!" I tell Frat Cat. "We'll come back for you tomorrow."

"How long have you two been together?" she asks, and I freeze. I'm figuring now isn't the right time to say we're stepbrothers. Maybe calling us his daddies wasn't the best choice of words.

"Oh, we're not. We're…" What are we? I want to say *everything*.

"It's new," Ash sweeps in and saves me. Right. Not like I have to give her any details.

I bend over the table, getting close to the kitten. "We'll come get you soon. I promise we're not abandoning you."

When I glance at Ash, he's smiling.

They charge me way too much money for today, but I pay it because Frat Cat is worth it. As soon as we're in the car, Ash asks, "To the store for kitten supplies?"

It's late, and I love that he doesn't try to put it off. He knows I wouldn't have the patience. This time it's my turn to grin at him. "You know me so well."

13

Ash

BEING A CAT dad wasn't on my bingo card for the week, but neither was my stepbrother hoovering up my cum in the back of his car.

Yet here we are.

Since we adopted Frat Cat, Colin and I have been tending to his needs, helping him through his recovery. We've always been good about caring for Colin's rescues together, but this time, maybe because of what the vet tech said about us looking like a couple, or because of what began in the car, it feels more coupley—taking turns giving him his meds and watching him to make sure he's eating and drinking enough. We're not just physically taking care of him, but emotionally too. He's had it rough, been all on his own, so he needs extra love, which Colin and I have plenty to give.

Between being cat dads and dealing with school and work, we've had our hands full, but we've gotten our fun in too.

Exchanging playful, flirty texts.

Making a game of feeling each other up discreetly around the other guys in the house.

Clearly, we stumbled upon something at that gas station.

It was more exciting than a live stream. It brought me to fucking life, but also made me a little cum monster. It seems to have had the same effect on Colin— at least, I assume that's what explains our epic jerk-off sessions—one downstairs late while everyone was asleep, the other in the shed out back. Both times, he was as cum-hungry as before, getting every fucking drop in.

Colin makes it easy not to overthink any of it. Or feel like there's anything wrong with what we're doing. I can just enjoy every second. Lap it up like he laps up my cum.

When Friday arrives, the house is setting up for the TaskFrat Challenge after-party. The event will be at Sigma Alpha, but after, everyone will be rushing here to get their drink on.

I head downstairs with Frat Cat wrapped in a towel, meet Marty and Lance outside, where they're positioning the bar in the yard.

"Is that cat gonna be your excuse to get out of help-ing out?" Marty asks as I offer some scritches to our new fur baby.

Our wounded kitten leans into my touch; he's

warmed up to me quickly.

"His babysitter is on the way, so you guys will have a whole five more minutes without me."

Marty rolls his eyes. "Wish *I* could have a five-minute break."

"Sometimes we all wish you'd take a longer break than that, Marty," Lance teases, which makes me laugh.

"That was harsh," Marty says.

"Truth hurts."

Marty shakes it off. "I don't know why you and your bro decided to become cat parents when that thing would eat your gerbils in a minute."

"I've taken the necessary precautions. Really, now I have three critters to protect from Payton's python."

Marty shivers. Snakes and spiders are not his thing, and Colin has had to keep him from killing either more than a few times while we've lived at the Alpha Theta Mu house.

Marty's unpacking the box of liquor when he shoots a glare at Frat Cat. "You filled out your pet wai—"

"I swear," Lance says, "if you ask him about the pet waiver again, I'm gonna kick you in the nuts."

Marty flinches. "It's a rule to make sure our insurance covers shit."

"They filled it out the night they found him. They just haven't told you because they like how it's grating on your nerves."

"Little fucks."

I'm in stitches. Marty is so fucking easy to work up.

"Afternoon, boys." Colin's voice makes my skin prickle, and I turn to see him approaching. He's been tucked away in his room today, working on a paper. And I must admit, the brief separation has made me needy.

"Oh, good, you can make up for your slack-ass brother," Marty says.

"Uh-uh. I'm not having this," I tell them. "It's your turn with the baby anyway." I hand Frat Cat over to Colin and head around the bar. "Here, you guys pass me shit, and I'll get everything set up."

Marty passes me the liquor from the box, and Lance hands over the cups and bar paraphernalia.

While we do that, Colin steps behind the bar with me. He massages Frat Cat's neck. It reminds me of all the moments like this, throughout our lives, when I've seen him tending to his animals. Nursing them back to health. He's a good cat dad.

I continue packing the bar when I feel a hand on my ass, then a gentle squeeze.

A jolt of excitement rushes through me as I look toward Lance and Marty, then at the guys around the yard.

Behind the bar, no one can see what Colin's up to.

He's a naughty cat dad.

This is what the past few days have been like since we

messed around in the car—touching and caressing each other discreetly, waiting for Marty to notice and say, *"Oh my God, you weren't fucking kidding!"*

As much as I love this game, I'm pissed Colin's in the better position to grope me.

His thumb strokes back and forth, his hand creeping lower. I push my ass back for him, savoring his touch, since I feel like I've been starved of it all day because of a stupid fucking essay.

"So who did you get to babysit that cat?" Marty asks.

"Do you know Miranda from Phi Kappa?" I ask. "We're friends from Math League in high school."

Marty's expression twists up. "Someone not interested in seeing all the frats of Alpha Theta Mu make asses of themselves in skimpy outfits? There's a first."

"I think her girlfriend understands why that's not really her thing."

"Oh, right," Marty says. "Guess that was a shitty assumption for me to make."

"Don't worry. We expect it from you," Lance teases, which makes Marty burst into a laugh.

"Fucker."

"Colin, will you be coming tonight?" Lance asks.

"I hope I'll be coming." He gives my ass another squeeze. All this attention on my ass is new.

I glance over my shoulder, and he sports a smirk.

Don't suggest anything you wouldn't follow through

with, Col.

Marty pushes to his feet and glances over the bar, making Colin pull back his hand.

My heart sinks.

"Looking for something?" Colin asks, sounding annoyed that we were interrupted.

"Where the fuck did Payton put all the gin?" His gaze meets mine, and he winces. "Jesus, Ash, you've been getting some sun. Need to up the SPF."

I glare at Colin, who knows why my cheeks look like this, and he gets a good chuckle out of it before my phone buzzes. Miranda's arrived, so I take Frat Cat out to her, giving her the info the vet tech provided before handing him off with his crate. Then I get back to the guys.

Colin and I manage to keep our distance and focus on helping out rather than messing around, and after we all finish up, Lance gives me and the other TaskFrat guys a fifteen-minute warning.

Fifteen minutes—that's all I fucking need.

I tail Colin, who acts surprised by his stalker before slipping into his room and making like he's about to close the door on me, but as I push in, he's all smiles.

I kick the door all the way open behind me and tackle Colin, forcing him back onto his bed.

"Fucking ass," I say as I mount him, straddling his leg, placing my hand against his crotch. I check the doorway before rubbing him firmly. "Making me get all hot and flustered in front of the guys…"

His gaze cuts to the door like he's waiting for someone to walk by, then turns back to me.

"And after not spending any time with me all day," I say like the greedy fuck I am.

He closes his eyes, resting his head against the mattress. "Fuck," he mutters.

His crotch is a rock already, and I slide my hand under his waistband.

We're in plain view. Anyone could come in at any moment and see us.

Thank God.

"Why didn't I ever know what a little perv you are?" he asks as I grip his girth and give it a good pump. He growls through his teeth. "You tease. You know you have to leave soon."

I pull my hand back up and lick my palm, sliding back under his sweatpants to wet his dick.

I lean close, inches from his lips. "You coming to see me at TaskFrat tonight?" I whisper.

"You know damn well I'm gonna be there."

"Not just there…to see *me*," I clarify.

"Of course it's to see you."

Why does that feel so fucking good?

I reward his dick with another stroke, then glance at the door, listening, my senses ready to detect anyone heading this way. I'm torn between the fear of getting caught and the excitement of what we're getting away with. Why is this so electrifying?

I continue stroking him, and his eyes roll back like this is the best anyone's ever jerked him.

"You like it too," I say. "Knowing that someone could walk by at any minute and see your pervy bro jerking your fat cock?"

He knows I already know the answer to that, so he just rocks his hips.

"Or I could stop?"

"Don't fucking stop, Ash."

I snicker, enjoying this power I have over him.

Colin cups my ass cheek, gripping firmly.

At first when we were groping and fondling each other, he would go for my cock, maybe my side or the small of my back. Why's he so interested in my ass today?

It brings forth fantasies I've had the past few days, since I learned what he could do to my fucking body.

A part of me is sure it's my wish, not his. Another part of me knows in my goddamn soul it's what he's thinking right now. "You keep grabbing my ass today. You don't just want to come in my hand, do you? You want to know what this tight hole feels like."

How could I not think about what that cock would be like inside me? How he'd feel?

Fuck, if that's how we felt just messing around, I know it'd be good.

How did we go from chill stepbros to me wanting to use him like a fuck machine?

"Yes," Colin says. There's a high to knowing, once again, that I'm fucking right about him.

"Would you be as good to my ass as you are my cock?"

"You know I would," Colin says, and I hear it as a promise. "You know I'll be the best you ever fucking had."

I lean close to his ear and whisper, "You're damn right. You said you love making me feel good. Fuck, you know how good that would make me feel? Do you want to hear me begging you to fuck me harder? You have any idea what it'd do to me if I came while your thick cock was slamming against my prostate?"

"Oh fuck, Ash."

A *creak* from a floorboard in the hall catches our attention, and I move like lightning, freeing his cock and rolling over on the bed.

Colin looks like he's recovering from a tackle, eyes wandering like he doesn't even know where he is, and I feel like I've just shaken out of a horny trance, this primal desire Colin's unlocked in me.

Lance pops his head in. "Come the fuck on, Ash. We gotta get ready. We need to be out of here in ten minutes."

There's panic in Colin's expression. "He needs, like, five," Colin says, his words nearly a threat, the look in his eyes desperate, pleading.

I'm hard too, but there's something exciting about the hunger in Colin's eyes.

"Be right behind you," I say as Lance heads off.

Colin doesn't waste time. As soon as the coast is clear, he rolls on top of me. He straddles my leg, seizing my wrists, reminding me of when he used to pin me when we wrestled around, except this time, our hard cocks are pushing up against each other.

"What the hell?" he says. "You can't just go after working me up like that. We can make it quick."

"Come on, Col. It'll make it more fun. Leaving you like this now so that when you're watching me at TaskFrat, you're jizzing yourself thinking about what you're gonna do to me later."

His gaze is wild, feral. "This is definitely cruel."

I lean up and bite his chin gently, then whisper against his flesh, "And as we've established, you like when I'm cruel."

As I pull away, the panicked expression twists into that familiar grin.

"I want you thinking about me, Col, about this. About what you want to do to me all night long. I want every fucking second of your mind to be occupied with all the dirty things you want to do to me. And how you'll make up for me leaving you like this."

He leans down, licks my cheek, then bites into it.

Like when he was eating up my cum, his movements seem beyond his control. A rush of desire overtakes me, swirls of sensation radiating through me, and I gasp.

"This is what I want," I tell him. "You to be so fucking horny, you're not even thinking when you fuck me."

When the hell did I start saying things like this to my stepbrother?

He takes a few deep breaths, which slam into my skin, when the *creak* outside the door returns. Colin leans back just as Lance heads in.

"I knew I should have pulled you out the first time," he says, unfazed by Colin having me pinned down, which really isn't terribly suspicious for us. "Enough roughhousing. You gotta get your contacts in before we go. Come on, Ash."

Colin crawls off me, and Lance takes my hand, practically dragging me off the bed.

"You can kick the crap out of your brother later," he calls out, and I glance over my shoulder, enjoying that determined look in Colin's eyes, which are right on my ass.

Damn right.

14

Colin

THERE'S A GOOD chance I might end up at the hospital today for being too hard for too long. I might get down to half a chub, but then my mind goes straight back to what it felt like to have Ash on top of me...beneath me...all the dirty, sexy things he said to me. He's fucking filthy and I love it, and the second I hear those words in my head, all the blood rushes to my groin again, making me uncomfortable in my joggers.

And it's hot. It's like he's mentally edging me all night. That's not something that would have ever entered my thoughts before we started doing this, but the rock-hard erection between my legs says I'm very much into this.

I adjust myself. Maybe I can sneak into my room and jerk it real quick, but no, Ash wants me needy for him, wants me hard and thinking about him all night, which sends a zing up my spine.

"Fuck." I wiggle around in my computer chair, and

when that doesn't help, I press my palm against my dick and give it a quick rub.

"I want you thinking about me, about this. About what you want to do to me all night long. I want every fucking second of your mind to be occupied with all the dirty things you want to do to me. And how you'll make up for me leaving you like this."

"Dude. What the fuck? Close the door if you're gonna jerk off." Troy sticks his head through the door.

Oops. Ash definitely got his wish. "What are you doing here?" I ask.

"Had to stop by and grab something before I go to TaskFrat Challenge." He was with Atlas earlier, so he hadn't been around when Ash and the guys left.

"I'll dip with you guys. Give me just a sec."

He cocks a brow. "You're going to go like that?"

What would he say if he knew I was going this way because it's what Ash wants? That I know how hot it will get him, which in turn gets me hotter than the surface of the fucking sun? It's not like Troy would care about the stepbrother thing, considering his situation, but this dynamic Ash and I have going on...well, it's not your everyday romance.

Romance? Shit? Why the fuck did I think that?

"You let me worry about my dick, Troy. I'll be getting this taken care of later."

"Who are you hooking up with?"

153

I wink, which is cheesy as fuck, but I don't care. "Wouldn't you like to know?"

"Nah, I'm good," Troy teases, making me laugh.

He goes to grab his shit, and I throw on a shirt, adjust my dick as best as I can, then meet him downstairs.

Atlas is waiting for us, all floppy hair and scowl like aways, though really, I've learned it's more an act than anything. Not that Atlas isn't grumpy—he is. But he also has a big heart he likes to hide from others.

"Why isn't the challenge here?" Atlas asks when we get outside.

"There's a TaskFrat committee, and they come up with locations that work based on the challenge. Tonight they're doing an obstacle course, so they needed the frat with the biggest yard."

"Fucking frats." Atlas shakes his head, and yeah, the frat thing can come with its problems, but Alpha Theta Mu and the other Peach State frats are as legit as they come. We don't fuck around with any of the bad shit. We want to party, have fun, and…okay, now I want to watch Ash participate in his challenges, but that's only a me thing.

I hear the music playing as soon as we get close to the house. Two guys are standing at the gate, taking cash to let anyone in. I grab money from my pocket and hand it over.

The yard is pretty full already, the course set up. The

way they have it planned is one person from each frat moves through *all* the obstacles, but there are members from every frat at each stop to complete the activity with the main guy. Ash is our main guy, of course, because he's a competitive motherfucker and good at everything. He's fast, strong, compact, and smart as fuck. My little bro is the full package, and everyone knows it.

I spot him instantly, my eyes automatically drawn to him. He's shirtless, while Marty helps him put on his temporary Alpha Theta Mu tattoo. All the guys wear one for their specific frat. Ash doesn't have his glasses on, and I can't decide which way he looks hotter. He's hot no matter what he's doing or what he's wearing. Funny how quickly I've gotten used to thinking things like that.

He's in shorts, and the muscles of his arms and chest glisten like they put something on him. My dick begins to throb again. Yep, definitely going to end up hurting myself today.

We stop by a group of people, but I'm not paying attention to anything they're saying. I can't keep my eyes off Ash...off his ass. The thought of being inside him, of getting to fuck that perfect peach, has me nearly coming in my pants already. Fuck, I want him.

"You're Ash Fuller's brother, right?" My eyes flicker to the girl who asks, Ash's name the only thing that can pull my attention away from him.

"Yep."

"He's really hot. You should hook me up." She laughs, and yeah, she's pretty as hell. I'd want to fuck her if I wasn't into Ash, and she's his type, but the hairs on the back of my neck rise, an uncomfortable feeling settling there.

"No, he's…busy."

He's busy? What the fuck is wrong with me?

"I can see he's busy right now. And I don't want to marry the guy. I want to have sex with him." She frowns, probably wondering what the hell I've been smoking. That makes two of us.

"Oh look! It's about to start." I leave the group of bewildered people behind and work my way to the front so I have a good visual on Ash. My reaction to her wanting Ash is…concerning. It feels different from when I'm protective of him with guys like Brenner. But then I figure it makes sense because we're doing…whatever it is we're doing. The Brenner stuff has been pre-hookups. Of course I wouldn't want him to be with anyone else when my dick will be buried in his ass tonight.

"Thank you for coming to TaskFrat Challenge," Jake, one of the frat presidents, greets us.

My gaze darts toward Ash, who is looking right at me. Goose bumps race down my arms when he smiles at me and palms his cock discreetly, just for me. Ash wants me hot for him all night, wants me here just for him, and damned if I don't feel the same. That's why I didn't want that girl to think she could have him. I love having his attention focused on me, on how I can make him feel and how fucking hungry for him he can make me. It's the best kind of rush.

Jake rambles on—dude never fucking stops talking—and I just watch Ash. Sneak my hand down my body and cup myself, give my cock a firm stroke on top of my joggers where anyone might see.

A random guy beside me bumps my arm. "Sorry, bro."

"No worries," I tell him, watching Ash. His gaze isn't letting me go as I raise one hand to my pec, trying not to be too obvious when I rub my nipple with my thumb, then pluck the hard nub for him. All just for Ash. Is there anything I wouldn't give him? Anything I don't *want* to give him? I don't think so. I'd fuck him right here in front of everyone if he wanted me to. The thought makes my balls tighten.

"Ready!" Jake shouts, and Ash is forced to pull his attention away from me, but he knows I'm watching him. Knows I'm hard for him and that later tonight I'll let loose all my pent-up want on him, fuck him so hard that he forgets what it's like to be with anyone else.

"Set…TaskFrat!"

There are three guys in line for the slip and slide, Ash at the end since he'll move to the next obstacle. The first guy in each line runs, dives onto the tarp, and slides to the end where they grab the first glass of beer and chug it.

Lance is our first guy, and he's in second place when he finishes his drink and slides back toward the line, but I have no doubt Ash will catch us up. Lance taps Payton, who goes next, sliding down, drinking, and racing back.

A fucking hurricane couldn't uproot me, couldn't pull my attention away from Ash as he slides, all fucking wet and hot, muscles and body so damn tight. I want to lick the water off him, lap it all up the way I do his cum, want to paint his body with both our loads and spend the day licking him clean.

Ash chugs his beer, then moves on to the next obstacle. He grabs the Hula-Hoop, and I swear if I were the whimpering type, I'd be whining at the sight of him shaking his hips as he walks down a path toward his teammates while keeping the Hula-Hoop going.

Ash can work his fucking hips. He's going to work them with me tonight while I plow his tight little hole.

I palm myself again, can't help it, don't fucking care if anyone sees.

When he makes it through that challenge, an "Oh fuck," slips out of my mouth when I notice what's to come. Bro beside me looks at me and frowns, but then turns away again.

Mitchell, one of our other frat bros, is bent over a chair, a balloon pinned to his ass. Ash grabs his hips, starts thrusting against him—hard, powerful thrusts, just like I'm going to do to him tonight—trying to pop the balloon between them.

Is it wrong that I'm both turned on as hell but also want to rip Mitchell away from him and be the one bent over for Ash? I have to bite back a growl at anyone else getting to feel him like that.

Ash pops his balloon first. Mitchell collapses to the ground laughing, and Ash moves to the next obstacle. I get harder with each one he accomplishes, my need for him building higher and higher, just like he wanted. Just like I want too, because with each passing second, my body tingles for him more, the control I have over myself getting harder to maintain. What will it feel like to be inside him? To hear him beg for me to fuck him harder and faster and know that no one has ever given Ash what I can. It's like I'm fucking invincible when I'm with him.

At the end, when Ash throws his hands in the air in victory, I'm rushing over to him. Everyone is around him, congratulating him, but he's watching me, wanting me. When I pull him into a hug, everyone around us, I rub my hard cock against him, a promise for what's to come, right in front of everyone, who are none the wiser.

"Good job, bro," I say for everyone else, then whisper in his ear, "I'm going to fuck you so hard you forget your name."

"You better," he replies before he's dragged away

from me, and all I can do is stand there and watch him go, flying high just because Ash is. I love nothing more than to see him shine.

I watch as everyone celebrates with Ash, but eventually I'm tired of waiting. I push away from the tree, walk over, and grab him.

"Let's go home," I say, turning so he can jump on my back, not caring that he's going to get me all wet.

"In a hurry?" He smirks.

"You know I am. I'm fucking dying here."

Ash grins, sexy and wicked, loving what he's doing to me, and I'm loving it too. "Good. That's how I like you best...going wild for me."

"I've been doing that ever since you followed me to my room." Maybe longer.

He jumps onto my back, and as soon as he's situated, Payton says, "Party at the Alpha Theta Mu house!"

Oh yeah. Fuck. Is he going to make me wait until after the party to have his ass? Or maybe I'll fuck him while everyone is around, plow him where anyone could overhear or walk in and see us.

A stampede of college kids storm the gate, ready to get their drink on.

"When do I get your hole?" I ask.

Ash chuckles. "When I think you've suffered enough."

I growl in response. His legs tighten around me, dick

pressed into me. The only words I have to give him are the truth. "I can't fucking wait. I want you so fucking bad, couldn't take my eyes off my stepbro the whole time. Wanted to fuck you in front of everyone just so you can see how much I want you."

"Huh?" someone beside us says. I don't recognize the guy.

Ash laughs when I say, "Nothing," on a quiet snicker of my own.

15

Ash

I'M A FUCKING sadist.

It's not my intention to torture Colin, but now that the party's really going, I can see how much it's killing him not to slip away with me and give me the pounding I need. I'm surprised I managed through the challenge with just a semi, considering I was basking in his attention, knowing his gaze was fixed on me.

Everyone's drinking and dancing in Alpha Theta Mu's yard. We're surrounded by our crew, but Colin barely gives me an inch. He's got that determined look in his eyes, like any minute he might scoop me up and carry me off to fuck me in the bushes.

I can't blame him—the only thing I'm using my brain for right now is to run through scenarios.

But there are too many people packing the yard for us to slip away into a corner even for a few quick gropes.

A few Sigma Alphas I competed with swing by for a chat, when one of the guys says, "This is Dax. He's my brother. Visiting from out of town."

I recognize the guy from back at the challenge; he nearly overheard Colin talking dirty to me, about how he wanted to fuck me with everyone watching. Dax brushed it off, but the way he's eyeing me, a big grin across his face, I can't help wondering if he heard more than he should have.

"That was wild," Dax says, shaking my hand. "Great work. Impressive. So you're with…" He checks my temporary tattoo. "Alpha Theta Mu?"

"Yeah."

He shakes hands with Colin too, and Colin's friendly, trying to make conversation, but I can tell he's as distracted as I am.

"Are you guys a couple?" Dax glances between us.

So yes, he must've heard us.

"Oh my God," Marty's voice comes from nearby. "What the fuck? They're stepbrothers, for Christ's sake."

Dax's forehead creases. "That didn't really answer my question, but okay, sure."

Colin and I exchange a knowing look, unable to keep from grinning.

We dance for a few songs, the gang getting a bit wild and doing Jell-O shots.

Colin still can't take his eyes off me.

Or keep down that raging hard-on he's sporting.

I don't know how much longer I can keep this up

either, as I'm salivating over it.

I dance over to him. "Maybe we should go inside and see if there's someplace we can creep into?"

"Best idea you've had all night." Colin moves close so that his lips are near my ear and whispers, "Unless you want me to fuck you right here in the middle of a crowd."

I chuckle. "Doesn't seem like such a horrible idea."

We share a laugh before sneaking into the house, on a fucking mission.

People are dancing in the living room, but it's not as busy as outside. And sure, we could run to either of our rooms for a quick fuck, but where's the fun in that? It's more exciting when there's an even greater chance of us getting caught.

I'm like a horny Terminator, running diagnostics for the naughtiest place we could fuck, when an idea springs to mind. I don't share it with Colin, just lead the way. He follows me through the living room, into the downstairs hallway. I guide him to the end, checking the door.

Bingo.

Alpha Theta Mu's converting the space into a weight room, but since we don't have it set up yet, it's the perfect discreet corner to play around in during a party.

The light that creeps in from the hall reveals gym equipment the guys have packed inside—bench press, cable machine, rower, stationary bike, treadmill, dumbbells. Once we get it up, it'll be pretty impressive.

"Nice use of our dues," I say before Colin spins me toward the wall. Seizing my wrists, he pins me, my back against the wall. I surrender to him fully as he presses his cheek against mine, breathing me in, pushing that hard cock against my waist. We push together, and I swear, even under his pants, I can feel him getting even harder.

"Fuck," I mutter, quivering as his body is tight against mine, his lips caressing my cheek.

Fire rushes from my face through my body as he licks across my skin, then kisses my neck. I roll my head back against the wall, my cock straining in my shorts.

He releases one of my wrists and reaches down, cupping my balls, gripping firmly as his tongue explores my flesh before he offers a soft bite.

"Colin," I say in a breath, and he grabs the waistband of my shorts and yanks them down. He releases my other hand and turns me to face the wall.

My shorts fall to my ankles as he shoves up behind me, pressing his pelvis against my ass so I can feel his girth behind his pants.

"Look what this ass has been doing to my cock all fucking night long," he says. "You proud of that?"

"Yes," I confess.

"I bet you are, my little perv."

I could get used to him calling me that.

Desire surges through me.

My skin prickles with sensation.

But there's dread in my belly. "Please tell me you came prepared. I meant to grab a condom and lube, but Lance was in such a fucking hurry."

When he doesn't reply right away, a knot twists in my chest. Fuck no. I could just go upstairs, but I don't want to wait another second to take my stepbrother's cock.

Colin snickers. "Like I wouldn't have come ready."

I glance over my shoulder as he retrieves a condom and mini bottle of lube from his pockets, and I'm so fucking relieved. It's like we've been wandering the desert for days and we just discovered water.

"Well, don't leave me hanging," I say.

"I *should* leave you hanging after you left me blue-balling like that, but you're lucky all I want is to have my cock in you right now."

As he readies himself, something catches my attention. I step out of my shorts and slip away from him.

"Where the hell do you think you're going?"

I turn back to him, snatching his cap off his head and putting it on mine backward. "Just trust your little bro."

I walk over to the bench-press rack, which is placed near the wall, with the barbell bar locked in the safeties. Resting my hands on the bar, I push my ass back, glancing at Colin, who's got the condom rolled on.

His gaze is fixated on my ass, his dick twitching upward.

"You make me feel like this is the first ass you've ever seen."

"Maybe the best, but definitely not the first." Colin winks before glancing to the open door, ensuring we're still on our own before joining me at the rack. He pumps lube from the mini bottle, quick to offer some for my hole.

Always fucking thinking of me.

Always so damn selfless.

Always so damn Colin.

The care he takes makes it seem like he's done this thousands of times before.

I enjoy the sensation of his fingers sliding around the rim, thinking about how much better it'll be when it's his cock.

When he's got me nice and wet, he rubs lube over his condom.

The anticipation is fucking killing me. "Give it to me, Col. Every fucking inch."

I grip the barbell bar, rock my hips back. I want to know what he'll feel like inside me. How long it'll take him to get it all the way in. How it'll feel when my stepbro's cock is wedged against my prostate.

He strips off his shirt, discarding it to the side and throwing the bottle of lube on top. Then he grabs my hip with one hand and my ass cheek with the other. He presses the head against my hole, pushing in.

Fuck, he's so hard.

But he's slow and cautious, taking his time to make sure my body's ready for every inch.

He's only getting started when he whispers, "Oh, yeah, even better than I imagined."

"Ditto," I confess, glancing over my shoulder. He wears a cocky smirk, like he knows what his cock is gonna do to me.

Then he gives me an inch.

And another.

I push my hips back, steadily working with him until there's the jolt I've been waiting for, like he's pressed a button attached to every nerve in my body, sending a rush from my pelvis to my face and fingertips. They're fucking vibrating with life as he slides right along the spot, and I arch my back as I fall into the high, basking in the sensations he stirs until he's buried deep, his hips resting against my ass.

He wraps his arms around me, tugging me close as he bites against my shoulder. "Jesus fucking Christ, Ash. You weren't lying about how tight it is."

I chuckle. "Are you proud of how fast I took you?" I ask, taking breaths as I adjust to that thick girth. "Are you impressed with your little stepbro for being able to handle a cock like that?"

"Very," he breathes against me, and another jolt of excitement pulses through me.

We stay right there, perfectly still, my muscles relaxing for him, and he must feel I've eased up because he starts offering the subtlest of thrusts, which my body eagerly welcomes.

"How's that?" Colin asks.

"Just right."

I close my eyes, facing the wall, enjoying each rub up against that sweet spot, losing myself in the web of nerves radiating with pleasure and excitement.

"Better keep it down," he whispers, and I realize I was moaning, as though it was only the two of us.

"Fuck, good call," I say as he offers another thrust that makes my whole body tremble.

I reach up and place my hand on the back of his head, running my fingers through his hair, encouraging him as he speeds up. With each thrust, I can feel his hunger, his need, his body making up for that time I deprived him of.

"I'd feel worse for being cruel if you didn't make it feel so damn good. Give it to me, Col. Give me what I need."

He moves even faster, though I notice he's keeping his hips from slamming into my ass and clapping—and possibly alerting others about what we're up to. I firm my grip on the barbell bar, the rack trembling with each deep push.

"You're just wishing someone would walk in and catch you taking my cock, aren't you? Wishing they would see how good you are at this? See how fucking hot you look as you take it?"

My chest and cheeks radiate heat as I sneak a glance at the open door.

I grip the back of his head, turning to see him over my shoulder.

I've always known Colin was a sexy fuck, but seeing the desire in those serious blue eyes as he fucks me, that intensity in his expression as he really gives it to me, knowing he wants to do this for me... He looks like a fucking god.

His face carved from stone. That chiseled jawline.

That sexy mouth.

I lick my lips, and I'm tempted not to say my wish, but no more Step Don'ts. "Col, kiss—"

I barely get the word out before he lurches at me, taking my mouth. It's his. He doesn't let up drilling me as he fucks me with his tongue and cock, and my body's never felt so alive. Every nerve on edge. The pressure mounting so goddamn fast.

We're heat and thrusts and wet tongues, not even existing in time and space, just spiraling through a roller coaster of sensations.

But a sound catches my attention, and I freeze up.

Fuck.

Colin and I turn at the same time to the door, where someone stands. Holy hell. We should have been more careful, shouldn't have gotten so lost in that kiss.

It takes me a moment to focus before I realize who it is. "Dax?" I ask, still with Colin buried inside me.

"Uh...sorry. I have to admit I did hear you guys back at Sigma Alpha, and I...well...I didn't know if that was just dirty talk, but I thought maybe...and then I found you. And it was so hot, I just...fuck...maybe I read this all wrong."

He's so innocent in his awkwardness, and Colin and I are frozen in place, neither of us knowing how to react to this surprise.

"I'm just gonna..." Dax signals behind him. "Unless you guys need a lookout? No? Keep up the good work. Okay...I'm out."

Wait. He heard us. Came to find us. He thought this was hot. And now he's offering to be our lookout?

I glance at Colin, a wicked impulse shooting through me. No...no way we can do that.

But that mischievous smirk plays across Colin's lips. He winks before turning to the door. "Hey, Dax?"

Dax spins around, still near the doorway, like he was hoping he might be summoned.

"A lookout wouldn't be such a bad idea," Colin says.

"Seriously?"

"As long as this stays in this room," I say.

Dax slips inside, settling along the wall. "Not a peep from me."

Something comes alive within me, reminding me of what I enjoyed about the live streams. Yes, it's fun with the door open, almost getting caught, but there's something else I like—having this guy seeing me taking Colin's cock.

I glance at my stepbro, who beams. "Come here, my little perv."

I snicker before he takes my mouth again.

I fall back effortlessly into his kiss as he begins thrusting, my body trembling as he really drills into me. Now I feel like I have something to prove. Not just to Colin, but to our guest.

I push my ass back, meeting each of Colin's thrusts, our kissing becoming frenzied as he hammers away at my prostate.

But I can do better than this.

"Pull out," I whisper into his mouth. "Just for a second."

"Oh fuck. You're killing me. I'm getting so close."

I love having someone else witnessing Colin's need for me. How much he fucking craves my body.

"I promise I'll make it worth it, Col."

His jaw tenses, like he's having to summon the strength before he pulls out. I spin around to face him, then grip the barbell bar behind me. Colin clearly knows what I want because he doesn't waste time. He hooks his arms around my thighs, hoisting them into the air. I wrap my legs around his hips, and he navigates his way back inside me. My body welcomes his cock, already trained to open up for him, and I brace myself on the bar, feeling the workout as he picks up the pace, really throwing his weight into pounding this ass.

I peek at Dax, who strokes his crotch as he watches us going at it.

I roll my head back, reveling in this moment.

Letting him watch Colin have his way with me.

Letting him enjoy my pure, unfettered pleasure of taking this massive cock like a fucking pro.

I bask in the sensations Colin stirs, locking gazes with my stepbrother, and he stares at me as if I'm the only thing in the world that matters to him in this moment. A servant to my pleasure.

"This is it, Ash. It's all about you. How good you look taking me. How hard you got my cock. How obsessed I am with your pleasure."

It's all too much for me: The pleasure that cock is giving me. The heat of having a guy seeing how wild my body drives Colin.

The pressure climbs so fucking fast. I wish I could reach for my cock to jerk off or ask Colin to do it for me, but as the pressure becomes unbearable, I realize I'm not gonna need my fucking hands.

"Col, I'm about to—"

He keeps his thrusts good and steady. "Do it, Ash. Show him that beautiful load you got." As soon as he says the words, he grits his teeth like he's not gonna last much longer either.

One push more from his cock flips the switch, and I start to call out when Colin's lips crash down on mine, blocking the sound before he grunts, as I feel the warmth rushing across my abs and chest. Since I'm not stroking myself, it takes longer for it all to spill out, leaving me suspended in this exhilarating high as Colin's thrusts become a series of erratic, wild movements, and I know he's coming in me.

It's just the two of us, lost in the moment, lost in each other, our tongues licking, lips smacking, teeth biting. I'm so lost in the ecstasy, I hardly realize my arms are trembling before my muscles give and I release the barbell. "Fuck," I mutter, but Colin's arms are around me in no time, gripping firmly, holding me in place. Keeping me right next to him.

Keeping me safe.

I hook my arms around him, pulling as close as I can to him, as if trying to merge our bodies.

"Fuck," Dax says from beside the door, which makes me chuckle into Colin's mouth. I feel his grin against my face.

"Oh shit." Dax's voice sounds distant as he says, "Hey, guys, sorry, this room is off-limits…"

Colin glances toward the door. "We picked a good lookout," he says, and I roll my head back, unable to contain my laughter.

I really do love the way we're weird.

16

Colin

EVEN THOUGH IT'S been a few days, I can't stop thinking about what it felt like to fuck Ash, to be inside him, feel the tight, hot grip of his ass as my cock slid in and out of him. I get hard just thinking about it, so I slip my hand down my shorts and give my dick a couple of squeezes. Frat Cat sees my hand move and immediately darts for my arm.

"Stop that," I tell him as he pounces around on my bed. "Daddy is busy."

Frat Cat jumps onto my chest and nuzzles my face, and okay, I can't be annoyed with him anymore.

"Why are you so cute? I can't stay mad at you. Hey, maybe that's why I can't stay mad at Ash either."

I lie there with Frat Cat, giving him some love. I had school earlier, then did a couple of hours' shift at the law firm. Homework is next on my list, but instead I'm thinking about Ash.

About fucking him.

About the high we felt with the door open.

About the way he nearly shot to the moon when Dax came in and started watching.

I mean, I did too. I wouldn't have thought of doing any of these things before, but they're an incredible rush. I like someone's eyes on me or knowing they could interrupt at any second, but more than that, I love what it does to Ash. Love being the one to give him pleasure and allowing him to explore this hidden desire of his. Seeing the bliss wash across his face and knowing it's happening because of what I'm giving him in more ways than just physically. I've fucked a lot of people, but none made me feel like I was skyrocketed to a whole new universe, simply because of how turned on they got about the situation.

As great as it is, part of me feels it's not enough. I want more, want to give him more, want to make every one of Ash's fantasies come true, even ones he doesn't know about…aaaaaaand, there goes my dick again.

I set Frat Cat beside me and roll to my belly, grabbing my laptop. I have no idea what I'm going to search: *How to turn your stepbrother on even more? How to bang your stepbro's brains out?*

I settle on exhibitionism, which gives me all the shit I already know, but it's interesting reading about other people who get off on it and why. Not that you need a reason for any kink, but it looks like my little perv's hobby isn't quite as rare as I thought.

I google *exhibitionism in Peachtree Springs*.

Random links pop up, most of which don't help me at all, and I'm about to close my search when I see PeachFlex.

Frat Cat chews on my T-shirt while I click. It's a local bathhouse, and honestly, I didn't even know we had bathhouses around here. I would have assumed they would be reserved for the lucky people in cities like Atlanta, but apparently, our college town is pretty fucking sex positive.

My eyes scan the pages—viewing rooms, steam rooms, hot tubs, and room rentals, which I assume is standard shit, but what the fuck do I know about this? It's not something I ever imagined myself doing, but I can't deny the way my boxer briefs feel tighter, the way my cock grows, heat flushing my prickling skin.

I think about the feel of Dax's eyes on us, of Ash's legs wrapped around me, eyes glazed over with lust when I told him how much it was all about him, how obsessed I am with his pleasure. And that was just with Dax in the room with us. What would it feel like to take him in front of a room full of people? For them to see what's mine? For Ash to make them all so fucking wild with need as they crave the hole that's wrapped around my cock? Or hell, I'd give him my ass too if that's what he wants. They can all be jealous of his beautiful dick pounding me.

A moan slips out just as the door opens. Frat Cat jumps off the bed and runs toward Ash, who cocks a brow when he sees the screen.

"Are you doing naughty things without me?" He picks up Frat Cat and closes the door. I know it's silly, but I love seeing him with our kitten, love that Ash only took him in because he knows how happy it makes me. That's what we do for each other.

"I'm planning naughty things I want to do with you. Come here."

He sits on the edge of the bed.

"I can't stop thinking about how hot the other night was…showing you off, making sure you know how much every-fucking-one wants you."

"Jesus, Col." He presses down on his bulge.

"It's true. I love the feel of touching you, of fucking you while everyone else admires you and wishes they were me." Because there's no doubt in my mind that's exactly what Dax was doing. He wanted to be inside Ash. And what that does for Ash…it gets me off more than anything else. His reaction, the way it stimulates him, makes me fucking feral.

"I feel like I might have corrupted you," Ash teases.

"Yeah, but do you regret it?"

"Not even a little bit."

I snicker, then nod to the screen. "Have you ever

been?"

"No, but I hooked up with a guy who mentioned it. I guess it's not a huge shock that it's the same guy who told me about Manzturbate."

A guy that makes me growly, but if he'd never told Ash about the app, we wouldn't be doing this. And I really, really love doing this with him. "Would you want to go? Show all those men how good you are?"

"I'd be so fucking good." He climbs toward me, and I roll to my back, Ash straddling me. "Jesus, you're fucking hard." He grinds down against my dick.

"And you're not?" I cup his bulge. Sometimes being with him makes me feel like a whole new person, one who doesn't have to ever hold anything back. Who can explore new parts of myself, parts he shows me exist, and I never have to worry about being judged.

"Yeah," Ash says, "but I think I'll make you wait for it."

I immediately miss the weight of him when Ash plops down beside me.

I groan. "You're a cruel, cruel brother."

"The cruelest," he teases. "Now come on. Let's check this place out. I'm definitely interested in trying it. The other night with Dax was even better than the live streaming."

"And getting head at a gas station?" I pump my brows, and Ash chuckles.

"That too. Being the center of attention like that…"

I wrap an arm around him and nuzzle close. "Now imagine just as many, if not more, people than on the live stream, being in the same room with you…seeing your huge fucking load in person."

A tremor runs the length of him, radiating into me. I swear we're both vibrating with need.

"And knowing that I'm giving it to you…that they can look but can't touch… Hell, if you're anything like me, you haven't even wanted anyone else since we started this." Hooking up with anyone other than Ash isn't even a blip on my radar.

"No shit. You too?"

"How could I want anyone else when I have my little perv?"

His eyes nearly roll back at that, his reaction making my dick throb.

"I can't even enjoy swiping on Tinder anymore," Ash says, "because I'm so busy thinking about my stepbrother's dick. Think you broke your little perv."

"Oh, I broke you?"

"It's okay. I don't want to be fixed." Ash licks my lips, and I take his mouth again.

When we pull away, he's chuckling.

"What?" I ask.

"I have a feeling we missed a really important Step Don't. Pretty sure stepbros aren't supposed to kiss…and they're definitely not supposed to fuck."

"I think we might have to move those to the Step Dos column…or maybe make a new list for Step Musts."

A wicked smirk plays across Ash's lips. "I guess I should start thinking of naughty things to add to Step Musts."

We share another laugh, when my stomach growls.

"You eaten?" he asks.

"No, but I am a little cum-hungry."

"You're my cum monster is what you are. Come on. Let's go down and make dinner. Then maybe I'll feed you dessert when we get back up here."

"Can I have dessert first?"

"Come on, Col. You know I like to make you work for it." He heads for the door, and I lie there a moment, watching him go, with the biggest smile on my face, then adjust my erection and follow him downstairs.

Payton, Marty, and Lance are in the living room, with books and their laptops.

"You guys cooking?" Marty asks.

"Yep," I reply.

"I mean…I could use a break." He closes his laptop, followed by Payton and Lance, all of us going into the kitchen.

It's a group effort making spaghetti because that shit goes far.

"Where did you guys disappear to at the party the

other night?" Lance asks.

Heat rises to my cheeks, my gaze darting to Ash. I might be slow on the uptake sometimes, but I'm figuring the best response here isn't *fucking Ash in front of Dax.*

"Colin and I were putting on a show for this guy Dax."

My eyeballs nearly pop out of my head, but Ash looks serious as ever. It's not that I care if anyone knows we're hooking up. I don't. And I know Ash well enough to know he has something up his sleeve.

"What do you mean, a show?" Marty asks.

Ash shrugs as if it's no big deal. "I was showing him some of the Frat Challenge stuff, and Colin was helping. We ended up showing him how the gym renovation was going too. The equipment's scattered all over, but Colin still managed to show off."

"You should have said something," Payton replies. "I would have come and lifted with you!"

"Colin lifted enough for all of us."

Damned if my dick doesn't stir again. The little shit is going to get it later.

"Don't let him fool you. Ash was showing all his skills. Dax was impressed with him."

"Well, not *all* my skills. I have some I haven't shared yet."

I bite back my laugh, but no one seems any the wiser.

"Dinner's done." I try to steer the subject in a safer

direction, otherwise I might end up fucking Ash in front of the guys instead of anyone at the bathhouse.

I make Ash a plate first, just because I like doing things for him, then my own. We all end up at the table together, talking shit and eating.

"Did you see that the next movie in that superhero franchise you like is coming out?" Payton asks me.

"On Friday. Fuck yes. I want to see it."

"We should go," Ash replies, and I nod.

"We can do dinner first too. There's that hibachi restaurant you wanted to try that's by the theater."

Ash twists noodles around his fork, and it's much hotter than it should be. "And that ice cream place you like too."

There's a flutter in my chest. He knows it's my favorite.

"Aww. The two of you are so wholesome, planning your date," Lance teases.

"They aren't Troy and Atlas. They're not dating each other," Marty grumbles.

"But they are wholesome," Payton says. "I swear you two remind me of one of those old TV shows where everyone in the family is perfect and gets along great."

I suck spaghetti noodles the wrong way and start coughing. Ash pats my back.

Wholesome my ass. My nape prickles, a new wave of lust sweeping through me. I like knowing they see Ash and me as one thing, but really, he's my little pervy stepbro, and I can't wait until the next time I get to show him off for others.

17

Ash

AFTER I FINISH up at my internship, I return to the frat, take a quick shower, then head back to my room. I tend to Darwin, Sagan, and Frat Cat before spending more time than usual at my closet. It's a warm spring day, so I can wear a polo or a tee and bring my jacket with me for when it gets cooler tonight.

I grab a tee, then second-guess myself.

Did I pick it because Colin mentioned he liked this shirt on me? Or did I start to like it more once he said that?

I chuckle; I'm being ridiculous.

But I kind of like overthinking going out with Colin tonight.

Between school, parties, and work, we've been so busy, we haven't had a night like this in a while. Just one-on-one time with my Big Man.

Hibachi, ice cream, and a movie is our thing— something we did plenty in high school. Of course, tonight's gonna be different with everything we've done together since the last time we hung out like this.

Before he blew me.

Or fucked and kissed me in front of a guy.

Or suggested fucking me in a bathhouse for people to watch.

And now that he's planted the idea in my head, my imagination has run wild. I thought the live stream was hot, but that sounds epic. Not just being fucked with people watching, but being fucked by Colin with people watching.

I love what we're doing and what we're talking about doing, but I'm curious what a night out looks like with all that's changed between us.

I throw on my shirt and a light jacket before there's a knock on my door.

I suspect it's Colin, so as I open the door, I keep to the side so he won't be able to see the collar of my tee under my jacket.

My stepbrother stands in the hall, smirking as his muscles flex in my favorite shirt of his—a sleeveless navy-blue shirt that hugs that chest and torso, emphasizing those impressive biceps. It's the shirt I've told him to wear when he's trying to impress a girl.

"You dork," I say. "Like I don't know why you wore that."

Colin's smirk spreads into a smile. "What are you

wearing?"

"Nothing."

"Perfect. That's what I'd prefer."

I chuckle as I open the door and unzip my jacket so he can get a better view.

Colin's eyes light up, and he checks down the hallway before slipping into my room.

As he steals a kiss, I rest my hands against his cheeks. He squats down and hooks his arms around my thighs, hoisting me in the air like I'm fucking weightless before pushing me up against the wall.

His lips are firm against mine. I didn't realize how much I missed his mouth until it was slammed up against mine again.

Fuck, what his body does to me... It didn't use to be like this at all.

When he touched me, my skin didn't come alive.

I didn't ache with hunger for more licks and kisses.

I didn't think about him taking me out and fucking me in front of strangers.

As Colin pulls away, his gaze shifts to my shirt again. "We're so fucking cheesy."

"You like when we're cheesy."

Colin's gaze wavers. "Well, we didn't specify when we made plans, but considering what we've been doing, is this a da—"

"Don't you fucking say it."

We both know this is date-y, but do we have to say the fucking word?

He's smiling as he opens his mouth like he's about to.

"If you say it, it's definitely not one."

"One what?" His eyebrows tug closer, really bringing the drama in his feigned confusion.

"You know damn well what you were gonna say."

"I don't think I do. Maybe you should tell me."

Why is my face so hot right now? But he's being so fucking adorable, my body can barely handle it.

"You were gonna say the D-word."

"D-word?" Colin says, searching around. "Wait, did you think tonight was a...a date?" He's really hamming up his performance.

And I give him a good tease. "Now I know why you didn't get the lead in that Arthur Miller play senior year."

"Oh, this is so embarrassing. You thought when we said hibachi and ice cream and a movie... Fuck, I never know when I'm sending the wrong signals. I don't know how to break this to you, but I'm just here for the Ash-hole."

I snicker; I can't fucking help myself. I know he's just joking around, and I fucking love it.

"I guess I'm an agent of chaos." Colin moves close, his lips millimeters from mine. "That must be so hard on you to have thought you were gonna get a date with all this and find out all you are is my naughty plaything."

He licks my lips before coming in for a kiss, pressing his weight against me, his tongue teasing mine, desire pulsing through me until I gasp. As I roll my head back, his mouth runs down my jaw to my neck. He makes his way back up until his lips are by my ear. "You think maybe we could just be friends and hang tonight? Then fuck around later? No strings?"

Colin bites at my earlobe, then sucks gently before pulling away, looking so fucking proud of himself for his performance.

I wish I wasn't grinning so hard, but when he's good, he's good. "To be clear," I say, "I know it's kind of a date, but we can agree that's a stupid word, so can we just go out and have fun?"

Colin shakes his head. "You are fixated on me. I feel like I'm leading you on, but maybe if we go out together tonight, I can help you understand that's just not happening. You're not even my type. I like nerdy guys." He studies me. "Brunettes with hazel eyes…who wear glasses."

"Interesting that you just described me to a T, though we both know you prefer blonds."

His gaze settles on my bangs. "I must've been mistaken."

And…he's got me laughing again.

"Don't worry," he goes on. "I'll help you through this, bro."

I don't fight it. "Yeah, I'd really appreciate your help through this, bruh."

"Perfect. Now come on, Ash. You got our table reservations for six thirty, and we don't want to be late for our *date*." He really emphasizes the word, which I admit doesn't sound horrible coming from his mouth.

"I fucking give up."

"Figured you would," Colin says before offering another kiss.

And really, though I doubt many people would get it, this might be my favorite way to start a date with Colin.

A sound catches our attention, and I turn to see Frat Cat pawing at his leg.

The meds the vet tech gave us have really helped, and he's been moving about quite a bit.

"You didn't drop the baby off at the sitter's already?" Colin asks.

"The babysitter's down the hall."

His brow rises.

"I was gonna ask Miranda again, but Marty insisted."

"Marty? Really?"

"He's taking to him pretty quickly. Think Frat Cat mellows him out a bit."

"You hear that, Frat Cat?" Colin asks. "We gotta roll

to your sitter's."

"You're gonna have to set me down for that."

"Do I?" he asks, carrying me to the door.

"No, I need my wallet!"

Colin backtracks, watching out for Frat Cat as he heads to my desk and grabs my wallet, then heads into the hall, Frat Cat following close behind. Fortunately, we don't have far to go before he finally frees me. Marty's looking at us like we're out of our minds as we're in stitches at his door.

After we walk him through instructions for watching our kitty, Marty says, "You know most cats are pretty independent, right?"

"He's just a baby," I say. "And he likes lots of affection."

"Especially scritches," Colin chimes in, "and if you stop petting him for too long, don't worry, he'll remind you."

Marty rolls his eyes. "You two have the most spoiled cat I've ever met. But don't worry, he's in good hands."

We don't doubt it, so we say goodbye to our precious fur baby before heading out.

We take my car to the hibachi restaurant, where the host seats us at a table with two other couples. We get our usual—Colin, steak, chicken, and shrimp; just chicken for me. As the server grills, he singles out Colin to catch some of the meat and veggies in his mouth. He aims to get Colin to miss a few times, but the guy clearly doesn't know my brother, and unsurprisingly, Colin pulls off some Hail Marys. Once the performance comes to an end, we enjoy our meals, catching up about our day, before Colin heads to the restroom. When he returns, he plops down in his seat, relaxing back the way he does when he's full.

"I warned you to make room for ice cream."

Colin glares at me. "You really think I'm not gonna be able to take down a couple of scoops? Please. I'm gonna be stealing some of yours when you're only halfway through."

That sounds about right.

The host stops by our table and passes out checks; he sets one down in front of me with my debit card sticking out. I slipped it to the host while Colin was in the restroom.

My stepbro glares at me. "Oh, really?" he asks, placing his hand on his chest. "You know I was gonna pay for this."

"Nope. I'm treating my stepbro tonight."

"You sneak," Colin says, his brow creasing. "You've been planning that. Someone's been committing Step Don'ts again."

"I think you'll find that the amendment to Section 1.3 of the Official Step Don't Policy states that exceptions include surprises like birthdays and special events."

There is no such official document, but we did agree on these things initially when we made our rules because as much as we don't love secrets, we both love surprises.

He's still glaring at me.

"Besides," I add. "I was able to cash in some of those tokens from Manzturbate, so my followers are sort of paying for tonight."

"Your followers? I didn't realize I was dating a celebrity."

I laugh. "It didn't cover the bill, but I figured it'd be funny if our first date was sponsored partly by the money we made the time I showed you the app."

The playfulness in his expression shifts to something more sincere, and he does a double take. "Yeah, I like that."

Mentioning the live streams brings to mind the bathhouse. Getting other people to watch us. It's something that's been buzzing in the background since Colin brought it up. But there's something else there too.

"I've been thinking about that thing you mentioned. A lot."

"Yeah?" Colin asks.

"I do wonder...what if we went and did something like that, but no one wanted to watch? I had the same thought about the app, and that was never an issue, but it crosses my mind."

Colin studies my expression. "I can't imagine anyone

not wanting to watch what you do."

I laugh, and I'm fucking blushing again.

"What you looked like when you were streaming or when Dax was there…it's like you're performing. Like you were born to do this. It's captivating, and it'll be just as captivating when you get around even more people. And now that I know what you're worrying about, all I can say is, I can't wait to prove that little nasty voice in your head wrong and let my little perv show everyone who's boss."

My cheeks are still warm now that he's settled my nerves but stimulated my interest even more.

"Thank you for dinner, Ash."

As he takes a kiss, his words really sink in, quieting that annoying voice in my head. And when he pulls away, he says, "But ice cream's on me."

"I mean, future dinners and ice cream, since I'm just an intern. I'd have to make a lot more videos to afford to wine and dine you."

"Well, you'd better get to work."

We share another kiss, then grab our things and head on to the ice cream shop.

"Which do you think tonight?" I ask as the person in line ahead of us finishes up with the clerk. Nearly every time we come here, I get hung up on fudge chunks or peanut-butter cups or both, and we have a bit of a game of Colin guessing which I've decided on.

"Hmmm," Colin says. "Peanut-butter cups."

"Ooh, you don't know me at all."

"Really?" Colin asks, because he's usually on point.

I shake my head. "Can't get it right every time." I approach the clerk, ordering the vanilla scoops and, "Just peanut-butter cups on top."

I sneak a glance to Colin, who glares at me. "*Fucking knew it*," he mouths.

This is what I like about being out with him. It's so easy. So fun. We always laugh.

We find a spot near a counter by the front of the shop, and as we settle on some stools, I say, "I like this. I was thinking earlier about all the times we did this in high school. You know, like going to the mall for dinner, ice cream, and movies. Heading around to different stores and just cracking jokes. I remember you were on a roll in a Spencer's with the sex toys, and I was laughing so hard, I thought we were gonna get kicked out or I was gonna pass out because I couldn't get air in."

"We've always had a lot of fun."

"We have. And it's kind of strange, but I keep wondering if this thing we're doing will make anything different. I guess it's been like everything else. Like it's so much the same. You're still my big silly stepbro, and now there's these added perks."

"And you like the perks, don't you?" Colin asks. "Get over here and let me give you some of my mint chocolate."

As I lean toward him, he shoves a spoonful in his mouth, and I pull back, bursting into a laugh.

Yep. Same old Colin, for sure.

We finish the ice cream, hit the movie, then head back to the frat, winding up in Colin's room. He attacks me with another kiss, pushing me up against the wall by his desk, his tongue tasting of the mints we popped after the movie.

When he pulls away, he says, "Well, the baby's got a sitter, so maybe we shower and then snuggle up, watch some Netflix?"

"Is this your sneaky way of trying to keep me here to do naughty things with you?"

"I'm sorry. I assumed you knew I was gonna do naughty things with you before we snuggled. Because as much as I'm eager to fuck you in front of a crowd, tonight you're all fucking mine."

He sounds so fucking greedy for me. I love it.

"Good. Wouldn't have it any other way," I say, and Colin beams.

"I had a really good time tonight. You really know how to date the fuck out of a guy." He winks, feeling so slick for sliding that in.

Hope he looks just as full of himself when he's sliding something else in later.

18

Colin

"CAN YOU SHOW me that play again?" Amelia, one of the girls who takes my football lessons, asks.

It's almost over for the day, and I find myself bummed about that. I hadn't realized how much I need this. It's a welcome break from school and my job at the law office. Not that I don't love what I do or not looking forward to what my future holds. Law is definitely what I want, but I've always been in love with football too. I'm not good enough to go to the pros, but I hope to keep football in my life, even if it's just doing things like this.

"Of course," I tell her, though I'm not sure why she's asking. Amelia has the best head for football in these lessons. She sees the field in a way most kids wouldn't at her age—girl or boy.

I go over the play again, explaining what her team-mates are supposed to do and then how she makes sure to get them the ball, and unsurprisingly, she nails it.

"Thanks, Coach Colin!" She sends a smile my way.

I tell the kids to practice it again, just as my phone buzzes. I tug it out to see Ash's name on the screen. It immediately makes me smile, and not for the first time, I'm grateful he's in my life. How lucky were we to end up with a stepbrother who became our best friend? And on top of that, the benefits are fucking incredible.

When we fucked after our date the other night, we'd done it standing up in front of the window, me whispering in his ear how fucking good he is for me, how hot he is, and teasing about someone seeing us—Marty or one of the other guys driving up to the house, and there I was, fucking my stepbrother at the window.

My load had been similar to the ones he shoots, my balls so fucking full for him. It had been the perfect end to a perfect night. The best date of my whole life has been with my stepbrother. Hell, it feels like I've been dating him maybe even longer than I realized.

Ash: We gonna bang tonight?

I grin. How can I not? Everything about Ash makes me feel good.

Me: Yep. We're gonna fuck too.

"Why are you grinning at your phone so much?" Amelia asks, my face immediately flaming as I shove my cell into my pocket.

"Was that your girlfriend?" Jacob asks.

"He doesn't have a girlfriend," Amelia snaps, then looks at me. "Do you?"

Um…what is happening here? Our conversations at

practice have never gone this direction before. "No. I have an…Ash…" I have an Ash? What the fuck does that even mean? He's my stepbro. My friend. My favorite person. I felt all these things before we started hooking up, and it's all just intensified since. But it's not like I can tell them that, even though Ash does feel like he's mine. Like he's always been mine, even before I let myself see it.

"What's an Ash?" Oscar asks.

"He's my person. Can we talk about football now?" That's a whole lot easier than dissecting my feelings with a bunch of thirteen-year-olds.

"Amelia has a crush on Coach Colin!" Oscar teases.

"I do not!" She charges him, and I have to bite back a smile when she tackles the little shit. Oscar is a good kid, but sometimes he likes to give Amelia a hard time. I guess today she's retaliating.

"Okay, that's enough." I pull them apart before Amelia kicks Oscar's ass. She totally would too. "Practice is over for today. Do you two want me to talk to your parents about running laps before you go?" A fact about me when it comes to kids and animals—I'm all bark and no bite. There's not a chance in hell I'm making these kids run extra laps, but they haven't caught on to that about me yet.

Four eyeballs go wide. "No, Coach," Oscar replies.

Then I remind myself that even though I like to be a

big kid myself, I'm the adult. While I hate feeling like a hard-ass, I'm not supposed to let them get away with things like this. "You know what you did is inappropriate. You can't just tackle each other when you're mad."

"Yes, Coach," Amelia grumbles.

"And, Oscar, you shouldn't tease people. Or tell stories about them."

"But it's—" I give him an eye, and he stops. "Okay, Coach."

"Go on now." I nod toward the others, and they scamper off.

Amelia gives him a dirty look. She's small for her age, but tough and full of heart. She reminds me of Frat Cat. Speaking of...

Me: Did you feed our baby?

Ash: Ding, ding, ding, we're sorry, your number cannot be completed as dialed...

Me: Haha. Very funny.

Ash: Yes, Daddy Colin. I fed him.

Me: Good boy...

I'm eager for a response while the kids are cleaning up. I should be helping, but I want to know how Ash will respond.

Ash: That only has an effect on me when we're fucking.

Me: Liar.

With a goofy smile on my face, I shove my cell into my pocket for good. I help the kids finish cleaning up, then talk with the parents real quick. It's a gorgeous day, the sun high in a perfectly blue sky, so I sit at a picnic table beneath one of the trees, just as my phone rings. The corners of my lips tilt up. I'm assuming it's Ash, but instead the screen says *Mom*.

My smile still grows. I miss her. "Hey, you."

"How's my favorite guy?" she asks.

"Good. I just finished teaching a football lesson."

"I love that you do that. My boy is so sweet."

"I mean, I'm not going to argue with you. I'm pretty awesome."

Mom chuckles. "Still the same goofball you've always been, I see."

"You expected me to change?" I tease.

"Are you kidding me? I hope you never change. And your father and Lauren?"

I love that she asks and legitimately cares. It's weird sometimes when I think about the fact that my parents divorced. On paper they should have been perfect for each other. They were friends, knew one another their whole lives, have the same hobbies, and are even similar when it comes to how they treat people and show their love. In a lot of ways, they're more fitted than Dad and Lauren, but for whatever reason, they didn't work. It just wasn't meant to be. You never really know when that will be the case.

"Same as always," I tell her. "Dad's working on a book, Lauren is conquering the world, but they're happy."

"And my son? Are you happy? What's new?"

Ash pops into my head. Our date, the sex, our up-coming trip to the bathhouse, which we're sure to do soon. Talking with him. Laughing with him. Making him happy, and how that makes me feel like I'm walking on the fucking moon. "Everything is perfect. Better than ever, maybe. Did I tell you me and Ash found a cat? We named him Frat Cat."

"No! You didn't. What happened?"

"We got home, and I heard him crying outside. We took him to the vet, and there was no way I couldn't keep him."

"Is it a house cat for everyone?"

"No, just ours."

"The two of you alternate whose room he stays in?"

I probably shouldn't tell her that Ash and I sleep in the same room most nights. But I actually, maybe, kinda want to…? Never mind. What the fuck am I thinking?

"Yeah. We went and saw a movie the other night too. We had hibachi. I know you love it as much as I do."

"What else have you two been up to?"

I give her the G-rated version of our recent shenanigans. Mom listens well like she always does, asking questions in all the right places.

When I finish, she says, "You really lucked out in the

stepbrother department."

I did. Even more than she knows. "I was thinking maybe he could come to North Carolina with me when I come to visit this summer." I used to want him to go with me all the time when we were kids, but it never happened. And as much as I love seeing Mom, it was torture being away from Ash. I remember once, Mom saying she worried we were too codependent, but I never cared about that. What matters is that we work, we fit, and despite kissing and fucking, nothing else has changed between us—only that it would be even more miserable to be away from him now.

"I'm sure Ash has better things to do than wanting to come and see your mom, but he's always welcome here."

My heart rate slows. I hadn't even realized it had picked up until Mom said yes. "Thanks. I'm sure he'll want to go. We can show him around Raleigh."

"You really love him."

"I do."

There's a short pause before she says, "You're a good big brother, Colin."

"Ash is good to me too." The best.

There's another delay in response, but then she says, "Things worked out the way they were supposed to. I'm glad you guys are such close friends."

We talk for a while longer before ending the call. I'm on my way back to the frat house, when Ash calls.

"Miss me?" I ask.

"Your cock maybe," he teases, and I beam. I love how much Ash likes riding my dick. He's vers, but just like I'm cum-hungry for him, he's dick-hungry for me.

"It's yours."

"I know," Ash replies. "Wanna hit the gym with me?"

All sorts of naughty images pop into my head when I think about the last time Ash and I were around gym equipment together, and it almost gives me wood.

"Bet. Want me to meet you?"

"I'll come get you," Ash says.

I change when I get home, grab some water and a towel for each of us, then wait for Ash.

He picks me up about five minutes later. As soon as I climb into the passenger seat, I lean over and kiss his cheek. "How was your day?"

"That was very boyfriend-y."

Oh, well, I guess I can see that. Still, "Have we been boyfriends for like ten years, then?"

"You didn't kiss me hello and ask about my day like that." With a small smirk, Ash drives off.

True, but... "Would it be so bad if we were boy-friends?" I didn't plan the question, not even sure if I'm serious... And I realize that I am. But I don't want to push him.

"What? Have you been thinking about this?"

"No. I would have told you. I wouldn't commit a Step Don't that way, but now that I said it, I'm thinking about it. So would it be bad?"

Ash glances my way as if trying to sort through what I said. "No."

"Good. I'll keep that in mind."

Ash laughs. "You'll keep that in mind?"

"Well, if we do become boyfriends, I should probably ask you properly. We went on a date already, so it feels like the next step."

"What if I ask you first?"

I grin. "That works for me too. Like a promposal. Now I expect that, FYI. You better come complete with flash mob."

Ash laughs. "We're ridiculous."

"We're fucking awesome."

"Truth." Ash parks at the gym, and we head inside. It's fairly busy, so I follow Ash to the machines. "It's leg day."

My gaze immediately shoots to his ass. It really is the best ass I've ever seen. "My favorite day."

"Now you see why I asked you to come."

We start out at the leg press. "Go ahead." I nod toward the machine, letting Ash go first. I don't take my eyes off him as he adjusts the weight and begins pushing with his legs.

"This one isn't sexy," Ash says.

"It is when you're the one to do it."

"You like watching me work out?" Ash's leg muscles strain slightly.

I look around to see if anyone is close enough to hear. There are people near, but I think I can play this game we both love so much without getting into trouble. "I can't stop thinking about fucking you on the bench press...how Dax couldn't take his eyes off you. There's a guy in the corner looking at you right now. Bet he'd love to see you shoot, would love to see my cock pumping in and out of your tight hole."

"Jesus, Col." He adjusts himself. "Would you show him how well I can take a pounding?"

"Fuck yes," I reply before he gets up and I take a turn. When Ash is at the machine again, I nod toward a woman. "She wants you too. I bet she wonders who I am to you, if she can get on her knees and suck that pretty cock of yours."

His face turns pink. Just as he's about to reply, a guy walks by.

"Excuse me." He uses the machine right next to Ash, so we have to pause our game.

We finish with the leg press, then leg extensions. When Ash heads to the leg curl machine, I bite back a groan.

Ash adjusts the weight, then lies on his belly, ankles hooked beneath the bar, ass in the air.

"That'd be a pretty way for you to suck cock in front of all these people," I tell him.

"You'd let me too. You'd let me pull out your thick cock and work a load out of your balls." I glance over, and several guys are close. If Ash's voice wasn't so soft right now, they would definitely hear us. "You'd do anything I asked, wouldn't you, Col? I have my stepbro wrapped around my finger."

My dick is taking notice, blood heading to my groin. I shift, trying to hide my semi. Somehow Ash has turned the tables. "Any-fucking-thing. Gladly."

He stands up, and with his mouth close to my ear, whispers, "I know you would, and that's so damn hot," before swiping at my lobe with his tongue and pulling back.

"I'm supposed to be driving *you* wild right now."

Ash chuckles. "I always come to win."

We each do a few sets on the leg curls, talking each other up, getting each other hot and heavy the whole time.

I know where he's going next before he makes it partway there: squats. I'm in so much fucking trouble, and I'm living for it.

"Can you show me how to do it?" Ash asks, as if he doesn't know, as if he doesn't have the world's best ass partly from his leg routine.

"Sure." I step up behind him. *Please don't let me get*

us kicked out. Please don't let me get us kicked out. "Feet shoulder width apart, and when you lower, you're going to poke your ass out. Try it with me once."

I feel the heat of his body against mine, see us in the mirror, flushed and turned on, and damn do we look good together.

"One…two…three." We lower, Ash's ass pressing against my groin. "I'm going to take you to the bathhouse this weekend, my little perv. I'll fuck you like this, from behind. I'd do it right here if I could, give all these people a show. See how many are here? That's how many people are going to watch you take my cock like you were made for it. Do you want that?"

"Fuck yes," Ash says. "Are they all gonna want a turn with me?"

"Yes. I bet every guy in here wants a turn with you right now."

We lower again, which is dangerous as hell, but damned if the prickle at my nape that worries about getting in trouble doesn't make my dick even harder.

"Friday?" I ask. "You want to put on a show with your stepbrother?"

Ash pushes his ass against me, rubs it, teasing me, before stepping away. "I can't fucking wait."

19

Ash

M Y NERVES ARE on edge.

We're really doing this.

We've teased so much about the bathhouse since Col first brought it up, but now we're standing in line at PeachFlex with seven other guys. I'm waiting for someone to recognize us from school, but it's a mix of ages. There aren't many bathhouses in Georgia, so I figure there are guys from all around who want to have a fun Friday night.

As we step up in line toward the receptionist checking IDs and handing out locker and room keys, Colin must sense how tense I am because he rests his hand on my hip, tucking his crotch up against the small of my back. Reminds me of earlier in the week when we were doing squats at the gym.

And suddenly, I take what feels like the first decent breath I've had in the past few minutes. It'll all be okay as long as I have Colin here with me.

When it's our turn at the front desk, we hand our IDs to the clerk, and he charges us for lockers, then gives us lanyards, keys, and towels.

This is it; it's really fucking happening.

The clerk buzzes us in, like we're entering a prison. We step through, into a locker room, where guys are stripping down. Just cock and ass all over the place.

Colin doesn't seem fazed, which isn't a surprise because during football season, this is what he's seeing all the time. I already notice a few glances our way, then between us, smirking like they wouldn't mind us tag-teaming them.

As we look for our lockers, we keep glancing at each other. I can't keep from smiling.

But I feel like a fraud. I'm just a big nerd, not some kind of sex god. What right do I have to be here?

I try to shake off my insecurity as we find our lockers and strip down. We purchased a lanyard upgrade for Colin, which has a clear compartment for condoms and lube—we read on some forums that was the right way to enjoy the experience. So we pack the compartment with the stuff we brought, then put our lanyards around our necks and towels around our waists before heading out to scope things out.

The locker room lets out into a lobby, where guys are sitting around, watching porn on a big-screen TV. There's an adjoining gym and a sign indicating where the saunas are.

I take Colin's hand and pull him toward a nearby hall.

"Where do you think you're taking us?" Colin asks.

"You're not the only one who knows where we need to go."

According to the forums, there's an area with viewing rooms, where guys can get in so others can watch. And it's funny that, even with my nerves, it's like my instincts are drawing me to them.

Colin chuckles. "Oh, I bet that was the only area that even interested you, my little perv."

Of course he knows this is the only place I even gave a shit about when we were looking at that stuff.

"Damn right," I say.

He's all smiles. "Lead the way."

I love how he lets me be the boss, until I need him to be my boss.

When we pass through a hall with private rooms on one side and stalls on another, I hear guys moaning, notice legs in the opening underneath. Another area has raised platforms and barriers with glory holes, where a few guys are blowing cock, really fucking going at it, like they're competing to see who can get their guy off first.

Colin reaches down and feels my crotch. "Mmm-hmmm," he says. "Maybe we should have done this sooner."

I reach over and feel his girth. "Like a steel rod," I note.

"I hope that hole's ready for it."

"Oh, it will be," I assure him as we round the corner into another hall, where guys are gathered around a few open doorways along the wall.

A rush of excitement courses through me, like right before I do the live streaming.

"This looks right," I whisper to Colin. There's the tiniest tremble in my belly as we near the doorways. About a dozen guys stand outside the first, where three guys make out on a matted floor, stroking each other's cocks. They're so fucking hot, they look like someone should have a camera out to shoot the porn they belong in. In the neighboring room, a beefy guy pounds a guy from behind, pushing him up against the wall, the guy calling out, which is clearly getting their audience worked up as they watch, stroking their cocks and muttering to each other about what a good bottom the guy is.

I can't help being envious, and as I turn to Colin, he steps up close behind me, whispering, "Don't worry. They just haven't seen what a good bottom you can be."

My cheeks warm. I'd be lying if I said I didn't need the encouragement.

And I'm glad Colin's so generous with it.

The next room over doesn't have anyone inside. Like

the others, it's matted, but there are mirrors on every wall.

"Well, that's fucking hot," Colin mutters as he assesses the space.

"They must not realize this room is open. It's clearly the best one."

"Maybe some other guys just left. Come on. We gotta put on a show."

I'm equal parts eager and anxious. Colin must be able to tell because he rests his hand on the small of my back, guiding me onto the matted platform.

This is happening. This is really fucking happening...

As we get inside, I notice a rail along one of the walls. "Remind you of anything?" I ask as Colin hangs his towel on a rack by the door. I strip out of my towel too and set it on another beside his.

There are already some curious gazes at the doorway, peeking in to see what we're up to.

I haven't really thought this far out. Figured Colin and I would just do our thing, but now the pressure's really on. And even with just these eyes on us, I notice my cock isn't even a semi, but Colin is still like a stone.

"You good?" he asks, cupping my balls.

"Just nervous," I whisper. "What if I'm not able to perform?"

He smirks. "Oh, precious Ash. I don't think we have

to worry about that."

He offers a kiss, slipping his tongue in. He just knows what to fucking do with that thing, and between that and the way he toys with my balls, it quickly becomes apparent I won't have any issues performing.

When he finishes massaging, his hand slides up to stroke me, and I take his cock in my grip. "You're so hard," I say between kisses.

"There's a way you can make it even harder."

I chuckle. I love that, even now, he's able to be Silly Colin, which reminds me again that as long as he's here with me, everything will be okay.

As I pull away from him, I notice guys crowding the doorway. I'm kind of shocked, considering they have two perfectly good shows going on next door, and Colin and I are just making out.

He glances over his shoulder, then back at me. "Everyone's here to see you get fucked," he says, which has my cock twitching. "So you ready to give your fans what they need?"

Between the audience at the doorway and Colin's chill attitude, I find it easy to let go of the anxieties I thought might overpower me.

And that eager part takes over, something feral in me lurching at him, taking his mouth, more aggressively this time. I nibble at his bottom lip, tugging at it between my teeth before releasing. Colin has his eyes closed, and I squat down, kissing between his pecs, trailing down his body as I get on my knees so that thick cock is in front of me.

I wet my lips before taking it in my grip and sliding my tongue along the side.

Colin moans as his hand rests on my head.

"Fuck, Ash," he mutters as I continue teasing him with my tongue.

"Look at this kid," I hear someone say outside, which only encourages me along as I continue working Colin's shaft, sliding my tongue along the side, then sucking along it.

"Fuck, you're killing me here," Colin mutters.

Makes me feel like I have him right where I want him. Just getting this dick on edge so that the only thing on Colin's mind is what he wants to do with it.

I slide the head into my mouth, running my tongue along the base of that cock as I open my mouth wider to take more of him.

I want to keep teasing him, but getting this much in, I become greedy, like I must get all of it in. I just go for it, gripping his ass cheeks as I demonstrate how far back I can take this thing. I want everyone to know I'm not an amateur with my stepbrother's dick.

"You can't do this to me if you want me in your ass too," Colin warns.

I don't just *want* him in my ass; I fucking *need* him

in it.

I force myself to release his cock, licking along the base like I need to promise it—not Colin—that everything'll be okay if it's patient and waits to see where I plan to put it next.

Colin kneels in front of me, taking my mouth again, pushing up against me so our cocks thrust together, our hands wrapping around each other. When he pulls away, he whispers, "Put your legs around me."

I rock back, putting my weight on my palms as I sit on my ass and do as he says. Once my legs are secured at his waist, he wraps his arms around me, lifts me up, and pushes to his feet.

"Fuck, yeah," comes from the doorway.

Colin looks real damn proud of himself.

"Show-off," I tease, which makes him grin.

He carries me to the rail along the wall, and as though we choreographed this, I reach back and grip on.

"You gonna be able to get in me like this?" I ask.

"Is that a challenge?"

"You know it is, Big Man."

He smiles. "Keep these legs nice and tight around me. I got this." He retrieves the lube from the pouch on the lanyard and starts to grab for the condom.

"Wait," I say.

He stops, as if my words control his every movement.

A wicked thought has entered my mind, but the

more I think about it, the more right it seems. "We both send each other our results after our STI panels," I remind him.

"Yes…"

"So unless one of us didn't share their last results or messed around with someone since then…"

His eyes widen. "You want me to fuck you raw?"

"Why do you keep using *want* when you know it's more than that? I mean, we were talking about a boyfriendposal the other day."

He licks his lips, and my body pulses with desire.

Now that I've said it, I'll fucking die if he wants to have me any other way. Of course, if he prefers to use protection, I'll respect that, but I love that I can read that expression and know we're fucking done with condoms.

Not just tonight, but for-fucking-ever.

I tighten my legs around him while he pumps some lube onto his fingers, then slides his hand between us, massaging my hole.

I'm thinking about what it's gonna feel like to have him in me, skin to skin…to feel that familiar sensation of him when he comes, but this time, without any barrier, just having him marking me, claiming me.

As he continues lubing me up, I relax against the rail, allowing myself to enjoy his tease before peeking at our growing audience. There must be at least fifteen guys out there now, and some are starting to crawl in to make room for the others, maybe get a better show for themselves.

When Colin's fingers pull away, he gets some more lube for his cock, tucks the lube into the lanyard pouch, then maneuvers himself against my hole. He licks his lips, this determined expression on his face, like he's on a mission now that he knows he gets to be inside me.

There's that pressure as he slides the head in.

"Fuck yeah, give it to him," someone mutters from nearby, echoing what I was about to beg for.

Colin's lips twist up as he obeys, guiding himself in.

My body welcomes him, and I close my eyes, allowing myself to feel every fucking beautiful inch. "Just like that, Col. Take this fucking greedy hole."

I don't know what the hell is coming over me, but between what we're doing and feeling Colin inside me like this, I'm so fucking hungry for him to be buried in me already.

He feeds me every sweet inch until I feel him sliding right up against my prostate.

The pleasure bursts through me so fast, I arch my back, feeling a warmth against my abs. I open my eyes, noticing the precum leaking. Colin swipes his hand through it and raises it to his mouth, giving it a lick, watching me like he wants me to see him feeding himself.

The guys around us are whispering to each other,

and I can hear how much this is driving them wild—
we're driving them wild.

As Colin finishes with his snack, he thrusts back that
final inch, my nerves shooting sensation through me,
forcing my mouth open as I gasp from the intensity of
the pleasure that's coursing through my veins.

"God, you're harder than usual now," I say. "Keep it
right there."

"Whatever you want, little bro."

He stills, and I rock my hips, sliding him in and out.

He closes his eyes, now his turn to revel in pleasure as
I tend to that cock that's been so good to me.

My arms are getting a fucking workout, but the way
he's holding me means I'm not having to put much
weight on them. I roll my hips, pushing in and out,
really trying to get him out to the head before slamming
down so everyone can see I'm not intimidated by my
bro's big cock.

The more we get into it, the more I'm able to speed
up my movements.

Colin fucking deserves this.

For understanding me the way he does.

For how good he is at giving me his cock.

For how good he's been at intuiting my desires.

Now it's my turn.

"You want to fuck me, don't you?" I ask.

"Oh yes. Fuck yes. Please, Ash."

"Not yet, but when you do, I want you to just lose your fucking mind. I want a fucking animal. Just take me like the hole that I am. Tell me you understand."

"I understand."

I stop my movements, leaving him hanging in suspense, his expression twisting up. "Fucking God, Cruel Ash."

But I can tell by the strain in his voice he's right where I want him, and I won't torture him anymore.

"Fuck me, Colin."

It's just what I'd hoped for, all this pent-up frustration and excitement slamming against me in a moment. His hands grip my thighs firmly as he pounds my hole like he's never fucking pounded it before, the slaps echoing through the room.

Sensation spirals through me. Intoxicating bursts on a spectrum of excitement. I'm fucking delirious with pleasure as my body twists and jerks with his movements, the rail revealing its age as it squeals.

As I survey the room, I can barely see straight, just faint images of eager eyes and smiles, men grabbing at their crotches to pleasure themselves.

All because of our little show.

"Just like that, Col. Drill me."

As he picks up the pace, really getting in me deep, my moans are so loud, it's like I'm calling out to alert the whole damn bathhouse about how good I'm getting it.

Colin leans close, taking a kiss. Our tongues work in a frenzy, and every kiss is a reward for how good Colin's giving it to me.

He kisses and fucks me until we're both thrusting together in a wild fit of chaos.

My arms are really starting to wear out, so I release the rail and hook them around Colin's neck, tugging him close.

"Fuck me...right here...on the floor," I tell him.

Colin's his usual cautious self, getting on his knees carefully. I can feel him starting to lay me on my back when I say, "I want to be on top."

"Gonna wear this dick out tonight, aren't you?" he asks before licking up my lips.

He chuckles, and I notice the sweat soaking his bangs. I run my fingers through them. "Just giving you a little break." I wink before sticking my fingers in my mouth, tasting his sweat.

His eyes widen with desire.

He pushes his legs out before lying back.

I take another glance at our audience. A lot of guys have moved into the room, surrounding us in a semicircle. Others are packed at the door.

Colin must notice too because he says, "And you were worried about...?"

"Shut it."

I love this, how we can be doing this in front of all

these guys, but we can still be silly, ridiculous Colin and Ash.

He thrusts up into me, and I roll my head back, really enjoying it, but I have other plans.

"No, no," I say. "Just stay still. Let me."

He obeys, and I get to work, rocking my ass back and forth. This hole is just to serve him. Just to get him to the end.

"Fuck, Ash...you feel so good. I love being in you like this."

"I love it too," I confess.

I rock back and really give the guys a show, letting them see how I can work Colin's cock.

Between everyone watching and the way he's striking my prostate, I know I can't last much longer. But I want to give these guys an epic finale. I don't want to let them down. Not when they were so good to come and watch us.

"Colin, when I say, just take me," I whisper. "Like a fucking wolf in the goddamn woods. Don't hold anything back. Have your way with me, please."

I don't know why that sounds like I'm begging when it's something I'm sure he's game for, but he looks me in the eyes, his expression serious as he nods, like he gets how important this is to me.

I pump his cock with my ass a few more times, waiting for the right moment, glancing around at my audience, reading the anticipation in their faces.

Feels like a gut instinct, something in sync with them as I whisper to Colin, "Now."

It's like a tornado tears through. I'm moving with Colin and the room's spinning before he's got me on my back on the mat. I hook my legs around him as he seizes my wrists, pinning them out to the sides as he gives me his all.

His mouth shoves up against mine—tongue, teeth going wild as he growls into my mouth.

I only break from kisses to holler out my pleasure as he drills in just the right place.

This is what I wanted everyone to see. Colin's fucking is all his desire and passion. He's worshipping me with his all, and they're free to enjoy watching what my body does to this man.

When he pulls back to give it even harder, I notice the guys at the door, two of whom I recognize from the show they were putting on in the neighboring room. Fuck, I was envious of them, and here they had to come and see what was up with us.

Colin tears into my hole like a sex beast, and my back arches.

"I'm about to—" he warns.

"Do it. I want you to come first. So I can have it in me when I shoot."

He leans back as he drills, that fourth-quarter sweat

just pouring off his bangs when he finally offers a series of jerks, his expression twisting up, assuring me he's filling me up.

It's all Colin deep in me. I'm fucking his now; he's claimed me in a way no man ever has.

And I fucking love it.

"Oh fuck yes," I say as he keeps thrusting. It's driving me wild with his hands binding my wrists at my sides so I can't end my agony with a stroke, but a powerful thrust from him takes me over the edge. I call out as my cum bursts from my cock, and I feel warmth streak across me, up to my chin.

Colin doesn't let it stay there long as he laps it up, still fucking the cum out of me, and I can hear the gasps and "Holy shit!" as everyone gets to see what feels like a never-ending load, as I just keep shooting in ropes across my abs.

Colin's lips are at my neck in no time, collecting some of the cum that shot up, and as he pulls out, he laps me up—surely everyone who's watching thinking how fucking greedy it is for one man to drink up all of me for himself.

"Take it all, Col. Every drop."

I lie still, reveling in satisfaction as he licks and nibbles, fucking worships every ounce of me for our loyal audience.

I was wrong about not belonging here. Feels like this

is exactly where I belong.

On this floor.

Filled with Colin's cum, with him eating mine off me.

With eager eyes taking it all in.

Blissed out and depleted, I could die in this moment, and I'm wondering how the fuck I could ever be happier than I am right now.

20

Colin

SO…I THINK IT'S time I acknowledge I'm hopelessly, head over heels in love with my stepbrother. Now that I finally see it, I realize it's something that was likely always there. It's in the way I'd always done anything for him, the way I love making him happy, and the way Ash can make me happier than anyone or anything else. For as long as I remember, if I had the choice to spend time with Ash or anyone else, he's whom I picked. Being around him feels better than being around anyone else. The jealousy when certain people flirt with him should have been a huge red flag, but everything with us has always been so natural that I didn't see it.

I always thought falling in love would be this big thing, this huge moment where everything shifts and the world around you changes, but with me and Ash, loving him feels like slipping under your favorite blanket on a cold day, like living in my own skin, so fucking normal that it's like breathing. We're always breathing, but most of the time it's not something we pay attention to or even notice when we're doing it, and that's what it's been like with us. Loving Ash has always been so easy, so instinctual, I can't even recall when it started, when those feelings weren't there.

"I love your daddy," I tell Frat Cat while he plays with his own tail. He stops and looks at me like *no shit, dumb fuck*, and I can't help but chuckle. Our cat is a badass and he knows it.

I grab a string and dangle it for Frat Cat.

The bathhouse last night was one of the greatest moments of my life. I felt like a king, like a king fucking a king with a room full of followers who worshipped the ground we walked on…well, fucked on. There's nothing like it, the rush I feel when I'm with him. Not even the sex stuff—just everything.

I want Ash to be mine in every way. Hell, I've belonged to him from the moment I saw him, and maybe it's time to make things official.

I pick up my phone and shoot Troy a text.

Me: Wanna hang?

Troy: I see you don't ask me to bang.

Me: That's kinda what I want to talk to you about.

Troy: Fucking me??? Do you want Atlas to kill you? I'm deleting this message now. *wink emoji*

Shit. I chuckle. I really should spend some time thinking about things before I say them.

Me: I didn't realize how that sounds. The banging

thing is with Ash. That's what I want to discuss.

Troy: I fucking knew something was up with the two of you! Come to Atlas's. I'm here by myself right now.

Me: Bet. Be right there.

After making sure the kitten has toys, food, and water, I close the door and head out. It's a quick drive from the frat house to Atlas's apartment. Troy opens the door as soon as I'm on the stoop, as if he'd been watching for me.

I wait for any nerves to come, any feelings of being unsure, and nope, I still want Ash and don't give a fuck what anyone thinks about it.

"I've been hooking up with Ash and I'm in love with him," I say the second I'm inside.

And oh shit. Did I just come out? I still haven't given myself a proper label, and while I don't need one for me, I know others do.

"Congrats, man. I'm happy for you."

I kinda love that Troy doesn't ask about my sexuality, because it's still something I haven't sorted out. "Wanna know something weird? It's not a thing I've even thought about much. I've always noticed guys, but never dissected what that meant. And I love boning Ash, so surprise! I guess I'm bisexual."

Troy chuckles. "There are a lot of things you can be—pan, for example—but if that's not something that matters to you, it's not something you have to figure out right now."

And it's not. Right now, I just want to talk to my friend about how to make things official with Ash.

I plop down in the armchair in the small living room, Troy taking a seat on the couch.

"How long has this been going on?"

"A couple of months," I admit, feeling guilty because I didn't tell him. I don't for a second think that's why Troy said it, but still. "I know I had my feelings hurt when you didn't tell me about you and Atlas right away, and now I did the same with Ash."

Troy holds his hand up. "It's okay. I get it. You don't have to apologize. You might have been bummed I didn't talk to you before I told everyone, but you still supported me from the start. That's what matters."

"Thanks, bro." Troy really is a good buddy. I'm so fucking lucky to have him.

"So…you and Ash…"

"Me and Ash. And like I said, I love him. I just realized it today, which means I gotta tell him." I'm not committing a Step Don't.

He chuckles. "There's not a part of me that's surprised. You've always been different with him. It would take an idiot not to realize you two are special to each other."

And that idiot is me. "You mean you and Atlas didn't wake up naked in bed together before you started hooking up?" I tease.

"Absolutely not, though it would have been fun."

"Yeah, well, I wish I could have enjoyed the benefits of it much sooner." We share another laugh before I sober. "I want to make it official with him. We joked about being boyfriends the other day but never confirmed if it was real or not." I feel like it's real. I feel like we've been boyfriends for a long-ass time, and I know it in my heart Ash wants it too. We're too attuned to each other not to be on the same wavelength with something this big.

"Let me guess, a simple date and asking him isn't going to cut it?"

I cock a brow at him as if it's the silliest question in the world.

Troy holds up his hands in mock defeat. "Just making sure."

"It has to be perfect."

"Do you have anything in mind?"

I shake my head. "I literally just realized I'm in love like an hour ago."

Troy leans forward, elbows on his knees, looking serious. "Then I guess we better figure it out."

I grin. "You'll help?"

"You know I will."

I clap my hands together, skin tingling. "Let's do this."

I HAVE TO get Ash out of the house. We picked a day when everyone is supposed to be out of the Alpha Theta Mu house, doing their own thing. Once Ash and I leave, all I have to do is shoot a quick text to Troy. He and Atlas will come over and set up the boyfriendposal Troy and I planned.

I open my bedroom door to head to Ash's, but as soon as I pull it open, he's there. "Oh. I was just coming to find you."

"I was coming to find you," Ash teases.

"I think I sorted that part out with you being at my door and all. And they say I'm the clueless one." I press a kiss to his lips.

"Wanna go grab some dinner with me?" Ash asks, and I say a silent thank-you to the love gods that he didn't come in here to tell me he has other plans or that he wants to stay home tonight.

"Fuck yes. I'm starving."

"Me too. Where's Frat Cat?" He frowns.

"Miranda has him." I didn't want us to have to worry about him tonight. Thankfully, Ash doesn't ask why I brought him to her.

I grab my cell, and we head out.

"Burgers good?" Ash asks.

"That works for me."

We're supposed to stay out of the house for an hour and a half, at least. If dinner goes a little longer, that's fine.

I try to be all incognito while I shoot Troy a text that I'm gone. Nerves make my belly tumble while I play on my phone and Ash drives. I want everything to be perfect. While it's not something he would expect, it's something I want for him.

"You're being quiet," he says as we pull into a parking spot.

"Huh?"

His brows pull together. "Are you okay?"

It's really hard to get something by a person who knows you as well as you know yourself. "Yes. I'm fine. Better than fine. I'm fucking perfect. Now come on. I'll give you a piggyback ride to the door."

A grin spreads across his face. Thankfully, I've managed to change the subject.

We get out, and I turn around for Ash to jump on. His arms and legs wrap around me, him feeling at home against my body. He playfully nibbles at my ear while I walk.

"You're going to get me hard, Ash."

"You think I don't know that?"

"You brat." But we don't keep the game up, don't really need to.

Ash slides off my back when we get to the door.

"Thanks, Big Man."

"You're welcome, my little perv."

Not gonna lie, I'm a bit distracted most of dinner. Strangely, Ash doesn't seem to notice. I can't stop watching my phone, wondering what's going on at the house, hoping Troy isn't running into any problems.

Ash is talkative tonight, so even though our food arrives pretty quickly, I don't have to come up with a reason to stall, keeping us here longer.

When the bill comes, I give the waitress my card this time. I'm about to text Troy under the table that we're leaving when Ash says, "I'll be right back. I have to go to the restroom real quick."

"I'll be here!" I say ridiculously. I'll be here? Where the fuck else would I be?

Ash chuckles, then disappears. The second he's gone, I call Troy because I'm freaking the fuck out.

"Everything is good?" I say instead of hello.

"Everything is perfect. Hurry up and get your asses home."

"We're about to leave. I'm gonna go before Ash comes out."

The waitress brings my card back, and I finish signing the receipt just as Ash comes back.

"I'm tired tonight," Ash says. "Is it cool if we head straight home?"

"Do you feel okay?" I stand up and tilt his face to look at him.

"Such a worrier. I'm fine. Let's go."

I try to hide my nerves the whole drive.

When we pull up, there are no cars in the driveway. A relieved breath wooshes out of my lungs.

My hands shake slightly as I open the door, and...

"What the fuck?" Ash and I say at the same time, before our gazes shoot to each other.

"Why did you say what the fuck?" I ask.

"There's a white aisle runner with flower petals in front of the door?" Ash says it like it's a question, and clearly, he's as surprised by this as I am, but it feels like there's more to it.

"Troy?" I say, stepping inside.

"Lance?" Ash says.

Our gazes dart to each other again. Something fishy is going on for sure. He's expecting Lance to be here, but Troy said no one was...

When wedding music starts playing, the pieces fall into place. Troy had something up his sleeve because this isn't what I planned.

"Shall we?" I hold my arm out for Ash. He hooks his through mine, and we follow the aisle runner and flower petals to the living room. They've moved all the furniture and added chairs like they would have at a wedding. A few of the guys from the frat are here, along with Brenner and Taylor. Streamers hang from the ceiling, balloons everywhere, and a banner across the back wall says: ASH AND COLIN...JUST MARRIED!

"This isn't what Lance was supposed to do," Ash says.

"Wait. What? I was going to say that about Troy. I had a whole thing planned. I was going to ask you to be my boyfriend."

He looks at me, heart in his eyes and a grin curling his lips. "I had a whole thing planned. I was going to ask you to be my boyfriend too."

Because of course we would plan the same thing on the same night. That's just how we roll.

Troy steps to the end of the aisle. For the first time, I notice two extra chairs, with homemade signs that say HIS and HIS. I'm assuming they're supposed to be like thrones, and the guys made do with what they could find.

"Are you guys gonna finish walking or what?" Brenner asks. "Because I'm salty I lost out on another hot guy."

I laugh, and Brenner winks playfully.

"I guess we should go," Ash says.

Arms still clasped together, we walk toward Troy, the music stopping when we're in front of him.

Troy clears his throat. "We're gathered here today to celebrate the union of Ash Fuller and Colin Phillips as boyfriend and boyfriend. Who gives these men away?"

Lance stands. "Frat Cat does." He's holding our kitten, who doesn't look thrilled. I take him from Lance and snuggle him close.

"Ash, do you take Colin, your stepbrother, to be your boyfriend?"

"Had to add the stepbrother thing in there?" Ash questions.

"Keeping it real." Troy snickers.

Ash looks at me, and though this is ridiculous and I kinda want to kill my friend, I see the emotions in my chest reflected in Ash's eyes.

"This won't end until you say I do," Troy reminds him.

"Oh shit. I do."

Troy gives me his attention next. "Colin, do you take Ash, your stepbrother, to be your boyfriend?"

"I do." I mean, weddings are fun.

"Is there anyone who objects to this union?" Troy asks.

"I do!" Brenner teases, but Taylor elbows him in the gut and they laugh.

"Try again with someone else. Ash is mine."

Ash flushes slightly.

Troy says, "You guys are looking at each other like you're gonna bone, so with the power of Alpha Theta Mu, I now pronounce you boyfriend and boyfriend."

Troy takes Frat Cat from me just before Ash's hands are on my face and he's pulling me close, taking my mouth in a kiss, surrounded by the cheers of our friends.

21

Ash

WE HAVE SOME drinks and dance, enjoying a...what is this exactly? A boyfriendposal reception?

Fortunately, most of the guys are finished giving us an appropriate amount of hell for the ceremony and are having their own fun, when I lurch at Colin, shamelessly kissing him in front of my fellow frat bros and Brenner and Taylor. I thought it'd be a quick kiss, but the way Colin pulls me in, his tongue sliding between my lips...I can't help myself.

"And now...I'm getting hard," I say between kisses before feeling his crotch. "You too, apparently."

Colin chuckles. "Maybe if you keep touching it like that, it'll go down."

I laugh before releasing him, mainly because as supportive as our friends are, they don't need to see me jerk off my stepbrother.

"And here I thought I was gonna outsmart you," I

say, "and pull off this great boyfriendposal."

"Outsmart me? I know you're smart, but that's pushing it."

"At least the guys know me well enough to know this had to end in dancing."

"I figure if they hadn't ended it like this," Colin says, "you'd still be dancing. Have Marty chasing you off the media console."

"Sounds about right."

"Someone say my name?" Marty approaches.

And I love the guy, but I'm gonna be pissed if he so much as makes a snarky comment. I don't want any hell during our special moment.

"Hey…can I talk to you guys for a second?" Marty asks, and the softness in his voice catches me off guard.

"Of course," Colin replies.

Marty moves closer, pressing his lips together. He looks so serious. Although, this is Marty, so no surprise there.

"I just…" He hesitates. "I know I can be a lot sometimes, and I don't always see things the way everyone else does, but I try. When you called me about you and Ash, I thought you were playing a prank, and if you needed me to be there for you and I wasn't, I'm sorry."

That's not what I expected.

"It's okay," Colin says. "Even though Ash and I were really hooking up, we were joking when I called you, so you didn't miss a moment to be there for me."

Marty takes a breath—maybe the first decent one since he approached.

"You're good, bro," Colin confirms.

"Very good," I add.

Marty smirks. "Good. Just wanted to be sure." He starts to head off, but stops, turning back to us. "Also, I think someone needs to clean the litter box. I can smell it."

Well, can't expect him to be a totally different person all of a sudden.

Colin and I sneak a look to each other as he slips away.

We enjoy another song before Troy steps in front of the media console. He lowers the music and raises the wireless karaoke mic. "Thank you, everyone, for making it today, but it's time for our guys to head off now."

"To the honeymoon suite!" Lance calls out.

I turn to Colin. "Oh, God no."

"That's right!" Troy says. "Time to get upstairs to your suite, which is the room without gerbils because they don't need to be traumatized when you consummate your boyfriendship."

The guys make some *oohs* to really play up the drama. "And by the way, Col," Troy adds, "apparently I still need to return that spare key to you from last semester when I swung by to grab your phone while you were at work."

He winks, and Colin mutters, "Fucker."

Colin glows with a grin as the guys cheer us on. And I guess we just gotta give in.

"Well," I say, "if we're going to the honeymoon suite, then I should probably carry you."

Colin winces. "*You* carry *me?*"

"I'm obviously the one with superior strength, so it makes more sense." I go for it, hooking my arms around him like Colin does whenever he scoops me up. I make what I feel is a decent effort, but then just grab his legs, straining until he goes on his tippy toes. The room erupts with laughter, and when I set Colin down, his face is about as red as mine as he tears up from laughing so hard.

"Act like we meant to do that," I tease, and he rolls his eyes before sweeping me right off my damn feet.

The guys are hollering with excitement again, Lance barking like a dog as Colin and I ascend the steps.

We thank the guys, and when we get to the second floor, I say, "You can put me down now."

"Uh-uh. I gotta take you all the way to our love nest."

"I think we've had enough cringe for the day."

"I feel like we are just one giant cringe at this point."

As Colin approaches his room, I nab his keys from his pocket, and once we manage to coordinate getting the door open, we discover what the guys have done to his room.

There are more decorations—hearts and roses and petals across the bed.

"Frat guys do know how to decorate, that's for sure," Colin says as he carries me into the room, tossing me down on the bed so I bounce. He hops on the edge, and my body bounces again with the mattress before he rolls over, getting on top of me, his lips crushing mine.

I don't know if it's because of how sweet it was that he thought to have a boyfriendposal for me too, or because of how awesome our friends are, or because we're finally away from the guys and I get him all to myself, but I'm frisky as fuck. Nibbling and biting. We roll around, and when I'm on top of him, I pull up his shirt, kissing down his chest.

"As much...as I love...the guys," I say between kisses, "I love this more."

I take his nipple between my teeth, then lick, but then I miss his fucking mouth, so I return for another kiss, when I notice his head angled down as he looks at me, not like he's enjoying messing around, but like something's on his mind.

"What is it?" I press as I crawl over him, gazing down at his pretty mug.

"What is it..." He drags that out, suggesting what's supposed to follow.

"What is it, *boyfriend?*"

Colin's smile returns, and he reaches up, resting his hand against my face. Instinctively, I lean into his hold. "Remember when our parents first got together?" he asks, and I nod.

"Mom was still really struggling with the divorce. We both were. Not about Dad and Lauren, or even because Mom was in love with him and wanted to stay married, but that the fantasy we all had about our family would never be real. I remember when Dad started bringing Lauren around, I saw how he would light up again, and I felt this pain. And then I felt guilty for that. I love my dad. I wanted him to be happy."

"Of course you did, Col, but that was a lot. He knew that."

"I know. It's just not how a developing brain processes that shit, right?"

"Too well," I say, reflecting on my parents' split.

"But I decided that I'd make the best of it, and then one day, Lauren brought you over."

"I remember that day," I say, rubbing my face against his palm.

Colin's lip twists up as he runs his hand up my cheek, until his thumb is over my temple. He strokes so gently. "Do you remember you wouldn't even look me in the eyes? And they left us together in the living room for a bit—I'm sure so we got to know each other. And I was trying to make conversation with you, just being friendly, and you had your head in some game on your iPad—"

"*Pokémon Gold*," I mutter.

He snickers. "Yeah. And I thought, this is gonna be a nightmare if they stay together and I have to be around this guy all the time. I figured I'd turn on the TV to have something to do, and do you remember what you did?"

"Asked if you liked Pokémon."

Colin's eyes widen ever so slightly, and I notice the way the room light sparkles in his irises.

"You showed me the different ones and which were your favorite," he says. "Even let me play a bit. And then you couldn't stop talking about Pokémon, and you were so excited to talk to someone about it, and just kept on and on, and I remember thinking you were the coolest kid in the world."

I laugh, not because it was particularly funny, but because it reminds me of what was going on in our lives at the time. "It was really hard back then. I don't feel like Mom or Dad were able to really teach me how to interact with people."

"No shit."

"Right? I was awkward. Didn't know how to make friends. And by the time we met, I had guys being mean to me on the bus. At school. There was a guy who wore glasses who called me four-eyes. I just didn't understand.

And when Mom and Dad were having more arguments at home, it felt like the kids got even meaner at school, like they could feel I was having a hard time. When we came over that day, I was so annoyed with Mom. I didn't want to meet anyone. I just wanted to stay home and hide. And when you were trying to talk to me, I thought, he's gonna realize who you are and be mean like those others."

Colin must feel how hard it is thinking about those painful times because he rubs my temple again.

"You looked so cool with your backward cap and your Nike sneakers," I say. "I didn't understand why you were trying to talk to me. I don't even know why, but I just looked over and thought, he seems nice. Maybe just try. Worst he can do is be an asshole. And then when we talked, you were actually interested in the things I was saying, and you were listening, and it felt so good. I'd never felt that way before. And I was so pissed when Mom said we had to go because we'd barely covered the second generation."

Colin grins. "Fortunately, you had plenty of time after that to educate me."

"What a relief. You would have been such a loser if it hadn't been for me."

Colin studies my expression, his jaw tensing. "I wish I'd known you were going through all that bullying shit a lot sooner. I would have protected you."

"I know that now," I assure him.

"Ash, you'll never know how much you helped me back then. Before the divorce, I was easygoing and chill. Laughed and smiled all the time. Didn't really need a reason. Then there was this heaviness to everything. I didn't really start laughing and smiling again until we met. Hanging with you made me feel like at least something good came out of that whole mess."

"I feel the same." I relax my weight against him, hooking my arms under his to pull him closer. "I remember how you and Steve gave these great hugs—and you did it as easily as saying hi, and it felt so good. Mom and Dad didn't do that, but fuck, those hugs made all the shit we were dealing with a little less shitty."

He wraps his arms around me, tugging me close. "I made you a hugger."

"You did." And I'm proud of that. "I can't imagine what my life would have been like if I hadn't met you that day."

"I'm glad we don't have to imagine that."

I lean close to him, taking another kiss, something deeper, more meaningful than the playful ones we shared when we first came into his room.

I couldn't have known that day how much that kid in the backward cap would come to mean to me. Couldn't have known how many years we would laugh and play, oblivious to what was in store for us. Couldn't have known that one day he'd be watching me live stream myself jerking off. Or that we'd be fucking around in a bathhouse together. Or asking to be each other's boyfriends.

Couldn't have known that I wouldn't be able to imagine my life without this amazing guy in it.

Gazing down at him, seeing that intense expression on his face, that familiar look in his blue eyes, I know exactly what I'm looking at right now. This beautiful man who has been here for me during some of the hardest times in my life. Who makes me laugh. This man who makes me feel so safe when he's around.

Who has the biggest heart of anyone I've ever known.

Colin.

My Colin.

"Ash, I—"

"I love you too." I didn't mean to interrupt him, but I couldn't help myself.

His forehead wrinkles. "You have to let me say it to say *too*."

I cringe. "Oh fuck. I'm sorry. I fucking made it weird and awkward. And here everything was just right and perfect. Can we have a redo?"

Colin laughs. "You can't redo that."

"But I knew you were about to say that, so you might as well have said it."

He shakes his head. "That doesn't count. But that actually wasn't what I was gonna say anyway." He says it in this dramatic way that lets me know he's full of it.

"Oh really? What were you about to say, then?"

"I was gonna ask if you wanted to watch a movie tonight."

I glare at him.

"Hey, you're the one who conned me into that date. I can't help that you're so obsessed with me, you have to like, proclaim your love for me."

I burst into a laugh. "Well, admittedly, I am kind of obsessed."

I wait for him to break the act, but he locks gazes with me.

He finally looks away. "I guess I should get some homework done or something." And at my glare, he smiles. "Of course I love you." He offers a gentle kiss. "My little perv."

"I love you too, Big Man," I say, surprisingly proud of myself for getting it right this time.

We seal it with another kiss as I relax against him, enjoying how it feels to be tight against my boyfriend.

Who loves me.

Whom I'm in love with.

My cock stiffens, and I slide my hand down him, cupping his firm ass, enjoying how it feels in my grip.

I don't know what it is about what we just shared, or

maybe it's just being on top of him right now, but I find my mind drifting to new places.

"God, you have a real nice ass," I say, giving it a squeeze.

"All those fucking squats and drills." Colin flexes it for me, and my cock pulses. "You like that?" he asks, doing it again before squinting. "Is my little perv thinking about fucking me right now?"

"Bingo."

"Mmm. Suddenly realized you got this tight virgin hole under you."

He's being playful, but now, fuck... I thrust slightly, not really controlling it, just some innate impulse.

He leans close to my face, until his lips are less than an inch from mine, whispering, "Does this mean I get to be cruel tonight?"

His tongue traces my bottom lip, his tease assuring me that this is about to get real fun.

22

Colin

REAL TALK: I'VE played with my ass a couple of times recently, trying to get myself ready for this happening. I want Ash to have my ass, want to know what it feels like to be stretched out by his cock and have that fat load of his coating my insides. But when I'm touching my hole, it doesn't feel as good as I can see it does for Ash when I'm dicking him down.

And I want that. Want it so fucking much that I'm shaking with need for it. As much as I love fucking Ash—it's absolutely my favorite thing—I want to feel it from this side, want Ash having his way with me because I know, fucking *know* he'll drive me wild. There's no doubt in my mind that there is a huge difference between teasing myself with my finger and having him.

"What?" Ash asks before nipping at my nipple and giving it a tug with his teeth.

"Just thinking about how it's only so-so when I finger myself, but I know under your deft hands, this night is going to end with me coming my brains out."

Ash gives me a wickedly mischievous grin. "Who said you get to touch that hole without me?"

I tremble, him being possessive of my body is really fucking hot. "Why don't you hurry up and get down there and show me what I was doing wrong?"

"I assure you, you know how to treat a hole. I just think it's because it wasn't me. You want to give me your ass, Colin. No one else." He kisses down my torso, each press of his lips like fire licking at me. "You know I'll treat you so good." More kisses. "Because there's nothing you wouldn't give me, is there?"

"Fuck no." I tangle my fingers in his hair, try to push him down my body toward my throbbing cock. "I'm yours. Got me under your control, Ash, and I fucking love it. It's where I want to be."

"Good. You have me under yours too." Ash hooks his fingers in my joggers and tugs them down, along with my underwear. My dick springs free, the head red, a pearl of precum already at the tip. Ash laps at it with his tongue. "I can't wait until I fuck a load out of you and I get to eat the whole thing."

"I thought I was the cum-hungry one." And I am, like I'm fucking addicted to it. Will swallow up what's in Ash's balls every day for the rest of my life.

"You are. You're my cum fiend, but you know I love the taste of you just as much. My favorite fucking meal."

"That's because you haven't tasted my ass yet," I tease.

"We should probably work on changing that."

I kick out of the rest of my clothes, then grab Ash, flipping us so he's lying on his back. I pull his pants down while he gets out of his shirt.

"Fuck, you're so goddamned pretty," I tell him, the sweet compliment tumbling out. "Your body is perfect. Your cock is so sexy." I cup his balls. "And Christ, I want to keep my face buried right here in your sac, just licking you and breathing you in, showing you how much I worship you." Because I do. I love everything about Ash and have for longer than I realized. Everything he makes me feel is too intense for words.

Ash's cock flexes against his muscular belly. "You make me feel better than anyone ever has…than anyone ever could."

I beam at him, pride surging through me. Healthy or not, that's what I want to be for Ash. That's what he is for me. "Good." I grin. "Now are you going to eat my ass or what?"

Ash chuckles, the sound of it one of my favorite things. "Come here, Big Man. I want you to sit on my face."

I mean, how can I argue with that?

I straddle his head, thighs pressed against his shoulders. Ash isn't a small guy, but I like that I'm bigger than him. I like that I can carry him and he's smaller beneath me, but also that he has me in his control. There's a rush to that I don't know how to explain.

"Fuck, look at this hole," Ash says, spreading my cheeks. "It's so fucking pretty. So tight. I can't wait to fill it up with my cum."

"Yes. That. God, I want it so much."

"I'll give it to you when I'm good and ready."

I'm the one who's supposed to play our cruel little game with him tonight, but I don't have it in me. I just want Ash, for him to treat me with whatever pleasure he wants.

He grabs my waist and pulls me closer so his face is buried right in my ass. He lashes at my rim with his tongue, the pleasure reverberating through me.

"Oh fuck." My eyes roll back as he keeps going, making a damn meal out of me. My whole body is zinging, each flick and press of his tongue making the whirlwind of satisfaction grow more and more.

I push back against his face, riding his tongue like my life depends on it. If just having my ass eaten feels this good, I can't imagine what it will be like when Ash finally fucks me.

"That's it…you like it, don't you? Like feeling my tongue in your ass."

"Fuck yes," I reply, then spit in my hand and stroke his cock. "You're getting my hole ready for this. Ready to stretch me open and fill me with your spunk."

"Bend forward and get me ready. Get me all slick and even harder for your ass," he demands before burying his face in my ass again. I'm too hungry for his cock not to bend forward and suck his dick between my lips. The taste of his precum bursts on my tongue, making me shake with even more need. I love the salty taste of Ash, the unique flavor of every part of him, but especially what comes from his balls.

I push back against his face, his tongue stiff as he pushes it inside me, but I'm not losing focus on the task at hand—his cock. The weight of it on my tongue drives me wild, the feel of my lips stretched around him, even the way I gag when he hits the back of my throat.

When Ash pulls back from my ass, I growl. I look back to tell him to get to work again, but he's sucking his finger into his mouth. The look on my face must say it all because he asks, "Is my boyfriend ready to feel my finger in his ass?"

"Yes. Fuck yes. Please put it inside me."

His pupils flare, and then he's tracing my rim and working the tip of his finger inside.

"This is so sexy, Col…seeing you this way, seeing your body open up for my finger, knowing that this is just the beginning and I'm stretching you out for my cock."

My cock twitches, balls tightening as I push back,

hungry for more. He slides it in and out while I ride his finger like the slut I am for him. When his finger moves just the right way, hitting my prostate, it's like an electrical shock to my pleasure receptors and I nearly shoot off him.

"Fuck. Do that again."

"Colin, meet your prostate. I knew the two of you would get along well," he teases, but I don't have it in me to laugh right now. I just want more.

"Do it again."

"Needy, aren't you?"

"Hell yes."

He rubs over it again and again, each time the pleasure building higher. Ash's mouthwatering dick is right beneath me, but I can't make myself move to grab it, to swallow it, not in this moment.

"Get on your hands and knees," Ash says.

I scramble off him, rose petals sticking to our skin.

Ash grabs the lube from the nightstand, slicking his fingers before settling behind me and pushing two digits into my willing ass.

He fucks me with them, and I push back to meet him, cock bobbing. I love fucking Ash. Will always want to fuck Ash, but I must admit, so far, it feels pretty fucking good from this side too.

"You're going to look so pretty on my cock."

"It's you," I say, then realize the words might not

have come out right. "This is what you do to me…make me want you so much. You make everyone want you so much, but you're mine. My boyfriend. Don't care if it's you pounding my ass or me owning yours, just need to have you. Always want you."

A wave of heat rolls off him, this desire-fueled blast of warmth, because my Ash loves hearing how much I want him and what he does to me.

"Hurry up and give me that perfect cock of yours. I want to work a load out of your balls, want all that cum to myself."

"Fuck. You're mine too." Ash slicks up his dick and pushes at my ass. "That's it…you can do it. Open up for me, Col. Show me how good you can take my cock."

It's uncomfortable at first. His dick is a whole lot bigger than two fingers, but I know that stretch, that pressure, it's what it takes to get Ash inside me, and I want it. "Fuck me," I beg. "Show me how good that cock will treat me. You're so good for me, Ash, so good to me. Always."

His blunt fingernails bite into my hips as his hold on me tightens. Ash makes short pumps of his hips, each one working him deeper and deeper inside me.

My hands fist into the pillows, the sound of his breathing lulling me, making me crave him more.

"Almost there. You're almost taking all of me. That pretty ass of yours is gonna swallow me up."

Yes. Please. Fuck, fuck, fuck, he keeps pushing in, until finally I'm full of Ash's cock.

"You're so tight." He reaches under me, wrapping his hand around my dick and giving it a few strokes. "You like taking your stepbrother's cock?"

"Hell yes."

He presses a kiss to my spine. "Your boyfriend's cock?"

"Yes. So fucking much. Now hurry up and fuck me."

Ash chuckles like I hoped he would, knowing I'm dying for this.

"I won't be cruel and make you wait…this time."

He pulls back and thrusts forward again, drilling me over and over and over. I take it, welcome it, feel my dick throb and swell, get harder by the second. Each time his dick moves against my prostate, I feel like I'm coming out of my skin in the best way.

Our bodies slap together, skin on skin. This is incredible, sharing my body with Ash this way.

He pushes me down and I go, Ash following me as I end up on my belly. He moves my left leg so it's bent at the knee, Ash straddling my right. He uses his hand to pull at my left ass cheek, opening me up more.

"I could watch my dick slide in and out of you all night."

"Don't make me wait that long to come."

"No edging for you?"

"I might die," I joke. "Or end up flipping you over and taking you."

"Oh, but, Col…then you wouldn't get your insides painted with my load."

"Oh shit." That was maybe one of the hottest things I've ever heard.

Ash keeps taking me that way, fast, then slow, working me up and making me feel like I'm losing control.

When he's had enough of me like that, he pulls out, my ass feeling way too empty. "Get back inside me."

"I will. Be patient. You'll get my load soon."

Ash flips me to my back and slicks my dick with lube. I spread my legs, pull them up, him shoving a pillow beneath my hips.

He pushes back inside me, my body accepting him hungrily.

Ash fucks into me, dick rubbing my prostate just right. Our gazes hold on to each other's, the dark strands of his hair wet with sweat.

"I like this." I wrap a hand around my shaft, jerking it. "Like seeing you…need you to see how much I want you."

"I want you too." He leans over me, tongue pushing into my mouth, kissing and fucking me with equal skill.

When he pulls back, I stroke myself harder, faster. Ash's hazel gaze turns frenzied as he lets loose, drilling into me. I'm not going to last much longer, balls so tight and high.

"You're about to get it, Col. You ready for my fat load?"

"Yes. Give it to me."

Ash thrusts again, cock jerking, and it's like that one pump into me unleashes any control I had left over myself. My back bows off the bed, cum spurting from my cock, hot jets landing on my stomach and chest. Ash's dick flexes inside me, his cum spilling deep, painting my insides just like he promised.

I come a whole fucking lot, but not as much as him, and I take it all, want it to leak out of my ass all night.

"Jesus, that was good." Ash pulls out when he's given me everything in his nuts, then laps at my jizz on my stomach.

"Kiss me." I pull him to me, take his tongue into my mouth, taste myself on him while we make out with my cum between us.

It feels almost impossible to move, but when he tries to pull away, I wrap my arms and legs around him.

Ash chuckles. "I was just going to get something to clean us off."

"Not yet. Need to feel you."

He snuggles in, doesn't try to go. He loves how much I want him, and I know Ash loves and wants me with equal fervor.

I stroke his back, feel us stuck together with sweat

and cum. "Was it enough?" I ask gently. I hadn't realized I wondered about that until the question left my lips.

"The sex?" He pushes up slightly so he can look at me. I nod. "Yes. It was incredible. I love the exhibitionism or teasing danger of knowing we can get caught, but I love this just as much because it's with you."

"I'm really good at sex," I tease.

"Who's the one that just made you come your brains out?"

"Both of us did that to each other."

I squeeze him tighter, and Ash licks the sweat off my skin, then asks, "It was enough for you?"

"You're always enough for me. Everything about you, and about what we do, is fucking incredible."

"We're disgustingly sweet."

I laugh. "I know, but I love that about us."

"I love you, Col."

"I love you too," I reply, knowing nothing can ever take me down from this high.

23

Ash

I STIR IN bed but can't move much since Colin's arms are hooked around me as he tugs me close to his chest, his legs entangled with mine, his morning wood resting between my ass cheeks.

In the days since I came inside him, we've shared plenty more fucks, like we're trying to wear our bodies down with the workouts.

I take a moment to enjoy just being in my boyfriend's arms.

The boyfriend I love and who loves me.

The boyfriend who gets me more than anyone in the world.

My alarm goes off, and I reach over to the nightstand, silencing it.

Colin's grip tightens around me. "No," he mutters before planting a kiss on my nape. "It's the weekend. Just stay here for a few more hours."

"We said we'd go to the Peach State Spring Festival

with the guys," I remind him.

His nose rubs against my neck as he shakes his head. "No, let's get Lance to tell them we died."

"Won't they be suspicious when they see us around campus?"

"I hear Wyoming's nice this time of year?"

I laugh. "I don't know that we need to move to Wyoming if we bail on the guys."

Colin groans. "Really? You think Atlas is gonna be totally cool if we slight his boyfriend?"

"In that case, I should start looking up flights to Cheyenne."

I move for my phone on the nightstand when Colin rolls, taking me with him to the opposite side of the bed. I love when he manhandles me.

"Fuck, Colin."

"If you say so." He pushes his hard cock against my ass, and I feel his smile against my neck. He reaches around, feeling my cock, which is a semi now, but as he plays with it, I get even harder.

"You're not getting any dick unless we get the fuck up and get ready."

"Cruel Ash."

"Damn right."

"I can be cruel too," Colin says before biting down on my shoulder and giving a firm thrust against my ass.

My face heats up as he pumps my cock.

"Oh hell," I mutter. "No, no. We're being good this morning. And you can spend the day craving this ass…and I'll give it to you later."

Colin growls. "I'd be so mad if you didn't make it sound so sexy."

"Let's take a shower."

I pry away from him, and we grab our things and head into his private en suite bathroom—a luxury afforded to him since he's a junior and star athlete. Mere mortals like me must use the communal one in the hall on our floor.

As cruel as I intended to be, I don't manage to keep from jerking off with him in the shower—that would require willpower I don't fucking have—and after we clean off, we brush our teeth and throw on some clothes.

When I step out into the hall, Colin snatches my hand and spins me back toward him, his lips mashing down against mine, one hand sliding under my shirt, the other around to my ass.

"Morning, guys," Payton's voice comes from farther down the hall, and we part to say good morning before glancing back at each other.

Colin winces. "It's getting more difficult to feel naughty with you around here since everyone knows."

"Yeah, last time we left the door open, Payton just walked by and shrugged. Doesn't really have the same effect."

As much as I love being out with my boyfriend and everyone in the house knowing about us, I miss some aspects of the sneaking-around-and-in-secret gig. It was fairly exciting and erotic.

"So we're in agreement," Colin says. "We gotta start fucking outside Marty's room?"

I burst into a laugh; my boyfriend always knows how to make me laugh.

"We'll definitely get a reaction then, but you know, if we can't do that here, maybe we need to make extra trips to a certain bathhouse in Peachtree Springs."

Colin nibbles at my bottom lip. "You read my mind."

We've only been that one time. Really, I've been perfectly content just fucking around with my boyfriend, and I haven't really felt like there's any hurry, since I know we'll have plenty of time for that.

After a quick make-out session, we head downstairs and find some guys are already in the kitchen. Atlas, Troy, Brenner, Lance, and Taylor—the crew we're heading to the festival with—lounge around, chatting over breakfast.

"Look who finally made it out of bed," Troy says as he spots us.

"Leave them alone," Atlas says. "They're in their honeymoon period, so they had to get off at least once."

Troy rests his hand on his chest. "Just once? I hope

not. If so, you guys have to get back upstairs."

"Shut it," I say, heading to the pantry for my grits.

We fix breakfast, catching up with the guys, when Marty and Payton join us. "Wait, is this our crew for the festival?" Marty asks.

"Yeah," I reply.

He glances between Troy, Atlas, Colin, and me. "We aren't crashing some kind of stepbrother double date, are we?"

That gets us all laughing.

"It can't be a stepbrother double date," Atlas says. "Brenner and Taylor are coming. And you, Payton, and Lance."

"Sorry," Marty says. "Just adjusting to the new normal."

"Don't be jealous because you don't have a stepbro you can smooch on," Brenner says.

"Well, who the hell needs stepbros when you have frat bros? Am I right?"

Lance chuckles. "Marty, did you just insinuate you want to smooch on other frats?"

"Yeah, it's called a joke."

"I'm sorry. I've been here for two years, and I didn't realize you did those."

"Shut the hell up," Marty says with a grin.

"I mean, there's gotta be plenty of that going on in here, right?" Brenner says, sliding onto the stool beside me. "I'm not really a frat type, but all these guys under the same roof... Shit has to be happening behind the scenes."

"There's some of that," Troy says.

"Not as much as you'd think...or hope," I add.

"That's not what I heard," Brenner says. "I hooked up with this guy Dax last month. He's brothers with someone at Sigma Alpha."

Dax? Brenner heard something from him?

Colin and I exchange a look.

"We met Dax at TaskFrat," Colin says, turning his attention to Brenner.

"What did he tell you?" Lance asks.

"That there are some hot guys at Alpha Theta Mu who can get real wild."

"Did he?" Colin asks.

"That's all he'd say, so I figure he must've had a three-way or some shit like that while in town."

"Or some shit like that," I mutter, sneaking another glance at Colin, who's smirking.

"He didn't get into specifics," Brenner adds, "but definitely played on my fratty fantasies."

It's nice hearing that Dax didn't run around blabbing about what we shared. Kind of like we could tell he was the right guy to share that side of ourselves with.

"I felt like everyone was straight when we were freshmen," Marty says, "and now everyone's falling out of the closet. We should have a board up on the fridge and just tick off as we steadily lose more and more straights. I feel like Lance, Payton, and I will be the last of the straights by the time we're seniors."

"If I find out it's you and me on the same side," Lance says, "I'll start sucking dick not to be."

"Guess it'll just be Payton and me, then. Right, Payt?"

"Sounds like Lance will need a dick to suck," Payton says, "and I'm always here for my bros."

As everyone gets to laughing, Marty rolls his eyes. "You all love me and you know it."

"Don't worry," Lance tells Brenner. "There's plenty of guys messing around under this roof."

"That's what I want to hear," Brenner says. "That guys are just running around, sucking each other off left and right."

"Well, some of us are," I say.

"Whoa, whoa," Marty says. "Too much info."

"I know you don't know Brenner well," Taylor says, "but you're just setting him up to say not enough info."

"Don't take my line!" Brenner snaps.

"Then don't take so long to say it."

I have a feeling this crew will have a great time at the festival. And I'm not wrong. When we get there, we hit up the arcade for a while, then ride roller coasters, hit the bumper cars, and take a spin on the Ferris wheel before some of us split up. Taylor wants to spend more time in the arcade, and Lance, Marty, Troy, and Atlas were gonna have another go at the bumper cars, but I'm still dizzy after that last coaster, so Colin and I head across the festival to a food truck we saw that sells wings and funnel cake—our favorites.

En route, Colin's hand grips mine.

I notice it's firm enough to let me know he's mine, but loose enough that I don't feel like he's dragging me around the place. Like so many things with Colin, it's just right.

"Aren't you glad I got you out of bed for this?" I ask.

Colin groans. "I don't know if *glad* is the right word. Think we could have had a perfectly fine day in bed." He winks.

"Maybe that's true."

"That was funny, what Brenner said about Dax. I bet they had a real fun night."

I laugh. "Right? But it was nice that he respected what we did enough to keep it secret."

"I had a feeling he was cool. It's nice to know we trusted the right guy with that."

"I agree." As I gaze at Colin's pretty mug, an impulse creeps through me, and I grab the back of his cap with my free hand, twisting it around to the front.

"I'm gonna have to start punishing you every time you do that."

"Punishing me? Oh, aren't we the kinky two? What did you have in mind?"

"Every time you do that, you're gonna have to clean yourself up after we mess around."

I glare at him. "It can't be a punishment if you wouldn't be able to follow through with it even if you wanted to."

Colin winces, leaning closer and whispering, "Then I guess it can't be no dick for a week either. I'm gonna have to think real hard about this."

"Careful, Col. You're not that clear-headed when you're thinking hard."

"Shut up and kiss me."

I grin ear to ear as I lean into him, accepting a soft kiss, enjoying that I'm still learning all Colin's kisses.

The soft ones.

The rough ones.

Every variant in between.

Wondering which ones I haven't identified yet, and eager to discover them.

As he pulls away, a voice comes from beside us. "Colin Phillips."

We turn at the same time. I don't recognize the woman, but I feel Colin tense up, so I pull my hand away from his, wondering if maybe this isn't how he wants someone outside our friends to find out about us.

"Mrs. Raeger."

"I thought that was you," she says, offering a hug.

Now that I've gotten a good look at her, she does look familiar, but I still can't place her.

"What are you doing in Peachtree Springs?" Colin asks.

"We're visiting Andy for the day. He figured we could come here. How's your mom doing?"

Oh, she's a friend of his mom's; that's why he tensed up.

"She's good. Busy right now. But it's been too long. Since she moved to North Carolina, we barely see each other anymore."

Now that she's been talking for a bit, I realize I do know her. She's dyed her hair blonder, but I've seen her at Steve's birthday parties.

Her gaze shifts to me. "Oh," she says, taken aback. "I don't know why, but I didn't recognize you right away, Ash. I thought you might have been…" She hesitates. "One of Colin's friends."

She seems flustered, which given what we were doing when she showed up, isn't a huge surprise.

Glancing between us, she says, "It's so good seeing you both. I should search for Andy and his dad. Tell your mom I said hi, will you?"

"Of course."

After she heads off, we continue a few yards, stepping into the line for the food truck, surely both of us considering the implications of our run-in with a friend of his mom's.

"Well…something like that was bound to happen," Colin says.

"I'm sorry. It does feel like we've been in our own little bubble. I probably should have said something about holding hands in public."

Colin glares at me. "What?"

"I just want you to do this at your own pace. You shouldn't have to be out before you're comfortable."

He moves closer. "Ash, I'm very comfortable letting the world know how I feel about you. And it's about time we talked to our parents about us…unless you don't want to talk to them about it."

"It's not a conversation I want to have with them," I confess, "but I knew that's where this was all leading."

He smirks. "It will be a weird conversation."

"You think they'll wonder about those sleepovers we had when we were teenagers?"

Colin laughs. "Probably."

It's finally our turn in line, so we order wings and a funnel cake. As I grab extra napkins, Colin says, "That whole interaction made me realize that we do need to have a serious conversation."

A serious conversation?

When I turn to him, his expression is so intense, it's making me nervous.

"If I'm holding your hand, Ash, you don't pull yours away. That's gonna be a big Step Don't from now on."

And he's got me laughing again. "Yeah, that's a good Step Don't."

"Also, no hogging the funnel cake." He grabs for it, but I pull it out of his reach.

"Now you're pushing it."

We share a smile and another kiss.

"Mmm," I say. "Well, maybe it's good that we ran into Mrs. Raeger. Guess it's time to have this conversation. Now everyone will know I'm yours and you're mine."

"Yeah, they will," Colin says, his lips tugging into a gentle smile—the sort of smile that soothes my concerns about sharing this with our parents. Awkward as it may be, I want everyone in the whole goddamn world to know how I feel about this guy.

And how he feels about me.

24

Colin

ASH AND I have been living in this perfect bubble, where it's either just us, or us and our friends, now that they know about us. It felt safe telling them, and I'd shout from the rooftops that Ash is mine, but seeing Mrs. Raeger was a wake-up call. I want to step out of this bubble we're in. I'm ready for our parents to know, but I don't want them to find out from someone else, not only because it's not fair to them, but because there's nothing wrong with Ash and me being together. Not telling them makes me feel like we think there is.

I make my way downstairs on Sunday morning.

Ash is sitting with Lance, Payton, and Marty in the living room. Frat Cat is on his lap in the armchair. I nuzzle Ash's neck from behind. "I'm jealous. I think Frat Cat loves you more."

"Aw, he loves his Daddy Colin."

"Oooh, that's hot. Say Daddy Colin again," I joke, earning a snicker from Ash.

"Please don't. I'm begging you not to say that again," Payton says from the couch.

"Go see *Daddy Colin*." Ash hands Frat Cat to me.

"Good boy," I tease, cuddling the kitten to my chest. Ash gets up from the chair, and I follow him into the kitchen. "What are you doing today?"

"You, I assume."

I chuckle.

"Though I'd rather you do me."

"That can definitely be arranged." I sit at the counter while Ash pours himself a glass of orange juice. I snag it and take a drink. "Oops."

"That was for you."

"That's sweet." He knows I like my OJ in the mornings. "My boyfriend is the best."

"Obviously." Ash walks around the counter and wraps his arms around my shoulders. "You can always tell me again, though."

Another laugh slips past my lips. "My boyfriend is the best."

Ash leans in and kisses me. "What *are* we doing today? Besides each other. Tomorrow is a busy day since we both have school and work."

"I have a Zoom with Mom in, like, an hour. I was hoping you'd want to join me so we can tell her about us, like we talked about. We can plan when we'll tell Dad and Lauren after that."

Ash nods, but then asks, "You're sure you want me with you? I don't mind being there. I just want you to be sure."

I frown. "I always want you with me."

The smile that stretches across his face is breathtakingly beautiful. It's wild to me that I can make him feel that way, but it's also the best feeling in the world.

"I guess we're lucky I feel the same."

"Come on. Let's get ready." I grab my glass of OJ and take it upstairs with us. We take a quick shower, get dressed, then hang out for a while, waiting for it to be time to meet with my mom. Frat Cat runs around the room like someone slipped him catnip.

"Are you nervous?" Ash asks.

I shake my head. "Nah. It'll work out. Everyone knows how close we are, and really, our parents just want us to be happy."

"Yeah, me too."

"We'll be okay, my little perv. I promise."

"I know." Ash pulls up the second computer chair, and we sit at the desk. I log in to Zoom. It's just a couple of minutes before Mom is joining. We have the same bright-blue eyes and the same smile, but my brown hair comes from Dad—Mom's being a more blond color.

"Hey, you," I say. Her gaze darts back and forth between me and Ash. "I dragged this guy to hang out with us today."

"I hope that's okay," Ash says, and I reach under the table, placing my hand on his thigh.

"Of course it is. How have you been?" Mom asks, and I let out a sigh of relief. I'd told him I wasn't nervous, and really, I'm not—or at least I haven't been until I saw the way Mom was looking at us.

Maybe Mrs. Raeger already told her.

Maybe I was wrong and our parents won't understand.

I push those thoughts aside while Ash gives Mom an update on his life—well, minus the biggest change.

When they're finished, I find Ash's hand, hold it in support, and say, "There's actually a reason I wanted Ash here with me today. This might come as a shock, especially since I haven't even told you I'm queer, but Ash and I…we're together now."

Mom doesn't answer right away, again looking back and forth between us—that same expression as when we first got onto the call.

Oh. She knew.

Mrs. Raeger already got to her.

"I know it's probably confusing," Ash starts. "Being stepbrothers makes things complicated, but I love Colin. He's been my best friend from the first day I met him, and now he's more. He's everything."

My heart bangs at my chest, running a million miles an hour. It doesn't matter that I've heard him say similar things to me before; every time feels like the first time, making a riot of butterflies dance around in my chest.

"Ash is everything to me too," I admit, our grip tight on each other.

Mom sighs, and I know that sound. Anyone who has a parent probably knows that sound, and it's not one we want to be hearing right now. It makes my heart slow down and drop to my belly. Just moments ago, it would've never occurred to me that we wouldn't have our parents' support. Maybe that's naive of me. Maybe it's not the way it works, but it's the way it *should* work.

"Mom?" I'm pretty sure Ash is holding his breath.

"That's my worry," she finally says, making my brows pull together in confusion.

"What's your worry?"

"How important you are to each other. From the moment you met, you've been inseparable—two peas in a pod. That's sweet. I know how much you mean to each other, and I hate to even mention it, but what if it doesn't work?"

I roll my eyes. "Why wouldn't it work? We love each other."

I feel Ash stiffen beside me, like maybe this is making more sense to him than it is to me. Like maybe my mom's not pulling ridiculous reasons out of the air, which is all I see.

"You don't think your father and I loved each other?

Hell, Colin. You've heard the stories. We grew up best friends, much like you and Ash." They'd known each other even longer. Played together, learned to ride bikes together. Shared their first kisses, their first everything, and then one day, they realized things changed. That they loved each other but weren't in love with each other and maybe never were.

"My parents too," Ash says. "They thought they would work, and they didn't."

"So? That doesn't mean it would happen to us. I can't believe you said that, Mom." I turn to Ash. "We're fine. Nothing is going to change between us."

Mom speaks before he can. "I'm not trying to hurt either of you. You know I love you both and will support you both, but I'm trying to be realistic here. You two are so important to each other. You're not just boyfriends and best friends, but stepbrothers. Have you considered what would happen if it doesn't work out? What you have to lose?"

"That's a risk in every relationship."

"But the stakes are higher here. I hate saying this. I'm not trying to be the bad guy, but romantic relationships fail often, even the ones that aren't supposed to, like mine and your father's, and what would that mean for the two of you?"

"You and Dad get along fine," I argue.

Why isn't Ash talking? Why isn't he saying anything?

"We do, but it was rocky at first, and maybe that's a risk you two are willing to take. I just don't feel like I'd be doing either of you any favors by pretending this can't blow up in our faces. You would be crushed if anything happened between the two of you."

She's right, I would be, but that's not a reason for us not to be together, is it? But then I think of Dad and Lauren too. If Ash and I broke up, would it cause problems for them? What if it has a domino effect, and things between us pull Dad and Lauren apart too? I would never forgive myself for that.

Family holidays, get-togethers, the bond I have with Ash, the way we never lie to each other… What if this messes up everything?

When neither of us reply, Mom says, "I'm sorry. Maybe I shouldn't have said anything, but I know how exciting a new relationship can be. We have all those good feelings, and you're filled with hope for the future, and I just think it's really important that you consider the consequences."

The air in the room is thick. I'm still not sure Ash is even breathing beside me. I let go of his hand, wrap an arm around him, and pull him close. I say a silent prayer that he comes easily. "We're going to be fine. Ash and I are different."

"And I hope so, but just think about it, okay? Both of you."

We nod, but neither of us replies. The mood is heavy, my chest tight. I was so excited to share this with her, to tell everyone that Ash is mine, and now I don't know what to think.

What if Dad and Lauren feel the same? What if this changes everything but not in a good way?

What if I lose my best friend?

My stepbrother?

My Ash?

I don't know if I could be like Mom and Dad, don't know if I could handle seeing Ash move on with someone else, not after finally having him.

"I think we'll go," I tell Mom. Maybe I should play this a different way, pretend none of it happened, but I can't talk to her right now.

"I'm so sorry, boys. I feel awful. Maybe I should have kept my opinion to myself."

"It's fine. Me and Ash are fine. I love you."

"Goodbye, Lacey," Ash says to her, a smile on his face that I know isn't real.

"I'll talk to you both soon, okay?"

"Bye, Mom." I end the session before she can say anything else.

Neither of us speaks for a moment. We don't look at each other. It's Ash who finally says, "I didn't expect that."

"Me neither." I grab his hand and tug him to the bed

with me. "Come'ere."

Falling onto my back, Ash comes down on top of me, holding me close. "She's right, Col. This could end badly. If somehow we had a bad breakup, what if our parents felt obligated to choose sides?"

"We won't," I reply, forcing the words from my tongue.

"I'm sure neither of our parents thought that either."

Everything Ash is saying is true, even if I don't want to believe it.

"I can't lose what we have, Col…what we had before this."

"We won't," I say, trying to make myself believe it.

"We can't guarantee that."

"We won't," I say again.

And now here I am, committing a huge Step Don't…because I'm scared. I'm worried that what my mom said is true, and I don't tell Ash.

25

Ash

I WAKE, EXPECTING Colin's arms to be around me, but he's not in bed with me.

He steps out of his bathroom, and when he looks to see if I'm awake, he grins, but I can tell it's forced.

"Morning, my little perv." He approaches and offers a kiss.

But like his words, something's off. It doesn't hit the way it did before our chat with Lacey.

Not that I can put this all on him; I'm off too. Our conversation with her really rattled us. She's not wrong, and we both know it.

Maybe that's one of the reasons we let it go on secretly for as long as we did. Kept each other to ourselves so that we wouldn't have to consider the real world and consequences. We could enjoy a Wonderland of emotion and passion, excitement beyond anything I thought I'd ever experience.

I'm smarter than this—we both are.

We've seen firsthand how that bright spark that bursts into an inferno can be extinguished. And now that we've been forced to face that truth, we're both shaken.

Colin's kiss lingers, as it normally does, and when he pulls away, he still doesn't take his eyes off me. It's all so familiar, but I can feel the difference, and surely he must too.

"Good morning," I say. "You heading out for class? Seems early."

"Was gonna head to the library to study a bit before."

"Oh, okay."

"I can feed Frat Cat before I go."

"I got it."

"You sure?"

"Of course."

Why is this normal thing weird today?

It's not the only thing. And I figure there will be more.

"I was gonna meet up with Troy for dinner." Colin hesitates before asking, "You wanna come?"

Now he's hesitating to ask me if I want to hang with him and his friends? Who the fuck are we?

A knot twists in my gut.

To the average person, I'm sure this isn't a horrible, nightmarish moment with their boyfriend, but for us, it feels wrong.

And it's not only him telling me he has plans with friends. That's not unusual. That's healthy. It's that in the days since our talk with Lacey, Colin's been acting strange…

"I'll get some homework done," I say, "but I'll be here when you get back."

Now I'm doing it too. Before our talk with his mom, I would have said yes without thinking twice about it. But now we're…different. I don't like it.

We're both trying to keep up like things are fine, but they're not.

"See you later," Colin says with a wink.

He starts to head out when I notice his hat in the sheets. "Oh, hey!" He whirls around as I toss it to him, catching it like always, though it doesn't have that spark to it. Just like so many of our rituals, it's been tainted.

"I love you," I say, unable to disguise the fear in my tone.

It's not that he's gonna leave me today. Obviously, that's not what any of this is about, but the thought of ever losing Colin…it's too much to bear.

He stops in the doorway, then comes back and places his hands on either side of my face. "I love you too," he assures me.

When he kisses me, I don't doubt that. I never would. It's not like he magically fell out of love with me over a few days.

He pulls away, and I want to ask him, *What are you thinking?* Talk to him like we would have before. Really get to the bottom of this. We communicate. That's our thing. I want to just say, *Let's stop being idiots and figure this out.*

But I'm too scared. I know he wouldn't commit a Step Don't. And really, I don't know that I could bear to hear that he's questioning what we're doing. That he's thinking we might struggle when he's in law school and I'm working as a TA for my master's. That he wonders if we'd make it through our high-demand careers, maintaining this magic we've always had.

We're Colin and Ash. I want to believe we could face anything together, but what if he's afraid we can't?

I wonder if he's scared of asking me that same question because it's not like him not to check in on me when he knows something's wrong.

After he heads out, I assure myself we're just off right now. *We'll be fine,* I tell myself. But I didn't have to keep telling myself that before.

Now, it feels like I have to keep reminding myself that nothing's wrong. And it's not like Lacey told us anything we couldn't have figured out for ourselves if we'd stopped to consider the long-term consequences.

I POWER THROUGH my day at school.

It's what I'm good at, where I thrive. I can distract myself a bit, and around three thirty, when I get out of my last class, I pull out my phone to check my messages.

Colin: I'll see you tonight. I love you. Everything's fine.

Oh fuck. I'm tearing up. Goddammit.

I hurry to my car, and as I get in, there are fucking tears streaming down my face.

I can't keep pretending everything's fine when it's not.

I'm not fine.

We're not fine.

He's still in class, and I don't know what the fuck to do, but I need to talk to someone.

I find myself pulling onto the interstate, heading to our parents' place. Since Steve works from home, he'll probably be there to lend me an ear.

I would never tell him what's going on with Colin and me, not without Colin present. But I need a warm hug and a friendly face. Someone to reassure me.

When I get to the house, I see his car isn't there. Steve must be out—maybe at the store or working on a chapter at Starbucks.

Mom's car is.

Fuck my life.

I key in the code at the front door, don't even bother looking for her. I head upstairs to my room.

Just need a good cry.

But then my feet take me farther down the hall into Colin's room.

The tears come again.

I crawl into his bed, burying my face in his pillow, hoping to get a whiff of him, but when I just smell Tide Free & Gentle, it stings that much more.

I'm in a fucking tailspin.

Why couldn't we have just enjoyed the fantasy a little longer? Why did we have to spoil everything by telling anyone?

I sniffle, trying to control myself. When I turn, I notice someone's sitting on the edge of the bed.

"Fuck," I call out, sitting up and crawling back to the wall, every nerve in me convinced there's a psychopath in bed all of a sudden. It takes my brain a moment to recover from the surprise. "Jesus Christ, Mom! What are you doing?"

She sits there, perfectly still, watching me as she brushes her fingers through a tendril that's fallen from her messy bun, which is how she tends to keep her hair on her days off.

Her face twists up. "Sorry, I heard someone come in and saw your car, so I tried to find you, and you were crying. I knew I needed to do something, but am I supposed to let you cry it out, or do I need to try and see what's wrong? And you saw me before I made a decision." She says it all so matter-of-factly. "Did something happen between you and Colin?" Surely she's wondering what I'm doing in his room. "Did you guys have a...fight?" Even as she says it, she makes a face like she can't imagine how that's possible.

"No. I mean, not really."

"Am I supposed to press, or would you rather wait and discuss this with Jeanie?"

Jeanie's my therapist who helps me with my relationship with Mom.

At my glare, she says, "Oh, this is a mom moment, isn't it? Um...well..." She searches around uneasily.

"What are you doing home?" I ask.

"Plea bargain," she says with a smile, shaking her fists at her sides in one of her awkward happy dances.

Why couldn't Steve be home? This is *not* her area of expertise.

"Maybe you can just message Sarah and see if she can come by and talk to me," I say, more than a little bitterly. I grab Colin's pillow, curling up with it, and Mom takes a moment. Why won't she just leave?

"I really thought I would be very good at this, Ash."

"Huh?" I turn back to her.

"I was valedictorian of my class. Summa cum laude at Princeton and in law school."

"Mom, this is not the time to brag about your CV."

"That's not what I'm doing. I was saying that I felt

invincible, and when your father and I were talking about having kids, it seemed like another thing I would breeze through. Win Mother of the Year. And then you came into my life, and I realized that some of these things that make me good in other areas didn't really make me very good in this one."

I'm surprised by this confession. Mom's not one to show weakness, a trait that's been cemented by her profession.

"When you were a baby and crying, it wasn't a logical experience. And intellectually, I understood that. I read all the books. I watched all the videos, but something about it just didn't click for me. And the same with your father. We both adored you, and we did the best we could, but it was clear you needed something neither of us could give you."

Her chin quivers and a tear stirs in her eye, but she shakes her head, fighting it back.

A crack in my mother's otherwise impenetrable armor.

A vulnerable side she doesn't usually show—not to me, that's for sure.

"I liked Steve when I met him. We had fun together. And he made me laugh, and that's all great. But I could have turned it off at any point. That's how I've always been with relationships."

Why the fuck would she tell me this about my stepdad?

"Mom, do you think this is helping?"

She rests her hand on the comforter. "Just listen. It wasn't until I introduced you to Steve, and I saw how good he was to you, and how you lit up when you saw him. How he gave you this thing I couldn't. Seeing him and Colin hug you so effortlessly, give you all this attention and affection that I didn't understand. And that was when it really switched in me. When I felt so much more for him. And of course, I fell in love with him outside of that, but I would be lying if I said that seeing how much he and Colin did for you, how they would have done anything for you, didn't play a big part in that, especially in the beginning. And to this day, I know it was the best decision I've ever made."

I'm shocked that, after all the sessions in therapy, she's finally sharing these details. And just as shocked that they're not only about her. That all this time, she has been thinking of me, just maybe not in a way I'd considered.

"Why are you telling me this?"

"Because I see my son's in pain. And I have a feeling I know why." She glances around the room again.

I wince. "What do you think is the reason?"

"Steve and Colin are a lot alike. Steve had a very obvious look when he fell for me, and though I might not pick up on everything, I was perceptive enough to see it on Colin the last time you were both over."

"You know?"

"I think it's really beautiful, Ash."

I cringe. "Don't lie, Mom."

"Lie?"

"Yeah, we were gonna tell you and Steve and Dad soon. We told Lacey first, and she was talking about all the things we needed to consider. The fact that it might not work out, and then what will we do? Colin and I were having so much fun, and we let ourselves get lost in each other. But he's gonna go to law school. I'm gonna stay in school to be a professor. We're both planning to go to school locally, but we've chosen high-demand careers, and it's not always gonna be as easy as it is now. I don't need a lecture."

"Well, Lacey was right."

I glare at her. "I said I don't need a lecture."

"You think it was wrong of her to bring up the practicalities you both need to consider?"

"Mom, you don't understand. It scares me to think of a life without Colin. It terrifies me. And we had such an amazing relationship, and a part of me is like, why mess all that up when we could be amazing friends forever?"

She snickers.

"Wrong reaction, Mom."

"I'm sorry. This is where we're both very similar,

Ash. So smart that we think everything can be boiled down to questions and answers. Life's not that simple. Not knowing the answers can't stop you from living."

Finally, she's starting to make some sense. "I'm listening…"

"I loved your father, and it didn't work out, yes. That's right. And I could have said, *Well, it didn't work out, and maybe no one else will either,* but I didn't. I got to know Steve and fell in love. And I know you think I'm just highly logical and that's all there is to me, like I'm a robot, but I understand love. It might not last forever with Steve. I hope it will, but that's all we have. Any of us.

"So maybe Colin goes to law school, and you become a professor, and it just can't happen. Maybe something happens and you wind up never speaking to each other again. Maybe you both get bored of each other and break up that way. Maybe you meet someone else, or he meets someone else."

"I really don't love where this is going."

She smiles. "Or…maybe it *does* work out. Because that happens too. I am a logical woman, and all those thoughts run through my head, but I've seen high school sweethearts make it to their deathbed, and from what I know of you and Colin, if I'm putting money on anyone, it's the two of you. And it's okay to be scared or worried about what might happen because that lets you know how important he is to you; it's the day when you stop being afraid of losing him that you need to worry."

Tears stir in my eyes.

She notices and says, "Really? I thought that was good."

"It was good, Mom. These are tears of relief."

She sets her hand on my shoulder and rubs...awkwardly. "There we go," she says. I glare at her, and she grins. "Come on. That's a joke. I'm not really that bad. Am I?"

"Just give me a hug like a normal mother."

She moves close and puts her arms around me, drawing me in.

"You don't think it's weird that I'm in love with my stepbrother?"

"Oh, Ashy...I don't know that anyone other than Colin is worthy of you."

I cling to her tighter.

Because it's just what I needed to hear.

It's what I know in my fucking heart.

26

Colin

I CAN'T STOP thinking about Ash. That's nothing new, but normally it's all happy thoughts—how fun he is or how good he makes me feel. The way his smile could keep me warm on the coldest of days and how good it feels to have him in my arms. The way he makes me laugh and feel like I'm important. How laughing with Ash is better than anything else in the world—okay, maybe tied with how good it feels to fuck him.

But all I can think about now is the way he looked at me when I left. The fear in his eyes that matches the fear that's lived in my gut, in my chest, and taken over my mind since we got off the Zoom call with Mom.

I'm not supposed to make Ash feel that way.

It's my job to make him feel better.

I always want to be the person who makes him feel better.

"T, I think your friend is broken." Atlas pokes at my arm with his finger.

Troy snaps in front of my face. "Hello? Colin? Anyone home?"

"Ha-ha." I shake my head, then lean back in the chair. We're at the square table in Atlas's dining room, the two of them flanking me. Books and laptops are laid out in front of us, but I'm doing a shitty job at studying for finals. Maybe equally as bad as being a boyfriend right now. Jesus, what the fuck is wrong with me?

"Maybe we should call Ash. He's like a shot of caffeine for Colin anytime he's in the room," Troy adds. I know he's trying to make me smile, but it's not working. I'm being a mopey idiot and I know it.

"No, don't call Ash."

"Uh-oh. Trouble in paradise? Not everyone can be as good together as me and T," Atlas boasts.

"Don't be a dick," Troy playfully scolds his boyfriend, who pumps his brows at him.

"But you think it's hot."

"Good point. Do it again," Troy replies.

I know Atlas isn't trying to be a jerk and really just wants to distract me or make me smile, but I can't do it. "Can we get back to me here? I'm freaking out, and the two of you are engaging in some kind of weird foreplay. You look like you're going to go at it on the table at any minute."

"Would be a good show," Atlas says. "Here, let me move some of this stuff first."

"Not as good as me and Ash." My heart flutters. "God, I love Ash." I bang my head against the table a couple of times.

"Um…maybe I should go. I'm not sure how good I would be at this." Atlas scoots his chair out from the table, but I snap my head up.

"Wait."

"Fuck. Almost made it." He sits back down. I know he's not being serious. This is just how Atlas is.

"What's going on, Col?" Troy sets his hand on my arm. "You and Ash are perfect for each other. I'm not sure there's anyone more fitted to be together than you." Atlas growls. "Other than me and A."

"That's better." Atlas crosses his arms, and okay, I smile. I can't help it.

"I know we are. Ash is my person. That's what makes all this so scary."

Troy's forehead wrinkles. "What do you mean? You're not the type to run from a commitment."

"No. That's not it at all. I'm not afraid of being serious with him. I'm afraid of losing him."

I glance back and forth between them, and they're looking at me like I'm the world's biggest idiot.

"This might be me being a dick again, but have you seen you and Ash together? Have you seen the way he looks at you? Do you know the way you worship the ground he walks on? I don't think you're going to lose him."

"What Atlas said, only not as douchey," Troy adds.

"But that doesn't mean anything. Not really. Shit happens. My parents were best friends growing up. They were each other's first everything, and they didn't work. And what happens if that's me and Ash? I don't know how to lose him. It would feel like losing a part of myself—fuck, like my heart or lungs or something I can't be without."

"So you're just going to pull away from him? Makes perfect sense. Solid plan," Atlas says.

I turn to Troy. "I'm going to kill your boyfriend."

"Do you want me to hold him down?"

I chuckle, though I don't feel it in my gut. "I know it's confusing, but we told my mom. I didn't expect anything but support, but she brought up all this shit, and now I can't stop thinking about all the things that can go wrong."

"You should try thinking about all the things that can go right." Atlas shrugs. "Seems more like the type of person you are."

Something about hearing him say that—maybe because it's Atlas and it's so unlike him, maybe because it shows that even he sees me, this guy who doesn't like to show he cares about anyone but Troy—but all I know is that it rings some kind of bell inside me.

He's right.

This isn't like me.

This isn't who I am.

Troy says, "I've known you for a long time, and you've never been the type to throw in the towel. I can't imagine why you would do it now, when all that's going to do is make you lose the person you love the most."

"I'm not throwing in the towel. I would never do that with Ash. I'd do anything for him. Anything to make it work with him. He's it for me. Forever. I...oh..."

"*Ding, ding, ding!* I think he's got it!" Atlas does a mock cheer, but I ignore him.

What the hell am I doing? Why would I keep this stuff to myself? Being scared is one thing—it's normal to be frightened when something really matters—but not sharing it with Ash is inexcusable. It goes against the essence of who we are. All it's going to do is put a wedge between us. The very thing I'm afraid of is the thing that I'm making happen...

"I gotta go." I grab my backpack and start shoving shit inside. I can't believe I've been so stupid. I'm *hurting* Ash because I'm scared, when all I have to do is tell him how I feel, and we can get through it together.

Communication is fucking awesome.

"Should I text the guys to leave the house tonight?" Troy teases, but I don't take the time to answer. I need to get home to my Ash.

I maybe drive a little too fast back to the frat house, hoping Ash is there. I can't believe I left this morning without making sure he knew everything is okay between us. Yes, I texted him later, but that's not the same.

Some of my tension eases when I pull up in front of the white, two-story house and see Ash's car out front.

I jump out of the car, and the second I'm inside, he's there, sitting on the bottom of the stairs like he was waiting for me. Ash shoves to his feet, his sweep of bangs slightly messier than usual.

"I love you!" we say at the same time, then laugh.

"Okay, we're kinda awesome," I add.

"More than kinda." Ash sits back down on the second step, and I join him.

"I'm sorry, Ash. I know I've been distant the past few days. It's not because of you. I've been scared…and I don't know why I didn't tell you that. It's what we do. What I do. I got upset at you for committing a Step Don't, and now I did the same."

"You're not perfect, Col."

"I want to be perfect for you," I admit. It's true. I want to be everything Ash needs.

"And you are. You're everything I want. Everything I need, but you'll make mistakes, and I will as well. I've been distant with you too. Neither of us talked to the other. We both stewed in our emotions and didn't do the one thing we do best…well, that and sex."

"We're fucking great at that too." We laugh together.

"Seriously, though. These things are going to happen, Col. That's what being in a relationship is, but we can't lose sight of who we are and what makes us *us*. That's how we'll stick together, how we'll make it work—by being open and honest with each other."

I nod, knowing he's right.

"I talked to my mom. I didn't tell her about us, but she knew."

Wow. Lauren knew about us? I'm surprised she saw it, but then maybe she sees more than she shares. "Is everything okay?" I reach over and grab his hand. "She didn't make you feel bad, did she?"

"No. She was great actually…well, as great as she can be. She supports us. She believes in us, but she also reminded me that this is life—maybe we'll work out and maybe we won't, but that's true of any relationship. That doesn't mean we throw in the towel now. We fight for each other, and we fight together."

I rub my cheek against his. "You be the realistic one, and I'll be the idealistic one, because that works for us. We fit together that way, and as the idealistic one, I'm going to remind you that we *will* work. That we *will* be together forever. We won't lose each other because that's not us, Ash. Together, we're the ultimate Step *Do*."

He grins, like seriously a smile so big that I think it might swallow his face. "That's so cheesy."

"Bet it made your pulse speed up. You can't pretend you don't love that shit."

"I love it from you...my Big Man."

"My little perv." I take Ash's mouth with mine. My tongue pushes past his lips, needily, hungrily.

Our mouths don't part as he moves forward, sitting on my lap and straddling me on the stairs. He grabs for my hair, knocking my cap off as we move together, swallowing each other's needy noises.

I'm pretty sure all the blood in my body rushes straight to my groin, cock going hard as stone behind my track pants. I grab his ass, pulling him closer. "Touch me."

"What if I don't want to? What if I want to make you suffer...wait..." He dances his fingers slowly down my torso.

"Please..." I don't care how fucking needy I sound for him. I am.

Just as he hits the bottom of my shirt, his hand pressing against my cock, the front door shoves open.

"Oh fuck. Not again. You two are the horniest sons of bitches I've ever known." Lance comes into the house, followed by Payton, and surprisingly, Brenner and Taylor.

"We were gonna have makeup sex," I tease.

"Very funny. You two don't fight," Payton replies.

"They probably fake-fight just so they can make up

301

again," Lance adds.

"I'm trying to get over the not-again part. Is this a thing you guys do? Walk in on them having sex?" Brenner asks.

"Only if you're lucky." I wink.

"I mean, if you're looking for an audience, I'd take one for the team. I think Tay has been curious lately. What do you say? Wanna have us watch you and Ash together?" Brenner pumps his brows at his friend.

"You're ridiculous, and I think there's something wrong with you," Taylor replies, but I swear his cheeks look slightly pink.

The group heads into the kitchen, and I give my attention back to Ash, where it belongs.

Chuckling, I press my forehead to Ash's, his hand coming up to cup my face. "You're going to make me wait now, aren't you? Just to be mean."

Ash grins. "You know me so well…and you fucking love it."

"Love it. Love you," I reply.

"I know…and it might not always be easy, but I believe in us."

There's a good chance my heart actually melts. "I believe in us too. Now let's go hang out with our friends, so you can sexually torture me before dragging me to our room and having your way with my cock."

Ash beams. "I can't wait."

"Me neither."

EPILOGUE

Ash

Early summer

LANCE AND I set up a fold-out table in the yard at Mom and Steve's place, while everyone else tends to their pre-party duties. Several Alpha Theta Mu guys are in attendance, but we're not prepping for a frat party—it's a surprise birthday party for Atlas.

Once Lance and I get the table up, we put a black cloth over it and place on top the speakers we borrowed from Payton.

"Okay, so the DJ stand's all set," Lance says as he syncs his phone up with the speakers. "Crisis averted."

"This is what happens when you Uber," Marty calls from the bar as he frantically pulls liquor bottles from a box he brought with him.

He and Lance ran a little late, and though it's not a huge deal, I'm sure this is like the apocalypse for Marty's anxiety. Lance and I don't intend to make him suffer, so we hurry over to help him through his mini crisis, unloading the box.

"That was cool of your mom to let Ellie have Atlas's surprise birthday here," Lance says as he passes me some mixers.

Ellie is Troy's mom and Atlas's stepmom. She's been friends with our parents since we were in high school, when Troy and Colin played for the football team.

"Yeah, it is. I was surprised my mom suggested it—she tends to be a bit oblivious to this kind of thing. And Ellie can't really do something like this at her condo, while we have the perfect yard for it."

"Can we have more work and less chitchat?" Marty says.

Lance glares at Marty, then shakes his head. "No."

Marty rolls his eyes.

"Troy just texted!" Ellie calls to us from the back deck. "They're almost here."

"Fuck," Marty mutters.

"Language, Mart," Lance says. "There are parents here." Marty's brow creases before Lance adds, "You self-centered bastard."

That gets us all laughing before Ellie says, "Oh my God. You guys, this is really too much. I can't believe you're doing all this."

"We're Alpha Theta Mus," Payton calls from the volleyball net he's setting up with Colin. "This is what we do."

I mean, it's a far cry from the usual parties Alpha Theta Mu guys are accustomed to. Atlas doesn't exactly have a ton of friends, though he's made more at our frat since he and Troy became an item. So really, it's those of us who are local, who live within a few hours of Mom and Steve's place. Ellie also invited Taylor's mom and Brenner's dad. Atlas is cool with them since Brenner and Taylor have been his crew since freshman year, but Ellie probably thought it'd be nice if it wasn't just her, Mom, and Steve hanging out with a bunch of frat guys all day.

And I'm sure Ellie was thinking it'd be low-key with just a few of us here, but like hell we're not gonna fucking bring it.

As we all head to the deck, Colin sidles up beside me. "How's the bar coming along?" He hooks his arm around me and kisses my cheek.

This kind of shit has become the norm for us. Shamelessly grabbing each other, kissing, holding hands in public. We're probably that annoying PDA couple who have our tongues down each other's throats a little more than we should, but it's probably not surprising that I enjoy that kind of thing.

Despite the little hiccup drama right before finals, I've been relieved with how things have gone right back to normal. No, better than normal.

The future is scary, neither of us knows what it holds, but I can't spend all my time stressing about what may or may not happen. I don't have all the answers, and I don't need them, not with Colin.

We head inside with the rest of the gang and gather in the living room. Colin's right behind me, his hips tucking close to my ass, his arm around my waist. I rock my hips back slightly, glancing over my shoulder, and he fucking beams but remains cool, not drawing any attention to us being a little naughty.

Brenner glances around. "Isn't Atlas gonna know something's up when he shows up here and there are all these cars?"

Taylor winces. "Bren, you think Troy told Atlas that it was gonna be a nice, quiet dinner over here?"

"He told him it's for Steve's birthday," Ellie explains.

Brenner chuckles. "Right...that makes a lot more sense."

"Yeah, it does," Taylor teases, and Brenner elbows him.

"Now that Brenner knows how surprise birthday parties work," Colin says, "can everyone shut the hell up because he's definitely gonna be suspicious if they get close and hear Brenner and Taylor running their mouths."

"And that's why we didn't drive here, right?" Brenner asks, which earns an eye roll from Taylor. "Kidding!"

We quiet before the door opens, and Atlas and Troy step inside.

Atlas's eyes widen as he glances around the room before we all shout, "Surprise!"

"Oh God," he says, needing a moment to take it in, and I can tell he's recovered when he shoots Troy a playful glare. "You sneak."

Troy shrugs innocently. "It was all Mom's idea."

"Thank you, guys," Atlas says. He hugs Ellie, then makes his way around the room. "You guys I can forgive," he tells Colin and me before he reaches Brenner and Taylor. "You guys, I don't even know how you were capable of keeping this a secret."

"You never know what you're gonna get with us," Brenner says before Atlas pulls him and Taylor in for a group hug.

After some food, drinks, games, cake, and presents, Lance blasts the music—at a more reasonable level than usual because of our parents—and we play some more games and enjoy some pool time.

Marty covers the bar. Payton ropes everyone into pool cornhole, including Mom and Steve, which is a fucking riot. This is so not Mom's scene, but she's doing her best to let loose.

Once things have settled down, Colin and I make our way over to the love seat, and I relax in his lap.

"Mom was texting earlier, asking if we could hop on a Zoom tomorrow," Colin says, and I can hear the affection in his voice. How much he adores Lacey.

"That'd be nice," I say.

Even though she brought up things we needed to consider, we both know it was from a place of love, and she's been nothing but amazing and supportive since, which is all either of us could possibly hope for. My dad was also supportive when we had a chat with him, but in his own way—as if telling him I was dating my stepbro was the same as telling him I won a TaskFrat Challenge. He's happy I'm happy, even if he doesn't totally get it.

"Gonna be a lot of Ubering tonight," Marty says as he approaches the pool with Brenner and Taylor, all still in their bathing suits.

"Hey, Bren, Tay," Atlas says as he and Troy swim over to us. "You guys conspiring to join the club?"

Brenner and Taylor glance at each other, obviously unsure what the hell Atlas is talking about, but Colin and I check over our shoulders—on the pool deck, Taylor's mom bursts into a laugh at something Brenner's dad said. "You are ridiculous, Keith," she says, her smile all teeth as he bows his head, snickering.

"My mom enjoys her single life too much for that," Taylor says, clearly unfazed by what appears to be a somewhat flirtatious exchange between their single parents.

"What?" Brenner asks, his face twisting up. "You wouldn't want to be my stepbro?"

Taylor glares at him. "You know that in order to join

their club, we'd have to be more than stepbros, right?"

That gets all of us laughing.

"You're right," Brenner says. "Wouldn't work at all. You'd be so clingy, and I need my space."

"*I'd* be the clingy one?"

"I know your straight ass doesn't get this, but in Queerlandia, I'm a fucking catch."

"Nothing a trip to the clinic can't fix," Troy quips.

"It'd be worth the antibiotic," Brenner claps back, earning some groans.

"Dude," Taylor says. "You're done."

"I think we're just getting started."

"Nope." Taylor tackles Brenner, diving into the pool with him, and they start wrestling around.

"Now this is my idea of a party," I tell Colin, who plants a kiss on my temple.

We celebrate into the night, catching up about how we've been spending the summer and chilling by the firepit for a while. Then everyone helps us clean before they start heading out. It's about one in the morning by the time Col and I make it upstairs to get ready for bed.

I hop in the shower first, and after Colin brushes his teeth, he joins me under the stream. He pulls me close, offering a kiss, and I can taste the fresh mint mouth rinse.

"Can't believe I had to keep my greedy fucking hands off you all day," Colin says when he pulls away briefly, before his lips attack my neck, licking, biting, kissing.

"You had your hands on me plenty."

"Not enough." As he says the words, his breath slams against my skin, making it prick to life.

I must agree with him there. As nice as it was to see the guys, it was cruel to see Colin running around in his board shorts for the past few hours.

"We might need to make a quick stop by the bath-house in the next few weeks," he goes on. "You've been without an audience long enough."

My cheeks warm. "Can't disagree with that."

"Maybe next summer we go on a cross-country trip, and I take you to all the bathhouses we come across." I chuckle, but—"Oh, you like that," Colin says. "Well, guess we know what we'll be doing next summer."

Fuck, this guy knows me.

When I first became interested in the live stream stuff, I remember judging myself, but seeing Colin not just approve, but explore it with me has made it easy to leave all those silly judgments behind. Just fully enjoy the experiences I'm lucky enough to share with him.

"I like you all horny like this," I say, grabbing his stiff cock and stroking. "Wonder what you'd be like if I waited until tomorrow morning to let you fuck me."

Colin pulls away, and I see the flash of concern in his eyes before he smirks. "Don't be cruel. You need it too."

I nibble his bottom lip. "I don't know that I'll be able to sleep if you don't."

He beams and takes my mouth again.

I stroke his cock, but he pulls it away. "What is this?" I ask.

"Uh-uh. We're not fucking in the shower again. I want you in my bed."

"Now who's being cruel?" I tease.

We finish up, dry off, and head to his bedroom at our parents' place, where we're staying for the summer. "Hey, Frat Cat," I say as we enter, and our baby walks over, requesting scritches, which we both give.

Since we took him in, he's grown so much, and his coat's shiny and smooth, his little personality as spoiled as it should be. After we've shown enough affection, he heads out of the room.

"Fuck, he really knows our nightly routine, doesn't he?" Colin says because we both know that as soon as we're finished up, he'll be scratching at the door to get in.

"Smart like his daddies," I say, loosening the knot in Colin's towel, pulling it away and tossing it onto the swivel chair at his desk. I push him back onto the bed.

"Oh, Ash is feisty tonight, isn't he?"

"With how you teased me in the shower, you're gonna get exactly what you deserve."

I nab the lube from the nightstand, then crawl on

top of my man, my knees on either side of him as I lube myself up, then his cock, before guiding him inside me.

Colin just lies there, letting my ass serve him. He moans softly as my body welcomes him.

"You've really trained me to take you," I say. "I love the way I just open up for you."

I lift up on my knees, then slide back down, rocking as I clench my ass, watching his expression, the way he rolls his eyes and opens his mouth. He starts to thrust, but I push my hand down against his chest. "No, no. Not yet."

He obeys, growling like it's taking strength and will-power to restrain himself.

I keep up my work. I know where I want to get him to. We've learned each other's bodies since we started messing around. I know every twitch of his brow, every shift in his expression. I've learned the little moves I can make to drive him wild, just like he's learned the ones that drive me wild. I can even tell by the way he fucks when he's about to blow.

As I rock on his hips, I lick my fingers and play with his nipples.

"Oh, Ash," he moans. "You feel so fucking good."

"You gonna be ready when I tell you to fuck the cum out of me?"

"Yes."

I feel him firm even more inside me, and a grin

sweeps across my face. "Like an animal," I tell him. "Like I'm just a fucking hole and you need to get the fuck off. Is that how you'll treat me?"

"I will. I promise."

I don't have any reason to doubt him; he's fucked me enough for me to trust he'll do just that.

"Now," I tell him, and that familiar storm sweeps me away as he sits up, hooking his arms under my legs, spinning me around. He's a fucking machine as he takes me on my back, hammering away. We make up for the lost time today, our moans and heavy breaths pushing through the brief moments when he doesn't have his tongue down my throat. Our fuck reminds me of wrestling matches we'd have when we were younger, as we toss around on the bed, though this is so much more thrilling.

Feels like he's taken me from every angle before he guides me onto my knees so he's fucking me from behind. With my hands on the headboard, precum dripping from my shaft, he doesn't hold back, really nailing my prostate.

As his movements speed up, I say, "I can fucking tell how close you are."

He reaches around, gripping my cock as his body pushes up against my back. "You're fucking close too, aren't you, my little perv?" He whispers the words into my ear, still thrusting and pumping my cock. His other hand slides around and toys with my nipple.

I'm overstimulated, struggling to think straight through the erratic sensations sparking off all over my body.

Heat radiates in my face as he whispers, "I'm gonna make you shoot when I do."

"I might be too close." I'm right on the edge, the pressure so intense, I can't imagine how I'm not blowing already.

"I fucking know you are. I'm just getting you right where I want you."

"You already have that."

Colin snickers, like he knows how true my words are, not about what we're doing, but about everything he means to me.

The pressure builds even more. Feels like my sensations are about to burst through my skin.

"Colin, it's too much. Please."

"Kiss me."

I turn as fast as I can before I feel his lips press against mine, and he fucks and pumps me, twisting his hand at the same time as he pinches my nipple just right.

The explosion sets off, a fucking hurricane of nerves tearing through me. I can't hold in my excitement as I start to moan, loud enough that Steve and Mom might hear, but Colin knows me well enough that he releases my nipple and places his hand on the back of my head, keeping me in place so that my moan enters his mouth, blocking the sound as I feel his final, powerful thrust slam up into me. As my moan settles, he grunts gently into my mouth while continuing to drain my load. The frenzy calms as we stay there, on our knees, our bodies puzzled together, our lips unwilling to rest with the rest of our bodies. I relax into the sensations of heat and tingling, staying with it as long as I can.

After we come down, I realize I made a mess on his pillow, so we change the case before slipping under the sheets. He cuddles me, my big spoon keeping me as close as he can.

"Another night fucking in our parents' place," I say, rolling to face Colin.

"Naughty boys that we are."

"Making up for all the times we weren't naughty." I position my hand near his chest, tracing my finger along his flesh. "All the times we were goofing around in high school when you should have been sticking that dick in me."

It's not the first time I've had the thought, especially since summer began and we started fucking around in this familiar house.

Colin studies my expression. "I think about that too. Like what if we had figured out all this shit sooner? We would have had fun, but then…"

"Then I realize it was perfect the way it was." As I say

the words, I finish drawing an imaginary star on his pec, and he grins, nodding. "Exactly."

"I—"

"I love you too," Colin says, making us chuckle.

I hook my arms and legs around him, pulling him close, rubbing my nose against his.

It was perfect the way it was.

Weird as we are, strange as our journey was, if we had to go back and do it all over again, I wouldn't change a damn thing.

THE END

Find Riley and Devon's Newsletters and
Social Media Accounts:
Linktr.ee/HartMack

BONUS SCENE

This fun, naughty scene takes place during summer vacation, after the epilogue of The Step Don't.

Colin

"WHAT ABOUT RIGHT here?" I ask Ash, who's attached to my back like a starfish. We're at a park, trying to find a good place to sit for our picnic. It's hot, and technically I shouldn't want to cart my boyfriend around on my back in this weather, but we both know I do. That I live for this shit. Being all the things that I can for Ash is the best kind of high, but that doesn't mean I'm not going to pretend otherwise.

"Hmm…"

I can tell exactly what he's doing by the tone of his voice, and I bite my cheeks to keep from smiling.

"I'm not sure… It looks a little bumpy."

"A little bumpy, huh? Well, we wouldn't want that. What about over there?" I motion to the left.

"Too sunny."

The smile pulls too hard at my cheeks, and I can't hold it back. I try, I really try, and maybe no one else would get it, but no one else has to get it because they aren't me and Ash.

"How is it that this whole picnic thing was your idea, yet I'm the one carrying you around?" I ask, as if I would want it any other way. He knows that too.

"Because you love me."

I heft him higher up on my back. His legs tighten around me, and...yeah, I'm in dangerous territory here. There is a good chance I'm going to get hard. He basically just has to look at me for that to happen.

"I do love you. And you love me. Hey, do you think we can find a place in this park to have sneaky, there's-a-good-chance-we'll-get-caught sex?"

Ash chuckles as I move toward a tree, then set him down. He immediately starts looking around, then bends and says, "A roly-poly." He lets it crawl around his hand, and I shiver.

"Can it be a roly-poly far away from me? But don't hurt it!"

Ash gives me that sweet smile, his eyes full of emotion, full of love, but also like he absolutely knows I'm ridiculous. It's a hot look. "You know I would never hurt it."

And he wouldn't. I don't even know why I said that. "Great. So now get rid of it."

He shakes his head teasingly, then walks away to keep the bug from trying to murder me. He does one more sweep, and when I'm fairly certain I won't be attacked by insects, we pull a blanket from the bag.

"Anyway…the sex?" I ask. The park isn't packed, but there are a lot of people here, enjoying their late-summer day. The grass is dotted with couples on blankets and people playing frisbee.

"You can't get enough of this hole."

"Am I supposed to? Because we can keep trying every day, but it's never gonna happen." While we do have sex without the exhibitionism we both enjoy so much, we've kept that a part of our relationship. It adds an extra rush we both love, and we feel lucky we get to share it together, that it's something we're both into.

"Naw. I like that you're addicted to my ass."

"And your cock." I sit down on the blanket, and Ash does the same.

"That too. And I'm sure we can find a place to sneak away if you want, but I was also thinking that today is the last day Mom and Steve are gone…"

She had a work conference out of state, and Dad went with her. After her conference hours each day, he's been working hard to get her to mentally clock out of her job and have some fun with him. And while she's trying to be more available for Ash, Lauren is still Lauren.

That also means we've had a whole week at the house where we can do whatever we want. I'm fairly certain we've scandalized Frat Cat with all the sex we've been having, and I can't help wishing we started doing this a long time before we did. "I'm listening..."

Ash begins to unpack our lunch, slowly, as if I'm not on pins and needles, trying to figure out what he's going to say. He really does have the best ideas, but then, I'm the genius who suggested I watch him jerk off on camera, so I'm pretty good myself.

"This whole thing started because of me on Man-zturbate, and we both enjoy being watched, so it would be the perfect full-circle moment if we ended the summer with the two of us online together."

My dick twitches beneath my shorts, and I push to my feet. "Welp, that was a fun lunch. Let's head home now."

Ash snickers in that mischievous way of his that tells me he has an evil plan. "Oh, Col. You know me better than that. Where's the fun in it if I don't get to be a little cruel first and draw it out for you?"

Blood rushes to my groin, to the point where the rest of my body is completely deprived. "I might die if I have to wait. Do you want to be responsible for that? Look, I can't move my arm. It hurts. Poor circulation in my limb due to lack of blood flow to the area. I think my legs are next." I try to make my arm look floppy, which earns me a joyful laugh from Ash. My heart thuds at the sound, so okay, maybe there's still some pumping through me.

"As long as it's in your dick, we're fine."

A light, fluttery feeling ignites in my stomach. God, he's so fun. Everything about him is. "Fine. You're a cruel, cruel man, Ash Fuller."

"Are you complaining?"

I sit down again and kiss him. "No, I'm not." And as much as I want to go back to the house and have live internet sex with my boyfriend, I also want to be here with him, talking with him, laughing with him, simply enjoying being together. I love everything about Ash, every moment we share. "So…what's for lunch? I'll need my energy for later."

Ash hands me my favorite sandwich, along with the sea salt and cracked black pepper chips I love and a Cherry Coke. It's exactly what I would have chosen for myself, each one picked because they're my faves, and just as much as I like to make Ash happy, he likes to make me happy too. We're literally the best boyfriends ever.

"You like it?" he asks.

"You know I do…and I also like you."

"Cheesy but cute."

"Not sure three words have ever described me more."

"I would also throw in *mine*."

My smile takes over my face. Because I *am* his. And Ash is mine. And after lunch, I'm going to show all those guys on Manzturbate just who gets to enjoy those big fucking loads of his.

Ash

AFTER WE RETURN home, I shower up first. While Col's taking his, I set up his bedroom, mounting my phone on a tripod I purchased so that I could make this a little more professional for my followers. I line up the shot, keeping out of it the rectangle of tape I've laid down on the bed.

Just as I finish making adjustments, Colin enters the bedroom, a towel around his waist.

"Mmm," I say, admiring his thick muscles, still glistening from his shower. "I like how your muscles get all bulky and sexy in the summer."

Funny to think of all the times he's walked around shirtless. Sure, it was hot, but it never had this effect on me. Now it's like my body has been primed, eagerly anticipating another touch, another kiss, another fuck.

Colin smirks. "I tell myself I'm bulking up for next season, but really, I just love carbs."

"They seem to love you too."

I approach him and take a kiss, enjoying the mint of his mouth rinse for a few moments before he grunts. "First you make me shower by myself, then you come in here and put on boxers and a shirt." He tugs at the hem of my tee. "You're really being extra cruel today."

I pull him close so our torsos are flush. "You know damn well you would have called me a sadist if we'd been in the shower, grinding on each other, and I made you save it for the video."

He shrugs. "I don't need to save any. I could just pretend to come in you. All I need to do is get hard and give a little…" He simulates his orgasm face with surprising accuracy, moaning, *"Oh, Ash, fuck… I'm gonna come inside you, Ash."*

I can't stifle my laugh, but funny as it is, the thought of him saying that has me blushing.

"Like hell I'm letting you fake it for me on camera!"

"I think we've tested my refractory period enough to know we'd be fine." He gives my ass a squeeze and licks up the middle of my lips.

I take another quick kiss but force myself to pull away and guide him over to his bed.

He assesses the tape I put down and shoots me a look, surely remembering the fun time we had ensuring we could fuck around and still keep our faces out of the frame.

"If we like this," I say, "we can try masks next time, but I like looking at that sexy mug when you come in me."

"That's not how it went down last night," Colin teases, and the heat in my cheeks flares up again as I think about how he took me from behind on the pool love seat.

"Well, I like to change things up too." I wink before heading over to my backpack. "Speaking of changing things up, what do you think of this?" I strip down real quick and toss on a crop top I picked up at the store the other day. "It's called an extreme crop top," I say, as it only reaches down just past my pecs. "I thought it might be a kinda Troy thing, but it looks hot."

I sneak a glance at Colin. He's got that wild-eyed look, like he's about to rush over and have his way with me. My ass clenches with anticipation.

"Guess I was right about it looking cute on me," I say.

"Cute doesn't really cover this." Colin approaches and slides his hands over my body. As his right hand reaches the hem of my top, he runs his thumb beneath the base, teasing my flesh.

As my cock stiffens, he says, "We might need to add these to your wardrobe." With his free hand, he grips my cock, then plants a gentle kiss against my lips before smiling. He offers a few gentle strokes, and I'm already precoming. "Don't forget you gotta save it for the stream."

He rubs his thumb gently just under the head of my dick, and I moan. "Really getting me back for being cruel, aren't you?"

"Don't worry. You won't call me cruel when I'm finished with you," he whispers, his voice a few octaves deeper than usual, making a pulse of excitement reverberate through me. "Now get in bed," he orders.

"I should put on pants. It's all about the tease."

He snickers, shaking his head. "Trust me, Ash. When people see you in this, they're gonna be jizzing themselves before we even get to the good stuff."

My cheeks flush, but the way he's ogling me, I don't question his judgment.

"Now don't make your stepbro any more impatient than he already is. Get on that bed, Ash."

I grab lube and a Bluetooth remote I purchased with the tripod for my phone, then hurry to the bed, getting on my knees and checking the camera screen to make sure we're good to go.

"Remember to stay inside the taped lines."

He winces. "Bro, I know how to stay inside the sidelines."

"Really? That's not what the ref said third game of last season."

Colin's lips curl into a wicked smirk that's sexy as hell. "I'm gonna make your adorable ass pay for that one. Now do I need to do anything to start this?"

"Getting on the bed would be a great start."

He glares at me. "You know what I mean."

"I got everything set up, Big Guy. Just get over here and fuck the hell out of me."

"Yes, sir." Colin tosses his towel into the laundry bin, then crawls onto the bed, getting on his knees behind me.

In the past, before recording, I would have a little stage fright, but today it's just eagerness welling up in me as Colin settles behind me, his hand resting on my ass, offering a gentle stroke.

"So…should we not speak?" he asks. "Is it recording audio?"

"The app has a voice disguiser I already turned on, but I'd avoid…how did you put it? *Oh, Ash, fuck. I'm gonna come inside you, Ash.*"

"Yeah, you're right. I should probably use your full name and social security number."

As I laugh, I glance over my shoulder. "I could kiss that snarky expression right off your face," I warn.

He taps the head of his hard cock between my cheeks. "Yeah," he says, admiring my ass. "I'm gonna enjoy this."

His gaze locks with mine. He has that determined look in his eyes that reminds me of when he's playing football. A confidence, a certainty in what a pro he is.

Along with my eagerness to share this on the stream, there's another familiar eagerness as I think about how good it's gonna be when he gets that cock in me.

He removes his hand from my ass and grabs the lube, readying himself. "Go ahead. Start the stream."

Another rush of excitement before I push the button on the remote and check my phone to see the screen shift to show the recording signal along with a comments box.

As the first of my followers start commenting, with one hand, Colin pulls my ass cheek aside, and with the other, presses his lubed fingers against my hole, massaging gently. He takes his time, working his fingers into me.

While I relax into his touch, the comments are already going wild. They're used to seeing me play around with myself, not having someone plow the fuck out of me. This is gonna make them lose their fucking minds.

Colin slips in, taking his time as he pushes deeper and deeper until I feel him right up against that spot.

"Fuck." I glance back to him. "You know what I want."

He slides his fingers out before pushing the head of his dick up against me, positioning himself before easing in.

He moves in steadily, inch by inch, my body opening up for him, just like he's trained it to do.

I turn back to the headboard and close my eyes, enjoying the sensation of his cock pushing in, sliding up against that spot before I feel his pelvis against my ass.

He rests one hand against my ass and the other grips my waist as he begins with gentle thrusts.

I turn to the phone.

I can't read the comments from this far away, but even if I could, they race by so fast, I doubt I could keep up. It's easy to imagine what they're saying, though.

Praising my big bro's thick cock…and me for being so good at taking it.

Each of Colin's thrusts takes me higher, pushing sensation from my ass to my fingertips. As he makes broader thrusts, I start pushing back, meeting each one as we work together, creating that effortless rhythm we always seem to find.

"Now we can really get this show on the road," he mutters.

The excitement he stirs with those words mixes with the excitement he stirs with his cock as he pushes up against my prostate again.

He leans forward, resting his hands on my shoulders before picking up the pace.

As he hammers away, I can't keep myself from calling out, my moans climbing with the pressure that swells in my balls as my boyfriend stimulates everything within me.

"Ah, that's real good," Colin says. "Doing a great job taking this cock."

He releases my shoulders, wrapping an arm around my waist and pulling back.

I follow him, rising upright, and he pushes his chest against my back, one hand greedily exploring my torso as the other slides up under the crop top, groping my pec before his finger and thumb tease at my sensitive nipples. He buries his face against my neck, kissing and licking, navigating up to my earlobe, which he takes between his teeth and gives a gentle tug.

It's sensation overload in a way that has my eyes rolling back as his hand slides down my torso and he grips my shaft.

I peek at my phone, my body on display for the audience as he starts stroking, a bead of precum dripping down to the sheets. As I twist my head, I notice Colin looking at the phone too. He walks on his knees, angling so my followers can get a better look.

"Fuck, you know me too well," I whisper.

"Damn right I do." Just as he says it, he starts fucking me harder.

I get lost in the storm that fucking around with him typically becomes as we adjust in different positions, as he finds just the right angle to fuck me. Each time I check, the comments are wild—this must be the most I've ever received. But as I call out, I'm not putting on a show, just reveling in everything Colin's doing to me.

I wind up on my back. Colin's got my ankles in his grasp as he goes in deep. I call out even louder, lost in sensation, delirious with the passion we've worked up.

It's like I don't just want everyone in the stream to know how good my boyfriend's giving it to me, I want the whole world to know.

Colin gazes down at me, like he's admiring how I look when I'm totally letting go, surrendering to him.

"You're so beautiful," he tells me before releasing my ankles. His lips crush down against mine, his tongue slipping between my lips.

I embrace every thrust, but I can feel something else too: the intense pressure that needs release...so fucking badly.

"I don't know how much longer I can last," Colin warns, gritting his teeth like he's doing his best to keep from blowing inside me.

"Let's finish with me on top."

It's another hurricane sweeping through the room as he hooks his arms around my thighs and I throw my arms around him in a familiar move as he rolls back. I reposition so I'm straddling his waist, bobbing up and down, each time making sure to go down until I feel his hips against my ass.

"I want them to see me milk it right out of you," I say as I speed up my movements.

Colin's expression twists up the way it always does when he's close. "Oh fuck...fuck..."

He grabs hold of my cock, strokes me, and it's too much.

"No, I want you to come first." I want it so bad, I'm practically whining.

"Trust me, I'm fucking coming."

Relief mixes with the explosion as a sharp thrust against my prostate sends me into a series of spasms, my body twisting and twitching with excitement as a thick load shoots across his abs, making it across his chest, up to his fucking chin.

Colin calls out like a fucking lion's roar as he finishes up inside me, his hips slamming up against me a few times as I enjoy the familiar sensation of knowing he's filled me up.

I roll my head back, sighing with relief before turning to make sure the stream got a good angle of everything.

I'm relieved when I see that not only is it an impressive angle, but the comments are lit up with plenty of emojis—fire, eggplants, peaches, and splashes.

Colin chuckles. "Oh, they fucking loved that."

As I turn to him, he's smiling, and I can't help but do the same.

"Now get down here and make a mess with me," he orders. I lean down, hooking my arms under his, really pushing up against my cum as we kiss again.

With his tongue playing with mine, his cock still shoving his cum deep into me, the live stream still rolling, all I can think is how totally satisfied I am in this moment.

"Okay," he whispers into my mouth. "Time to end the show." He nuzzles his nose against mine. "They don't get to stick around for the cuddles."

His words pull a laugh right out of me in that way

only Colin can.

I nibble at his jaw. "I think we need to clean up a little before cuddles."

"Eh, we can wash the sheets tomorrow. I don't mind being a mess while I watch you read all the comments we missed."

A mischievous smile tugs at his lips.

That's my dirty man.

My dirty Colin who knows me better than anyone ever could or ever will.

We kiss again, and I can't help thinking that as much fun as the fuck was, I'm gonna have just as much fun cuddling the fucking shit out of him.

ABOUT THE AUTHORS

Riley Hart

Riley Hart's love of all things romance shines brightly in everything she writes. Her primary focus is Male/Male romance but under various pen names, her prose has touched practically every part of the spectrum of love and relationships. The common theme that ties them all together is stories told from the heart.

A hopeless romantic herself, Riley is a lover of character-driven plots, many with flawed and relatable characters. She strives to create stories that readers can not only fall in love with, but also see themselves in. Real characters and real love blended together equal the ultimate Riley Hart experience.

When Riley isn't creating her next story, you can find her reading, traveling, or dreaming about reading or traveling, spending time with her two snarky kids, and swoony husband.

Riley Hart is represented by Jane Dystel at Dystel, Goderich & Bourret Literary Management. She's a 2019

Lambda Literary Award Finalist for *Of Sunlight and Stardust.*

Find Riley:

www.rileyhartwrites.com

Devon McCormack

Devon McCormack grew up in the Georgia suburbs with his two younger brothers and an older sister. At a very young age, he spun tales the old-fashioned way, lying to anyone and everyone he encountered. He claimed he was an orphan. He claimed to be a king from another planet. He claimed to have supernatural powers. He has since harnessed this penchant for tall tales by crafting worlds and characters that allow him to live out whatever fantasy he chooses. Devon is an out and proud queer man living in Atlanta, Georgia.

Find Devon:

www.devonmccormack.com

Made in United States
Orlando, FL
20 September 2024

51741645R10185